Bound
by
Blood

THE BLOOD BEGOTTEN
SERIES ~ BOOK 1

Steven Louis Turk

Flint Hills Publishing

Bound by Blood,
The Blood Begotten Series - Book 1
© Steven Louis Turk 2020
All rights reserved

Cover Design by Amy Albright

ʃFlint Hills Publishing
Topeka, Kansas U.S.A.

www.flinthillspublishing.com

Printed in the U.S.A.

ISBN: 978-1-7332035-8-6

Library of Congress Control Number application pending

THIS BOOK IS DEDICATED TO
BRIAN NIGHTINGALE

.

Chapter One

The aroma incited the creature's need to sample its deepest wanting. He raced through the maze of city streets and factory buildings until the scent led him to a set of winding railroad tracks just beyond the railway station. Trees and brush outlined the trail's perimeter, obscuring what awaited around its bend. He followed the path and found an old man sprawled next to the tracks, his body contorted in ways a body should not be.

The man strained against his body's desire to stay prone, but his strength abandoned him. He collapsed back to the ground and gasped, conceding to whatever fate had in store for him.

The creature drew closer, his thirst goading his primitive desires. But instead, he fought the urge and savored the moment. And like a predator that toys with their prey, he squatted down next to the injured man and watched the man's will cave and his pride yield to his whim. He felt a malicious satisfaction in stalking someone so helpless. He burned inside. The bouquet of blood prodded his craving. He longed to taste what sprouted from the man's wounds, to feel the viscous life-sustaining fluid on his fingertips. He reached out and touched the open gashes on the man's forehead. As soon as he grazed his quarry's skin, power surged through the monster's arms

1

and forced its way throughout his body. It pushed away his visceral need while a lifetime of memories, not his own, flashed in his mind. Stunned, he pulled his hand away. Phantom energies throbbed along the nerves of his arm and over his flesh. Its pulse refused his dismissive attempt to rid himself of the sensation as he scoured his arm with his palm. He wanted to claw through his flesh and dig into the core of the source of this feeling and rip it from his mind and body.

When these sensations diminished enough for him to function without disruption, the being noticed the man's tattered, blood-saturated shirt. And in morbid curiosity, he peeled apart the shirt's shredded remains, mindful to avoid skin contact between them. The wet cloth stuck like a doused beach towel and separated from his skin with a sickening moist sound. He flung the torn clothing aside and it hit the ground in a splattering thud. As he viewed the seeping torso wounds, he expected some inner reaction, but felt indifferent. This disturbed him. Had he completely lost his humanity? Out of some displaced sense of modesty, or compelled by an ingrained habit, he covered the man's fatally damaged body with the same wet, decimated rags.

"That doesn't look good," the creature said.

"I know." The man laid still and looked skyward. He flinched in pain and coughed up blood. The creature gasped, taken aback by the sweet fragrance that roused his primal compulsion again.

"Should I get you some help?"

"No thanks," he let out a snort that became a painful cough, "hospitals are for sick people."

"I suppose so." The creature gave an uneasy smile.

The levity passed and the horror settled back upon the doomed man's face, "I'm dying."

"What do you want of me?"

"Don't leave me here, like this." The man's breath went shallow and his voice faded to a whisper. "Don't let them dissect me and keep me in a fridge. Bury me, burn me. I don't care either way." He grabbed the creature's arm, "Promise me."

"I promise. Relax."

The creature took the man into his arms, transfixed his gaze deep beyond the eye's pupil, and penetrated his victim's mind. He found a vortex of torment within the dying man and placed him in a trance, a dark tranquility that overshadowed consciousness. As he sedated the man, his prey's neck arched back and exposed the pulsating nectar of desire. Surroundings dissipated, and the perfume of blood, so enticing and dulcet, intoxicated his mind and enraptured him with a visceral need to taste the forbidden more than ever before. No longer contented with pacification, his fervency swelled, his eyes turned crimson red, and his fangs jutted out in rapacious lust as he plunged through lurid flesh.

Enveloped in euphoria, he relished the virility that streamed into him, as if ecstasy was tangible. The act alone stimulated something buried in his repressed memories, something he believed unattainable.

He felt alive.

He hadn't experienced this since his change. And then, without warning, his elation slipped away as death poured in and took its place.

As he drained the last essence from the human shell in

his arms, he glanced up at a cloaked figure's silhouette gliding toward him along the tracks. He relinquished his grip and the entity faded from sight. This thing's presence hadn't stirred his danger sense, but a cold sensation penetrated his body and passed through him as quickly as it had made itself present. Although unharmed, he wasn't foolhardy enough to stay around. With unearthly speed he ran away, uncertain of where to go or what to do.

With his victim's body still in tow, he rushed back through the stagnant industrial shipping yards. Its concrete and steel barricade dampened the inner metropolis of Beshkno's resonance and captured the machine-driven stench of filth that permeated all within its confines. He slowed to a prowl long enough to collect his thoughts. With no immediate exit present, he searched for shelter, concerned over his vulnerability even though he appeared impervious to many of the dangers he had confronted since his recent transformation.

Seeking escape, he found no refuge within the labyrinth of buildings and his internal defenses warned him of an impending threat. He rounded the corner when waves of babbles and noises inundated his cognition, inducing vertigo. He tried to keep upright but swayed in place and then went to one knee.

"Nathan," a voice said, its origin hidden behind echoes and incomprehensible babbles.

Even with his bearings inhibited, he stood, the reverberating intonations skewing his head, and a foreign intuition manifested, revealing a new ability. He faded, morphing into evanescence and his wraith form transcended the heavens. He darted through the stratosphere and soared above the dense clouds that separated the starlit sky from the draped gloom below.

He flew in haste, not born from fear but of instinct, toward his hidden sanctuary in a cemetery long forgotten by the living, just past the dilapidated section of downtown. The overgrowth of weeds, moss, and wild vines covered the epitaphs on the tombstones and the untamed shrubbery, trees, and foliage shrouded all within the area's natural barrier in anonymity.

Within the recesses of the graveyard, he materialized in front of a mausoleum and opened the door with one hand as he held the man's remains over the opposing shoulder, and entered the chamber. He approached one of the vaults, shoved aside the stone slab on top of it with unearthly strength, and placed the body inside. He resealed the vault as sentiments vacillated between his culpability and the cold truth of his murderous deed. The old man deserved better than what he was given—a burial known only to the monstrous being that assisted in his demise.

As he pondered this, an ill cognition befell him, a sinking notion something terrible had happened. He dashed outside and leapt into the blurry overcast sky with steadfast intent. His bloodlust weakened his resolve and swayed him from his nightly vigil, *his unspoken promise to her.*

He descended into an elm tree, hidden from the commotion below him. Patrol cars congested the street, their lights illuminated the house outlined in yellow crime scene tape. Despite the late hour, eavesdropping onlookers stood along the boundaries of the normally quiet neighborhood and watched the turmoil unfold in the restricted space.

Although ten feet away, he could see and hear all activity in the house from his vantage point—a perch from where he observed her on countless nights—waffling on whether to reveal his existence or continue his secretive watch. But that decision, that choice, had come to pass. Cameras flashed in the bedroom as the scent of death, unnatural death, drifted out of the open bedroom window. The smell didn't stir his appetite this time. Instead, it knotted his stomach. His torment shifted from an emotional turmoil to physical pain. He peered in through the window in horror and watched the detective survey the crime scene from the foot of the victim's bed. A woman, sprawled out on a blood-drenched mattress with a vast crater replacing where her torso should have been, her innards strewn across the room. Her head dangled back and crooked, attached by threads of flesh that encompassed what remained of her neck.

"I guess we can rule out accidental death," Murray said as he entered the bedroom, the grey of his dress pants closely matching the streaks that had taken over much of his short brown hair. His shoulder holster made the unbuttoned collar of his yellow shirt hang loose. His black tie dangled askew. His shirt, sleeves unevenly rolled up, draped over his lanky figure. The shoulder holster held his Smith and Wesson .357 magnum. His belt held the speed loaders, Glock 22 .40 caliber handgun, and additional magazines. He looked like a scarecrow ready for war.

"Actually, she left her chainsaw on in bed and fell asleep," the young detective said, rubbing his face and blonde buzz cut hair, trying to keep sleep at bay. And yet by the look of his freshly pressed brown suit, one couldn't tell he'd been awake for over twenty-four hours. Cooper always looked sharp. Once a soldier, always a soldier.

"Tragic. Does insurance cover that?" Murray said through his clenched teeth that held his cigar.

"An insurance company that pays claims? Now that's funny." Cooper yawned and took more notes on his tablet, "Do you know how much trouble you're facing for smoking at a crime scene?"

"It isn't lit," Murray paused as he struck a match. "I.D. the victim yet?"

"Rachael. . ."

Murray looked down and his eyes widened. "Brooks?" he interrupted. "She must have moved."

Cooper scrolled through his notes, "Yup. Old case?"

"Right before you transferred. She just found out she was pregnant when her husband was killed. And if I remember correctly, she's about due."

Cooper shook his head, "Not anymore."

Murray sighed and put his cigar in his shirt's breast pocket where his badge dangled crookedly. "So, what do we have so far?"

Cooper read from his tablet. "This is confusing. Her position on the bed and surrounding bloodstain patterns suggests she was asleep when attacked. We found hair fibers in her hands, as well as defensive scratches, consistent with a struggle. So far, textbook. But here's where it gets weird. There are very large, bloody animal prints on the sheets and the floor. Photos have been taken and the lab is ready to bag and collect the rest after we're done."

Murray bent over the body from the side of the bed and

observed the edges of the neck wounds. "Torn skin. Definitely looks like an animal attack to me. Find any human prints?"

"None. And no signs of forced entry. The only indication of exit is here." Cooper pointed out the bloody animal prints leading to the open windowsill, covered in the same bloody prints.

"Out a second story window?"

"Didn't say it made sense."

"Regardless, there has to be a blood trail."

"K-9 unit's already on its way. This case, this whole scenario—an animal attack in a bedroom with an escape out of a second story window—it doesn't add up," Cooper said, yawning.

"It never does."

Both men turned to leave when Cooper stopped and gazed out the window as if searching for something.

"Find something?" Murray stepped back over to the window.

"No, I—have you ever had one of those feelings, like you swore you were being watched?"

Murray put his cigar back in his mouth, "Yeah, right before I found my first ex-wife's boyfriend hiding in the closet."

Beyond the branches and leaves, Nathan sat against a tombstone in the graveyard, mourning his immeasurable loss. At first, although drawn to its aura, this place made him wary. But over time, he grew accustomed and then dependent on its solace. And now, isolation no longer brought him peace, only stints of dwelling on days gone by. As much as he missed his mortal life, the only thing left that he held sacred had been stripped from him in a thoughtless gesture. This, and his lost humanity, compiled his unbearable misery.

He brushed his hands along the smooth grass blades, letting condensation cling to his pale, frigid fingers and palms. He raised a hand up and watched virgin dew trickle down the contours of his ghostlike skin. His bluish lips formed a slight smile and then receded as quickly as it had formed; his joy dimmed to bitterness as fragmented memories of his life with her rushed in. He clenched his fists, his nails dug into his palms, and he tried to contain the mounting rage and pain that followed. Tears swelled then burst forth, streaming from his ashen eyes until he had no more tears left to shed.

Don't carry such a heavy burden with you. Your mortal attachments will bring you nothing but misery, a voice said. The voice was being fed into his brain by either telepathic means or similar method. In any case, he wasn't listening to the disembodied voice's ill advice.

"Where are you? Show yourself."

I'm right here. You haven't looked with your true sight.

"What does that even mean?" He dismissed the question and said aloud, "Why should I bother?"

Because you know there's something amiss, and that without my guidance, you'll never find the peace your departed has.

"I never wanted any of this for her and now she's gone," Nathan whispered.

You will learn to let go.

9

"What if I don't want to?"

Don't let your thoughts linger on such things. Now rest, you've had a long night.

"And it's about to get longer."

As the night faded into sunrise, Nathan remained awake, defiantly mulling over his bereavements under a cruel and unforgiving light that weakened him but would not burn him into dust. In this moment, as erratic emotions calmed the tormenting seas within, sadness abandoned its station, and then malice, a thirst for vengeance, took its stead. *No,* forgetting she ever mattered and sleeping away her memory was out of the question, an impossible task. This was truly the darkest night he had ever endured.

Chapter Two

Steam rose from the coffee cup into the chilled, early morning air. Cooper took a sip, hastened his stride, and caught up with Murray as they headed toward the crime scene tape that blocked off the dank and unsettling entrance to the alley. The blood trail from the original scene led them to the outskirts of town, referred to as Dead Man's Land, a derogatory term used by patrol soon after several cases in the area went cold. Beshkno tossed this part of its city aside, abandoned the old and decayed to vagrants, homeless, and unwanted. Those who inhabited the ruins had no other choice but to stay and lived in perpetual fear of the criminal element that controlled the city. According to rumor, the crime syndicate was well informed and implemented brutal methods to maintain order. Those who spoke to the police or dared defy the criminal organization vanished, so cooperation was sparse at best. Many crimes went unsolved if an investigator's case brought them here—a void into which tracks faded and questions remained unanswered.

Uniformed officers gathered potential witnesses—the people who dwelled in the alleyways—into a group for questioning just next to the blocked off area. Murray took out a cigar and lit it. Cooper stopped and gaped at his partner, incredulous to the blatant defiance he displayed once again.

"Don't start with me," Murray said. "It's been a long shift and we've wound up in Dead Man's Land looking for evidence. We'll be lucky if we find anything here."

"Okay, okay, I'll ease up. But if you get suspended again, Laura won't be so nice." Cooper paused when Murray's brow furrowed at the mention of her, then continued, "You're still out? I thought you resolved all of that."

"We haven't talked. So, no. I haven't moved back in."

"But she told you to come home and you refuse to because. . ." Cooper's sentence trailed off into nothing. He knew he had gone too far already and didn't want to risk telling his partner that his pride had gotten in the way of principle.

"It's not that simple."

"All right, I won't say another word about it." Cooper let the subject drop.

"Murray! They said I couldn't get my stuff." A man limped over from the group of witnesses, ending the detectives' conversation. Murray closed the distance between the man and himself while Cooper set off to interview other potential witnesses.

"Relax, Carl. We've been through this before. Your things are safe, and if anything's missing or if we need it for evidence, we'll make sure it's replaced," Murray said, patting him on the shoulder. Carl drew back and downward, wincing in pain.

"Are you all right?" Murray noticed Carl's bruised left eye and swollen cheek.

"I'm fine."

Murray knew not to push the issue. Otherwise this potential informant would quit speaking and give him nothing. He needed Carl relaxed and chattering. He pulled a cigar out of his pocket and presented it to the beaten man.

"Here's something to make the pain more bearable then."

Carl snatched the cigar from Murray's hand and grinned as he put it under his nose, taking in the tobacco's aroma. Murray struck a wooden match and cupped the flame to light it. Carl stuck his prize into the flame and inhaled.

"Last night, did you see anything unusual?"

"Can't say that I did." Carl spoke around the cigar, smoke billowing from his mouth.

"Liar." Another man marched over from the group.

"Don't listen to him. He's nothing but a drunk," Carl said. The other man rushed over, enraged by the challenge.

"Hold on." Murray stepped in between the feuding men and turned his attention to the hostile man, "What's going on, Ed?"

"We've all heard strange noises in the alleys. They've gotten closer lately. And bolder. Like they don't care who hears them now. It's just a matter of time before—you know." Ed's voice trailed off. He looked away, kicking gravel and debris around. Murray studied Ed's odd behavior and realized whatever he saw frightened him more than he wanted to admit.

"Sounds like the booze to me," Carl said.

"He won't admit it because he's scared." Ed dismissed Carl's verbal prodding.

"When did you first notice these noises?" Murray

asked.

"It all started when he showed up." Ed pointed to a young, gaunt man huddled at the edge of the crowd. He hugged his chest to combat the breeze that cut through the young man's ripped up jeans and sleeveless shirt. Although difficult to discern through the layers of grime, an indistinguishable tattoo was on display on his right upper arm. The rest of his body, including his blond hair, echoed his arms—dirty and unkempt. But what Murray found most striking about the man was his gaze, a trait he found too often in young men in recent years. He couldn't have been much older than seventeen, and yet he possessed the stare of someone beyond his years, the vacant eyes of the young when the dark side of life tears away their innocence.

"Leave him alone!" Carl charged after Ed, Murray's grasp halting the assault. Carl scowled at his foe and continued clawing for him. Cooper and two uniformed officers hurried over to assist as soon as they spotted the ruckus.

"Stop," Murray said. "Ed, go with Detective Cooper. Carl, come with me." Murray took Carl by the arm, signaling to the officers it was okay, and walked out of earshot of Ed and the others and resumed their conversation. He hoped Carl was still riled up enough to slip up and reveal any indication of what happened.

"Sorry," Carl said.

"What's really going on between you two?" Murray relit both of their cigars.

"He won't give the kid a break. He wants him gone. And the others, they don't trust newcomers and Ed's been stirring things up, trying to blame him for everything."

"Who's the kid?"

"Kevin. Don't know his last name."

"What's his story?"

"Don't know. He doesn't talk much. I've been showing him the ropes, keeping him safe." Carl said.

"Is that how you got your limp and matching face?" Murray asked. Carl stayed silent and his expression gave Murray nothing, not even a flinch, but his eyes deceived him. Murray's question was rhetorical. "Better have that checked out at the clinic."

"I'll go to the clinic after I'm done smoking. Dr. Half Moon doesn't like it."

"Can't argue with that. She's smarter than we are." Murray handed him another cigar. "If things get too rough, contact me down at the station through patrol or however you want, just stay safe doing it."

As Cooper pulled away, steering with one hand and holding his cup with the other, he compared what little findings he had accumulated with Murray, "Other than the blood trail ending at the entrance, we found no physical evidence."

"Did anybody corroborate Ed's story?" Murray rolled down the passenger's side window and tossed out the butt end of his cigar.

"Not a one. Everyone claimed they either were asleep or didn't hear a thing." Cooper tipped his cup up and finished the dregs of his coffee. He put the empty cup into a stack of others still in the cup holder.

"Figures."

"Somebody will come forward. They always do," Cooper said.

"Unlikely. Did you see Carl? Half-beaten to death and he wouldn't say a word."

"Then why did Ed say something?"

"About what? Strange noises?" Murray lit another cigar. Cooper coughed and waved away the smoke. "The information was vague at best."

"Then why come to us?"

"He's scared. He doesn't want to say anything that will get him killed, but he wants help," Murray said.

"He knows we're going to increase our patrols around here now."

"Precisely, but it won't help our case, though." Silence and smoke filled the small space between the detectives, an introspective but troubling quiet. Murray continued, as if he needed to finish his final thoughts aloud, "I never found her husband's killer, or any solid leads to a suspect. The case went cold and I had nothing to follow up on. Everything about the case, his presence at the scene, the killer's method, it all seemed out of place."

"I'm not familiar with the case," Cooper said, his eyes still on the road.

"We found Nathan Brooks dead on an empty building's rooftop downtown among five other bodies, all known drug dealers or associates. It looked like a deal gone wrong. Except his presence didn't fit. We never found anything to substantiate any theory we thought of. The pieces didn't fit—the method Nathan died of—two of the men died from questionable means. Nothing made sense."

"What was so unusual?" Cooper asked.

"Nathan died from blood loss—a bullet wound to the gut and puncture wounds in the side of his neck. One assailant died from a broken neck, one from huge gashes to the throat, and the other two shot each other. Other than the handguns found at the scene, we never found out or were able to identify any of the murder weapons. And I never figured out why Nathan ended up there. The case left me with more questions than answers."

"No witnesses, lack of physical evidence, no indication of how the victim was taken there. What a mess," Cooper said, interjecting his thoughts on the matter.

"After a while, his wife only wanted to know *why.* She didn't care about any of the rest at that point. She wanted closure and I couldn't give it to her. I hate leaving cases unsolved. And so, here we are with another murder case without a solitary witness, no clear motive, and a blood trail that vanishes into Dead Man's Land."

"Don't worry," Cooper said, "we'll find who's responsible for this."

"That's not the point."

Rain clouds gathered in the inky sky and released a sudden, torrential downpour that drenched all below. Nathan stomped through puddles of anguish as they rippled on the sidewalk. He trudged along, drifting within the city uninhibited, giving free reign to the emotions that had manifested his sorrow into bloodlust. As virtue had taken its leave, he selected a weakened straggler amongst the herd of pedestrians and stalked her, studying her every inebriated move.

Lost in her drunken haze, the woman strayed from the safety of numbers and ventured into an isolated residential area, absent of light and activity from the lateness of the hour. As she searched for something familiar, she panicked, realizing how astray she had traveled. And in her haste, she stumbled through the vision-impairing rain and slipped on the wet pavement, falling into a saturated lawn. Her fingers sank into the mud beneath the grass as she clawed her way through the soaked ground, pulling herself to a nearby tree's slick trunk. Using the tree as a crutch, she struggled in her exhausted state and stood upright, recuperating from her fall.

He drew close, close enough to smell her inviting warm skin mixed with sweat and heady perfume radiating from her neckline's curves. Her heart pounded, fluttering from the eerie sensation that overtook her, and the rhythmic pulse beating in her chest quickened. The sound of it hastened his senses, and he felt its pounding, its beckoning call. Its thumping made his fangs protrude and invoked the still-fresh recollection of the taste of blood that coursed through her carotid arteries.

Terrified by whatever lay in wait behind her, the woman turned in apprehension and became blinded by movement too fast for her mind to register. She blinked, disoriented from her momentary lack of sight, and rubbed her eyes. She thought she caught a glimpse of something she couldn't identify, yet found nothing as she strained to see through the dense rainfall. She dismissed the notion, convincing herself that a raindrop blurred her vision, that her altered state of mind distorted her judgment. With a sigh of relief, she wobbled away.

Brushing aside his wet, dark-brown hair, Nathan stepped out from behind the tree she had leaned on and watched his prey leave unscathed. His memories intervened once again, superseding his instincts. He couldn't destroy such beauty when he gleamed into those radiant, steel-blue eyes that revived the deep-seeded memory of his beloved.

Rachael.

Her name, he remembered her name. Oh, how he missed the sound of it uttered from his lips. He spoke it aloud, taken aback by the passion he felt by simply saying her name and unable to fathom how he could have forgotten it.

Someone appeared from out of the darkness and approached the woman as she moved aimlessly through the rainstorm. Even by the din of the rain, Nathan knew the man was not of the living. His fluid, silent movement seemed unnatural even to the casual observer. He posed as a helpful samaritan, a middle-aged man in a grey trench coat, holding an umbrella. A chill crawled over Nathan's skin as the man grew closer to the woman, exuding his power over all within sight and beyond. Nothing stirred in the night, for nature had cleared all from death's encroachment.

The woman stopped in front of the man blocking her path, swaying in place, and then went still. He gazed into her eyes and told her of his hunger. She extended her wrist to him as an offering and he obliged her by taking her wrist and gently placed a kiss upon it. His eyes shimmered in the night, turning red as he wrapped his mouth around the appendage and bit down, watching Nathan while he displayed this deliberate act. Nathan's craving rose with the combination of the scent of blood amongst the rainfall and the visual accompanying it.

Nathan rushed over beside them, unsure what compelled him there. Was it a primal reaction? Or perhaps a lingering mortal inclination to save her? Either way, Nathan couldn't stop this even if he wanted to. His desire refused interference, and all involved, including the man's quarry, wanted this. The woman tilted her head backward, euphoric and breathless. The man released her wrist and took her in his arms as she arched back, her legs buckling.

"I believe it's time to get you home so you can rest and forget everything that happened tonight." The man's voice reverberated in a stir of echoes.

"That sounds like a good idea," the woman said. Her eyes remained fixed, in a trancelike state, clinging to the man.

"Who are you?" Nathan asked.

"After our guest is safe and on her way home."

As the taxi drove off, the man said, "Let's get out of the rain, shall we?"

"Something tells me I shouldn't trust you," Nathan said. "And since I don't know you, why should I follow you anywhere without at least asking your name?"

"Wise of you to question my intention but I ask you to follow me all the same. I can only promise that I mean you no harm. I won't force you to come with me or stop you from leaving at any time."

"You think your vague, unfounded promises will supersede reason?"

The man continued without acknowledging his statement, "My home isn't too far from here. I admit it's not as quaint as your place, but we'll make do. Come, we have much to discuss."

Nathan thought of every reason in the world why he shouldn't follow the viper into his pit, and still, he followed. He had experienced this being's might firsthand and realized if all went awry, how powerless he was against it. Despite this, he had to know.

In the heart of the city, they arrived at a luxurious, gothic-styled house. Adorned wood and stone-etched trimming and high peaks with guardian gargoyles edged along the rooftop. Inside, antique furnishings intermingled with modern appliances in an open, high-ceilinged spacious living area. The man hung his umbrella and coat on a free-standing coat rack next to the door as he entered. With his coat removed, Nathan saw that the man wore a tailored grey suit with black shoes that shined so finely they looked like they never ventured out into the rain. Nathan stood at the doorway, uncertain of his apprehension. He couldn't move past the doorframe, as if an invisible barrier prevented entry.

"Forgive me. Please come in," the man said.

Nathan felt the heaviness lift and allowed himself to advance through the doorway unhindered, "So much for your promises."

"I apologize for that. I forget the rules apply no matter the dwelling, even to our kind's domicile. Unless of course you enter a group's place, such as a brood, clan, or coven—

whatever term their group refers themselves as," the man said.

"Our kind?" Nathan asked.

"Vampires, Nathaniel. I assume you're either in severe denial or that I left you alone far too long. I hoped you would learn much of this on your own."

"You knew?" His mouth gaped open.

"It's complicated. I will explain all in due time. Pardon my miscalculation and my next comment, but do you know what you look like? You look as if you crawled out of your grave."

Nathan couldn't dispute the vampire's claim. He hadn't changed or bathed since his demise. His clothes dangled threadbare off his body and dirt coated his skin.

"The shower is this way. I believe I have clothes your size, or close enough to suffice," the vampire said, guiding him down a hall, through a bedroom into a bathroom with a walk-in shower with sliding glass doors and lavish, cream colored tiled walls and flooring with golden faucets and spouts.

The thought of a shower, regardless of his surroundings, sounded as wonderful to him as a man who's traveled through the desert and stumbled upon a water fountain. He stripped off his clothing, tossing them away in the trash, and stepped into the shower. He turned on the faucet that activated the three showerheads. Steaming hot water rained down on his encrusted pale skin and grime-laden hair. He lathered soap on his body and the heated water rinsed away the dirt, releasing tension he wasn't aware of. He dried off and stepped into the adjoining bedroom and found a cerulean blue suit with matching shirt laid neatly on the bed and a black tie and pocket square, both with a jacquard diamond pattern. The silken suit felt comfortable, soothing against his clean skin. It fit as if tailored for him. He returned to the living room where the vampire waited.

"Perfect fit. I knew it was your size. Please, sit." The vampire gestured to the couch.

"I thank you for your kindness but I'm ready for that explanation now." Nathan stood at the opposite end of the couch. He attempted to not sound ungracious. He failed.

"Your response demonstrates my point. Your mortal emotions run deep within you, clouding your rational senses. They will pass in time."

"Who are you to dictate what I need to know? I don't know what you want from me but I'm nobody's fool and refuse to play these games. I either get answers or I'm out the door." Nathan gestured at the door, his anger rose, and hate emanated throughout the room.

"Refuse and you merely play the pawn."

The comment triggered Nathan's breaking point. He turned toward the door, not wishing to continue such a futile conversation and fight a losing battle. The vampire stood, speaking at Nathan's back.

"Pardon my quip. Please stay. You're free to leave, as promised, but where will you go? Back to the graveyard? Your enemies will surely find you and I will not always be there to protect you." Nathan stopped momentarily, contemplating the reasonable argument for staying. The vampire stepped forward and put a reassuring hand on Nathan's shoulder. A chill of dark energy ran through his shoulder from the vampire's lightest touch. Nathan turned and stepped away as the vampire backed to the end of the couch.

"I have no enemies," Nathan said.

"None you're aware of. There are dangers you need to know before venturing forth alone, although I don't recommend it. Let's speak further about this before you make any rash decisions."

As much as it pained Nathan to admit it, the vampire's logic was sound. He came for answers and leaving without hearing what the vampire had to say accomplished nothing. If anything, he would only lose time if falsehoods were told. Nathan headed to the couch. His mind teetered with ambivalence. He sat on the opposing end of the vampire and asked, "Who are you?"

"I am Zander," the vampire said.

"How long have you. . ." Nathan's question trailed off.

"It's been centuries, even longer, longer than I care to remember."

"How did you become. . ."

Zander interrupted, "That's a long story, one for another time. What you really want to hear is why I brought you here."

"Along with some other things, yes. But first, I want to know what is with all the secrecy? Why not tell me all of this earlier?" Nathan asked.

"I won't tell you everything now. There are too many mundane details and I want you to concentrate on the important issues at hand. Think of me as your mentor, your guide concerning the world that's hidden from the living. What you don't realize is your importance in the scheme of the current situation," Zander said.

"Not an encouraging statement."

"I couldn't have said it better but you must know *how* dire so you can appreciate what I'm conveying." Zander paused and looked at Nathan, "Agreed?"

Nathan sighed, "I'll do my best but no promises."

"Fair enough," Zander nodded. "You may find this ludicrous, especially since, as you have stated, we don't even know each other. But there are forces working against you already and they would rather see you destroyed than undergo my tutelage. I kept you hidden to keep you anonymous, safe. But when you fed for the first time, your power spread throughout the city. Without you knowing, you exposed yourself. And now your enemies know of your existence."

"Really?" Nathan raised an eyebrow and his voice went deadpan, "And who are these enemies I've never met?"

"They're referred to as Seditionists. Their objective is for vampires to rule over humans. Don't underestimate them. You may not know them but they certainly know you and that makes them a dangerous adversary."

"What does this have to do with me?"

"Vampires have survived this long through incognito, hidden from most of mankind. Throughout our history, any time vampires reveal themselves, they are hunted down and destroyed. The Seditionists believe they are at war and recruitment is a priority. You're the kind of weapon they're looking for." Zander stood and paced around the room as he spoke. Nathan recognized the wrinkles in Zander's brow, the first real sign of emotion he had seen.

"Hold on a minute. You said most of mankind,"

Nathan remarked.

"Yes, certain government officials know of us. And like all political relations, promises and compromises are made. Agreements we uphold and indiscretions they allow."

"Such as?"

"The railway incident. I soothed things over with our contacts, explained to them that the death occurred by accident and that you fed on someone dying. No harm, no foul. Just try and feed without killing. Sometimes it's too late to contact these people. Try feeding on psychic energies. It's been effective for you so far."

"How?"

"Through touch for now. With training, you'll learn to channel your powers through other means."

"So, killing isn't allowed and I don't have to drink blood to feed?" Nathan said, confused. This contradicted any myths he had heard about vampires. Lore felt more believable than the truth.

"You have the gift of feeding either way. Not all vampires have that power and even fewer can sustain themselves. With training and practice, you will learn how to channel untapped energies and command them. When you touched the man at the tracks, other than the elation of feeding, did you experience anything else?" Zander asked.

"I saw images, memories of his. And then, someone appeared in a dark cloak. His presence frightened me, he felt so hollow," Nathan said as the thought haunted him.

"Vampires sense the presence of their own kind and others, although masking our presence is possible. But what you saw was Death collecting your victim's soul. Vampires reside in the realms of the living *and* the dead, even though we exist in the realm of the living. From time to time, we can see into the realm of the dead."

"Can we speak to the dead?" Nathan's tone, as well as his attention, rose.

"She is gone, nothing will change that."

Nathan stood rigid, clenching his fists. He had his fill of admonishment for one day, "I've listened to you and now it's time for you to answer one simple question—can we speak with them?"

Zander said nothing, and with that, Nathan stomped toward the door. Zander spoke at his back before Nathan exited, "In slumber, if you are powerful enough and have the ability to make it through the other side without getting lost. That's why some of our kind sleeps for so long, never waking, choosing to stay in a self-induced limbo or risk vanishing into the abyss of the realm. It's a dangerous journey. Don't head down that path, I beg you. Your pain will only intensify on a path you may never wake from."

Nathan paused and then stormed out, flying back to the serenity of the graveyard. He rushed into the mausoleum and closed the door behind him. He settled onto the slab he put his victim under, ready for slumber. He hoped it would work, contacting her this way. He had to try, had to see her, hear her voice, if only for one last time. But how would he explain what happened to him and why he never told her while she lived? These thoughts took him to a dark place, a place where guilt and misery manifests, burying itself so deep into the depths of one's self that it grows roots, ensuring its difficult if not impossible removal. And with these clouded thoughts, tenebrous sleep consumed him.

Chapter Three

As Cooper and Murray stepped into the Captain's office, Murray slammed the door shut, rattling the office's glass frame. Captain Deveraux sat at his desk, unfazed by the detective's overt act, and continued eating his lunch—a baked potato and iced tea.

"You wanted to see us?" Murray asked.

"Yes, please sit," Deveraux said, his soft, Southern drawl commanding respect while holding its refined quality. He stood, wiped his mouth, and cleared the food from his desk to a side table.

"What smells like bacon in here?" Murray asked, sitting at a chair in front of the Captain's desk, with Cooper following suit.

"My baked potato."

"Your potato?"

"I add salt, pepper, and bacon grease for flavor."

"Sounds disgusting."

"You Midwest boys always drown everything with cheese or catsup. Now that's blasphemy."

"Shows that neither one of you have been in the military," Cooper said. Murray leaned back in his chair, turned toward his partner and gave him a disapproving look. Cooper shrugged it off.

"Now you probably guessed I didn't call you in here to

discuss my lunch," Deveraux said.

"He's a perceptive one. That's why he's in charge," Murray said to Cooper. Deveraux ignored the comment.

"Any new developments in the Brooks case?" Deveraux sat back down.

"None so far," Murray said.

"No witnesses have come forward. We've been door to door around the surrounding neighborhoods but have come up empty," Cooper said.

Murray responded, "We're still waiting on forensics with the lab and autopsy reports but it'll be a while before we get anything."

"I might have something here for you to work with." Deveraux pulled out a file from his desk drawer and handed it to the detectives. He took out a comb and groomed his mustache. Murray skimmed over the file, then handed it to his partner as he scowled at Deveraux.

"There's no body, only a lot of blood. How is this related?" Murray asked.

"It's a lead that needs following up." Deveraux put the comb back in his drawer.

"The industrial park is next to the railway. It's worth a look," Cooper said to Murray.

"No, it's not," Murray said to Cooper and then brought his attention back to Deveraux. "Why don't you have forensics collect from the scene and be done with it?"

"I don't believe in coincidence when it comes to murder. See if we can connect the dots." Deveraux said.

"And after we pencil in this vague image in our book of connect the dots, we can color it with crayons and then Mommy can put it up on the refrigerator," Murray said.

Deveraux snarked, "You don't seem very enthusiastic about your new assignment."

Murray snatched the file from Cooper, sniffed it and said, "This smells about as bad as your potato." Murray stood and tossed the file onto the desk. Papers spilled out on the flat surface from where it landed, "Thanks, Quinton, for adding dead wood to my caseload."

Murray turned to leave until Deveraux said, "Please stay a spell. We have more to chat about. Detective Cooper, please excuse us. This is a private matter."

Without a word, Cooper scooped up the file's scattered contents. Murray shot daggers at Deveraux. His captain stood and leaned against his deck and returned the gesture. Both men looked eye to eye at each other, remaining silent until Cooper finished gathering the file and left.

"Why, oh why, George, must everything be so difficult with you? I had one request and you can't do that without seeing fault in it." Deveraux said.

"Whenever something doesn't make sense, I question it. Why stall my investigation? What did I do to piss the brass off now?" Murray asked.

"For starters, when in view of the public, you need to wear a coat or jacket to cover that arsenal you carry around."

"Old habit from my Gang Unit days."

"And again, I have reports of you smoking at crime scenes. I'm really trying to maintain departmental standards and give leniency, but I can't if you continue to ignore the rules."

"Don't start with that. I was trying to get a potential witness to talk. None of this has anything to do with the case." Murray leaned in on the desk, "Do you want this case solved, stalled, or buried?"

Deveraux collapsed back into his chair, "I really don't know what to do with you anymore. Ever since the first Brooks case, you think there's some great conspiracy aligned against you. You're as stubborn as a dog with a bone."

"We both know you're sending me on a fool's errand. Why? Someone pressuring you and now you're looking to save your own hide?"

"There are outside influences, I cannot deny that, my friend. But let's push those issues aside and get to the heart of the matter—that you believe departmental rules are only suggestions."

"The only thing that matters to me is solving crimes. When did you forget that? Since your promotion to a chair? Has that object sapped every ounce of being a cop out of your ass?" Murray's voice elevated into a scream. The tension had spilled over and a floodgate of emotions burst forth. His hatred for hypocrisy rivaled only his loathing of the media. In his view, for as many years as Murray had been on the force, reporters were there to leak information, stonewall access to witnesses, and overall, destroy investigations. But at least he understood why the news did what it did. Hypocrisy had no reason for being.

Despite Murray's tirade, Deveraux stayed calm, "Our job and the rules that govern them go hand and hand. You've never understood it and that's why you've never raised in rank."

Murray pushed away from the desk, "That's the difference between you and me. I didn't become a cop to fulfill any political agendas or take office." He slammed the office door as he stormed out, marched through the maze of partitions to his desk, grabbing his coat as he left.

"What was all that about?" Cooper asked, following Murray to the elevator.

"Politics," Murray said as he put his coat on while walking toward the elevator.

On their way out, they passed a large man who stood in front of a cluttered desk, his bushy mustache covering his upper lip, highlighting his droopy Basset hound-face. He spoke, "I heard you got called into the principal's office."

"Well, you know what they say," Murray said while he stepped in the elevator and turned toward the man, "you can't see the forest for the trees."

As the elevator doors closed, the man's smile, hidden under his mustache, drooped with the rest of his face and he yelled, "Screw you, Murray!"

"What was that about?" Cooper pressed the first floor button.

"Phillips was a star lineman for Nebraska, almost went pro until he got drunk and hit a tree."

"That could have been any one of us."

"True. But his ego caused his downfall. His teammates tried to stop him and he broke a receiver's jaw to get to his car. Messed up his knee and ruined his football career all in one night. And then, rumor has it that he claimed the accident was a hit and run."

"Hence the tree jokes."

"Exactly."

"Are we off to check out the scene?"

The elevator dinged, noting their arrival to the first floor.

"It's a dead end," Murray said. The elevator opened and Murray headed toward the front entrance with Cooper following. "I want answers before the trail goes cold. Tomorrow we shake a hornet's nest. Pick me up early. We're going to the farmer's market."

Although Cooper thought Murray's statement was strange, and despite the fact that Cooper had been partners with Murray for only a few brief months, he followed along with the plan without question. Cooper found that Murray had unorthodox methods but that they were effective.

As Murray flung the door open and exited the station, he stopped in his tracks and said with disdain, "Great."

A young woman hurried over to the detectives, almost tripping in her high heels and questionably short skirt. She flung her long, straight brownish-blond hair out of her face with the whip of her neck as she made her way, microphone in hand, through the people coming and going from the building. The cameraman tailed her with his camera already mounted on his shoulder, filming by the time they reached the detectives.

"No." Murray extended his hand out and blocked the camera. The cameramen stopped filming and lowered the camera.

"Really? Just no? Please, detective. Just a minute of your time," the reporter requested.

"Okay, Ms. Brewer. Just one minute." Murray turned to his partner and gave a devilish grin, the type that indicated he was up to no good. Cooper widened his eyes, indicating this was a bad idea, but his silent plea went unheeded. The cameraman raised the camera and the reporter began her spiel into the camera, turning to Murray. Cooper backed out of frame and wandered a few steps away, watching the inevitable mistake unfold.

"This is Sylvia Brewer with Action 9 News. I'm here with the lead detective in the city's latest homicide. Detective Murray, are there any new leads in the case?"

"We haven't made an arrest, but we have leads to a possible suspect and have collected evidence that may link the suspect to the scene and the possible murder weapon," Murray said.

"Really?" Brewer said, doubt bled through her voice and the corners of her mouth curled down in frustration. She had dealt with Murray before and hoped in vain this time would be different.

"Yes, I believe it was Professor Plum." Murray said.

The cameraman ceased filming and Brewer lowered her microphone.

"It was done in the bedroom and I think they did it with the candlestick but I'm not a hundred percent about that."

"Oh, that's mature," Brewer said.

"Coming from you, *someone like you*, that means absolutely nothing,"

"What have I ever done to you to make you dislike me? We both want the same thing—the truth."

"You wouldn't know what the truth was if it stood in front of you and hit you on the side of your head with Plum's candlestick."

"Would it kill you to at least act civil to me, if not professional?"

"If you want civil, talk to Captain Deveraux. He'll tell you how unprofessional I really am." Murray turned to Cooper, "Hey, you want to handle the rest of this?"

"I'm sure I can't do any more damage," Cooper said as he walked over to them.

"Don't underestimate yourself," Murray said as he departed. He went about ten feet and looked over his shoulder and yelled, "So long, Miss Scarlett."

"He's really a gem of a guy once you get to know him," Cooper assured.

"Yeah, a flawed gem," Brewer said.

Nathan's tangible senses were absent and all enveloped into a darkened abyss. He didn't know if he had vanished from the physical plane or if he had disappeared entirely, wiped from existence. Whatever this place represented, it existed somewhere far beyond man's reach or comprehension. There was no physical world to latch to here, no life nor death. He only subsisted as a spectral traveler on a passage through the unknown.

He waited for something to happen, like a latent epiphany that emerges from the recesses of some forgotten place and would deliver him from the endless, monotonous nothing that loomed over him. Unable to discern reality from dream, his perception of time abandoned its post, went aloof, and left him with his preoccupation, his sole companion on his lonely expedition. His mind focused to his only thought.

Rachael.

He could not, nor wanted, to erase her from his mind.

The mere inkling of this plagued his mind. He wanted a second chance, to make things right again.

Yet, his determination wasn't enough to overcome his despair. His thought turned against him and he imploded, unraveled within and under the immense weight of self-imposed guilt, lost his grip on his dwindling sanity. A numbing sensation crept around him, encapsulating his mind as it dulled and suffocated his awareness. Was this her fate also? Trapped alone in an eternity of emptiness?

Reality was a vindictive mistress, cold and unsympathetic. He slipped into despondency and stared deep into a chasm of morose memories, too agonizing to remember but too precious to discard. Fueled by thoughts of despair, his mind stagnated into a surreal numbness. Giving into its desolation, these festering ideals consumed him, trapped him within an inescapable stasis.

All looked bleak when a dim beacon glimmered in the void, beckoning his presence. The entity's arrival uplifted his spirit and drowned his smothering grief. Driven by the luster glistening through the sable, his wits turned vivacious and battled through dismal thoughts fermenting in the dregs of his mind.

The radiance of the glow waned for him. Its warm, soothing manifestation drove him to the expanding light. He struggled with how a minute entity honed such power as it widened its reach, enveloping the darkness around it. He gravitated to the light, feeling a sense of serenity pulsating from the source, never questioning its purity or inviting intent. Still, anything beat wandering in emptiness forever.

An indefinite amount of time lapsed as the light expanded and intensified into an overwhelming presence that blanketed the area ahead in a blinding, infinite lumination. As he moved from one extreme surrounding to another, fear of what lie beyond unsettled and skewed his perceptions. He dwelled far too long in the comfort of the dark and its shadow hid his vulnerability to where he grew dependent on its bleakness, like someone institutionalized that is discarded without thought or preparation back into society, inept and afraid of the ever-changing ways of the world, and dread overshadowed the elusive freedom he sought not but a moment before.

Between the ardent whiteout and pitch black, trepidation stifled any further movement, and his mind swirled in ambivalence. Both the light and dark summoned him yet he resisted their pull. Then a familiar wariness clung onto him and his indecision betrayed him as he fell back into the void. The mundane prison that had nearly devoured him lay claim to him once more and pulled him away. He gave in to the vacuum of despair, his stamina depleted and surrending to his fate as he withdrew from the fading light's radiance. His memories diminished and blurred and then paled from remembrance.

As he sunk back into blackness, an unseen force ceased his plunge and throttled him into the luminous white. The aura's extremes blinded him, testing his sanity. An emotional current built then purged his disturbing attachment to the dark. It penetrated his essence, stripped his defenses, and revealed his fears. Exposed by its power, he felt violated, mentally raped, and anger edged over him.

He tried opening his eyes only to close them instantly, the concentrated glow too intense to absorb all at once. He squinted and adjusted his vision to the bright climate.

Finally, he attuned his sight and opened his eyes, siphoning the brilliance around him. All lingering anger, fear, and uncertainty relented and withered into nothing.

He pressed through and the inaudible voice sounded out again, and guiding him on his trek. The light had shattered his darkened surroundings into pieces and a new backdrop faded into being, replacing the harsh contrasts between black and white. Grass shimmered on a picture-perfect rolling hillside decorated in wild flowers. Birds sang in melodic unison as butterflies and various other insects busied themselves in the field. Dew and jasmine filled the sweet smell of nature's backdrop.

This peaceful setting felt unreal and his mind insisted on rejecting it, questioning its verity. He found it all too convenient, most likely wrapped in the glamour of deceit. His ascension over the hill revealed what he sought. At the bottom of the hill he discovered a winding, dirt ravine coiled and twisted at a downward slope that led in the distance to a gothic, stone castle, its grim reflection shadowed by grey clouds on a vast purple sky. Thunder rumbled in protest as lightning flickered through the dark, purplish-tinged clouds. This was his destination, the passage to a reckoning, and he wondered at what price his obsession would cost him.

Nathan ventured through the ravine, his vision impaired as a jet stream kicked up dust that blew through the path ensnared with decrepit branches that bent and creaked in the wind. He reached the castle after what seemed as long as his travels through the dark and ascended the stairs. A pair of gargoyles flanked the tall, arched double doors of the castle that turned and watched Nathan as he approached. Both doors swung inward upon nearing the wooden monoliths and closed unaided as he passed through the threshold. The oval room, lit by several torches along the curved walls, captivated him with its spacious, ornate ambiance. Large marble pillars stretched up on an unseen ceiling. The multiple archways and ledges had faceted stonework carved in ribbed tracery, giving an impression of sinister beauty. Across from the main entryway, opposing dual spiral staircases reached up, angled as if joined somewhere beyond sight.

From the left, a black-cloaked figure glided through one of the many doors along the curved walls toward Nathan. A pale man removed the hood and said, "Welcome. We've been expecting you. I hope your journey wasn't too unnerving?"

"I didn't realize I was expected," Nathan said.

"But of course, I can see all in this realm for it is mine to watch. What did you think you would find?"

"I thought I'd see ghosts."

"And you have, in a sense, depending on your beliefs. One sees any number of preconceived forms I have when I escort them. Most become lost unless I offer my assistance."

"So that was you?"

The pale man nodded.

"Who are you?"

"It is of no consequence since you will remember little. But if it comforts you, a very long time ago I was called Lawrence."

"Why won't I remember?"

"Think of this place like a dream realm. One rarely

recalls their dreams, and if they do, they are fragmented at best."

"Fragmented or not, I've come to see my wife. Will you take me to her?"

"I shall, but I must warn you, you will find the experience bittersweet. Your stay will be shorter than you wish." The pale man proceeded to a door across the room.

"Why?" Nathan stood still and looked at the being heading toward the door. He couldn't move and didn't know why. There was something sinister in the man's statement.

The pale man stopped, turned his head around and said, "Because you don't belong here."

Nathan trailed behind until they reached their destination. The pale man opened the door. A bright light, a light more intense than anything he had experienced on his trip here, shone through. Its glare made it impossible to see into. Nathan tried to enter but couldn't pass.

"You can't go in. Call to her, she will hear you," the pale man said.

"Rachael!" The light seemed so bright that it consumed sound.

An echoing response came, "Nathan."

"I'm here. I miss you so much." Nathan's lip quivered and his body flushed and tingled.

"Nathan, find our son before it's too late."

"I'm so sorry," a skeletal hand grabbed Nathan by the shoulder and spun him around. The pale man's fleshless skull uttered at him, "It's time to go."

"No, wait!"

And then, all went blank.

Chapter Four

The weather yielded a mild-tempered morning with little breeze, and as a result, the farmer's market was unusually crowded. Murray pulled into the bustling parking lot across from the courthouse where the market was held, found a spot at the far end, and killed the engine. Cooper continued reading files on his tablet and sipped his coffee. Murray lit a cigar, inhaled, and puffed smoke in Cooper's direction. His partner coughed, waving through the cloud that hung around his head.

"That's breakfast, I suppose," Cooper said, coughing.

"You drink yours, I smoke mine," Murray said.

Cooper wrinkled his expression and nodded in disgust. "Thanks for sharing. Do you know what your lungs must look like?"

"About as black as your kidneys, so don't push it," Murray said. "You look worn out. Rough night?"

"Late night dinner date."

"She must be a keeper then."

"I hope so." Cooper lowered his tablet and put down his coffee in the holder, "It's only been a month, but I really like her. Our schedules complicate things, although I think it's worth it."

"If her schedule is as messed up as ours is, then it makes it easy. So, what does she do? Not another flight

41

attendant I hope." Murray said.

Cooper hesitated and then said, "She's a reporter."

Murray pushed his cigar into the ashtray, teeth clenched. "Let me guess, little Miss Scarlett, Sylvia Brewer."

"I wanted to tell you, but. . ."

"You've compromised our investigation," Murray interrupted.

"No, I haven't."

"Really? Explain that one to the Captain and let's see what he says."

"You're overreacting."

"You knew how important this case is to me, now it'll get yanked because you're sleeping with the enemy." Murray continued his rant, ignoring Cooper's attempts to calm him down. "Never trust the media. They're bottom feeders, every last one of them."

"I trust her over some of those crooked slime balls that we work with. Wake up, George. Nobody plays by the rules anymore—cops, reporters—nobody." Cooper had had enough of Murray's indignation.

"There's a big difference between cops and reporters. Any one of those so-called slime balls would take a bullet for you. Now find a reporter that would do the same," Murray said, his eyes narrowed and his brow furrowed in rage. Cooper returned the glower, rebuffing the scowl.

Vying for their attention, a man wearing Ray-Ban aviator sunglasses rapped on the driver's side window, prompting them to roll the window down. Murray hit the switch, lowering it just enough to hear the man.

"Hey, you love birds, I hate to break up your domestic

quarrel here, but the boss says the apples are going fast so you'd better hurry up," the man said, smirking.

"Tell him I'll be right there, Noodles," Murray said. He rolled up his window and opened the door as Cooper followed suit. The man walked away and disappeared in the congested humanity.

"Noodles?" Cooper asked.

"One of the captains," Murray said.

"Why the name?"

"Oh that. He's a trained chef. He makes great noodles. We'd better not keep the boss waiting." Murray and Cooper got out of the car. Cooper let the conversation drop, only because of work. This wasn't over by any means.

"Why are we here?" Cooper asked.

"Big Mike owns this city, legitimately and otherwise. I need to know if he's behind this," Murray said and walked toward the crowd. Cooper followed.

"But why would he tell you anything?"

"He won't. It's like poker. I have to guess if he's bluffing."

The detectives maneuvered their way to a stand surrounded by baskets of assorted fruits and vegetables. A large, imposing man standing over six feet tall leaned on the counter, engaging a customer as he completed their transaction. Though his oversized belly defiantly pressed against his buttoned-down shirt, his solid arms bulged out from his sleeves with muscular tension. The other man behind the counter had his arms crossed and watched around the booth, stone faced. Although opposite in stature, one could tell they were related by their facial features, olive skin tone, and dark hair. He looked in the detective's direction and whispered in the large man's ear. The large man nodded and gestured to the detectives, waving them over. Murray nodded and approached.

"Why would a mobster spend his Saturday selling fruit?" Cooper asked.

"It's an old family tradition. They do it in Kansas City and so they do it here," Murray said. Both men came around the counter to greet them.

"Good to see you." The big man shook Murray's hand and then hugged him like they were relatives.

"How are you doing, Mike?" Murray asked as he hugged and then pulled back.

"Weather's great so business is thriving," Big Mike said. "And this must be Bill Cooper. Impressive resume. Military police, tour in Iraq. Pretty young to make detective. Would have made your folks proud if they were still alive."

"Likewise, Mr. Spinelli, likewise." Cooper's body tensed and he tightened his jaw. Murray was right; this guy knew everything about him, and that made him feel uneasy.

Meanwhile, the smaller man shook Murray's hand but certainly didn't embrace in a hug, which made sense to Cooper. The man didn't look very friendly even as he shook hands with Murray. Up close, the man's profile didn't lie. His small frame revealed a sturdy, barreled torso and well-cut thin muscle. He turned and greeted Cooper, extending his hand. Cooper looked into the short man's unusual eyes. Their round, beady shape hardly showed his eye whites. Because of their deep black coloring, it made it difficult to distinguish whether he looked straight or sideways. He shook hands and then noticed the small man's abnormally long, boney fingers that wrapped around his.

"I'm Angelo." His fingers slithered around Cooper's hand further and then clamped down, tightening his grasp like a boa constrictor. Angelo stepped in closer, with Cooper's hand locked in a vise grip of a hold, and whispered into his ear, "I'm ambidextrous and I've got your gun hand."

Cooper lost composure briefly and his eyes widen. Despite his training, he had let his guard down and, in other circumstances, it could have cost him his life.

Big Mike and Murray, as well as the man in sunglasses who appeared from nowhere, laughed, bringing levity to the friction between the two men who now stared at each other, fury displayed on their faces. Angelo released his grip and stepped back. Cooper wiggled his fingers, urging blood flow back into his hand. His jaw stiffened even more, his ire at himself outweighing any anger he had at Angelo.

"You'll have to excuse my brother's unorthodox humor," Big Mike said, still laughing. Cooper stayed silent and continued his glower.

"No hard feelings," Angelo smirked.

"Of course not," Murray intervened. The detective's looks said it all; Cooper showed overt anger and Murray's composed stare indicated to him to let it go.

"And now, onto business. What brings you here besides a great deal on produce?" Big Mike asked.

"But you already know why I'm here," Murray said.

"It usually takes the department longer to get to me when these unfortunate things happen."

"The department doesn't know I'm here. I'm here on my own accord."

"Personal?"

"You can say that. Look, two crime scenes lead to your front door. You know what comes next: surveillance, pressure on you and your associates. It's bad for business and a waste of our time. Anything you can tell me to speed this up?" Murray asked.

Big Mike put his arm over Murray's shoulder and walked him to a clearing behind the stand, "Our families go way back, so I'll do you this favor. Let me tie up any loose ends and I'll make sure this all goes away. I can even put a big bow on it for you if you want."

"You won't have to if I get to them first."

"Fair enough."

"I don't need to mention that I won't hesitate to take anyone down if they get in my way."

"Hey, business is business."

Cooper was waiting in the car when Murray opened the back door and placed two full apple baskets in the rear seat.

"What in the world are you doing with all those apples?" Cooper asked.

"Half of them are the Captain's." Murray climbed in behind the steering wheel and shut the door. "He uses them for his famous apple pies. Is something wrong?"

"Why would you buy apples from a mobster?"

"They're great and cheap, if you know how to haggle."

Cooper sighed and asked, "What did you find out from Spinelli?"

"The good news is that we can eliminate him from our list of suspects. The bad news is that now it's a race. If we don't find this guy first, then all we're going to find is another blood trail ending in Dead Man's Land," Murray said. He started the car and pulled into traffic.

"He told you that?"

"In a way, yeah." Murray put a cigar in his mouth, "He talked too much. I think he didn't like this mess placed on his doorstep and now he wants recompense."

"Why is he so forthcoming with you?" Cooper asked.

"When I was in K.C., a sting operation turned bad. The Spinelli and Avella families had made a truce in order to conduct a business deal. At the last minute, right before we found out what the deal entailed, an informant told us that Paulie, Big Mike's father, was getting hit by a third party at the meeting place. We were already in position, so we had no choice but to stop it." Murray lit his cigar.

"I take it you stopped the hit."

"Barely. We gunned down the assassins before they got to him. Luckily, no civilians got hurt, but we lost Simecka and I blocked a bullet meant for Paulie. My vest saved me."

"You took a bullet for a mobster?"

"If I hadn't, there would have been a war that lasted for months."

"I can't imagine a worse scenario—saving a mobster while watching one of my fellow officers die."

"Tell me about it."

She had moved everything. Nothing remained as beforehand; he barely recognized the kitchen. She had torn out the wallpaper and painted the walls bright beige. Only the oak cabinets survived the remodeling. She rearranged everything to her liking, from furniture placement to where the coffee mugs resided—they had eluded him for the past fifteen minutes. He rummaged through items moving plates and strewing glasses and bowls around all the cabinets and across the counter below. He shoved canned goods aside, spices and cereal boxes tumbling in his haphazard exploration, accomplishing nothing but the destruction of a tidy, organized room in a matter of minutes. He continued rifling through cabinets until Laura walked in.

"Not even back a day and you've made a mess," Laura said, dropping her laptop bag and purse from her right shoulder to the kitchen table.

"Where in the world did you put the coffee mugs?" Murray asked.

"Over here above the coffee machine." Laura walked over to the opposite side of the kitchen and opened the cabinet above the coffee maker with her right hand and picked up two mugs by their handles with the same hand, "Some detective you are."

She placed the mugs upright on the counter and poured steaming coffee into the mugs. She loved the coffee maker's auto timer feature she set to brew fresh coffee upon her return from work. No waiting. Perfect.

Murray ignored her sarcastic remark, distracted by her radiant presence. He couldn't help but look over his shoulder at her as she poured the coffee, ogling at her from her high heels to her finely sculpted calves that peeked through her skirt's back slit. His gaze continued up over her backside to her long sleeved blouse that covered the scars on her shoulder from the gunshot wounds that rendered her left arm lifeless. With her brunette hair pinned up, the nape of her neck revealed her smooth skin that always smelled so sweet. He had been away from home far too long.

Regardless, her presence stunned him, made him swoon. Their marriage difficulties didn't consist of intimacy problems or a lack of physical attraction toward each other, far from it. But somewhere along the way, their relationship got damaged, and he didn't know how to fix it, salvage it. Hell, anymore they fought for no good reason. The tension between them stifled any meaningful communication they had. He was at a loss. And yet, he came back, like a lovesick teenager. He loved her, but did that matter? He had ended two previous marriages the same way, asking himself the same questions. Then again, his second marriage lasted no time at all and he didn't consider it valid. He should have had it annulled, but why bother? She hardly stuck around while they were together, let alone for the divorce.

Laura walked over, placed a mug next to him on the counter, and headed over to the kitchen table, grabbing her mug along the way.

She sat down and sipped her coffee. He took a hold of the mug—not by the handle—he never grabbed the handle for some strange reason he himself didn't understand, and tried the warm brew.

He took a sip and pulled the mug away, "That's hot."

"Coffee isn't hot enough unless you singe your lips on it. You know that, you big baby."

The delicious coffee tasted of actual flavor, unlike the crude, blackened tar he drank at the office or the wretched cups of toxic waste Cooper bought for them at the convenience store. No, this was the real thing. She purchased the beans at a specialty shop and ground them herself. She drank only the best, being a coffee snob and all. He never thought about that until now, facing her in the redecorated kitchen, her kitchen. Any input he expressed about the remodeling went out with the wallpaper, as if his opinion didn't matter.

"I see you redid everything to your liking," he said, his sarcasm bleeding through, despite his avoid-confrontation plan. He couldn't keep up the façade of idle chatter. What remained unsaid deafened the uneasy silence they had danced around so far. He couldn't help himself. After all, it was his kitchen too.

"Yes, I did," she said, annunciating those three words, telling Murray he screwed up when he made that comment. "You lost your say when you walked out and didn't return for three months."

"Laura, do we really need to go over this again?"

"We never talked about it in the first place, that's the problem. And repeating the same thing over and over again is the only way I can get through that thick skull of yours." Laura's anger seeped through the longer she spoke.

"Why call me then, if I'm so hopeless? So we can fight in person instead of over the phone?" Murray sat the mug on the counter.

"I called because I want you back home, for good. No more walking out when things get rough. And I want you home because I miss you, I love you. Don't you get it?"

"No, I don't. You say all those things and you show it by starting in on me and then you throw the remodel in my face. So no, I don't get it."

"Then I guess you never will. You've never taken the time to understand our relationship. It makes me wonder if you ever cared about us. You mean the world to me, and you're the only person that can hurt me the way you do." Her voice quivered and broke. Rage and sadness swelled in her eyes.

"Hurt you? I haven't been home," he said, looking around the room. "I figured you didn't want me around. All we do is fight."

"You're never here, in mind or body. If you're not out drinking, that is. If you're home, your mind is elsewhere, on a case."

"I'm a cop. Work is always on my mind. It's the sacrifice all cops make."

Laura picked up her mug and flung it at Murray. He ducked just before it flew by his head and shattered on the cabinet behind him. Ceramic shards and blistering liquid splashed on his back. He didn't expect such a reactionary response from her. She was usually the composed one.

"Save your sanctimonious ramblings for the rookies. Sacrifice? I lost the use of my arm in the line of duty. But I never, ever, took any of my work, no matter how emotionally draining, home with me. Now you get out of this house tonight and think about that. I'm going out to dinner and then to bed—alone!" She picked up her purse and stormed out, slamming the front door behind her.

"Well, that didn't go well," he said out loud.

Although comatose, Nathan's mind remained in perpetual thought; his essence pulled back through his travels by an unseen force, similar to that that drew him here. Incomplete as they seemed, erratic memories, past mysteries shrouded in hazy particulars of his fragmented fate, emerged as a haunting reminder of a nightmare come true. A frightful image burned into his mind—the night of his mortal death. He remembered being snatched from the streets, carried up to the rooftops in someone's grasp, blackness, and then a piercing pain in his neck. It paralyzed him completely, and he grew rigid under its clenching control over his body. When released, he dropped to his knees and crumbled into a fetal position, incapacitated. Blood flowed from his wounds, his life drained away. As he lay dying, his mind departed and gave way to anguish. Gunshots blended into the fading, muffled into the nothingness that followed.

He woke abruptly. His mind crashed through the beyond, back into the material plane and into consciousness. He opened his eyes. His pupils focused immediately and adapted to the dark abode. He outstretched his ashen arms and levitated to an upright position. A current of power swelled in him and reached out. His innate perception sensed the presence of danger that drew near.

He stepped outside and looked to the skies as moonlight beams flashed through the stark clouds that billowed past the luminous, full-harvest moon. Its gravity's pull fed his vigor that danced along his skin like static electricity. The satellite's ominous glow augmented the eerie ambiance that harbored the seed of dark suspicion. He stretched out a hand and released an energy that spread throughout the graveyard, divulging four figures in the distance advancing upon him. He felt their power extend across the environs. They pushed their own force against his until a stalwart between them mounted and created an energy surge that built until it imploded and bust outward. Its impact formed a rippling shockwave that sounded in a thunderclap and blew foliage and debris aside. Nathan staggered, gained his equilibrium, and awaited the other's next move.

Out from the dust and shadows, one of the four beings stepped into sight. Sinister mirth filled the air; the creature's laughter emitted a dark energy as he moved closer. The menacing noise saturated the night and resounded in a nefarious gaiety that enveloped Nathan and attempted to immobilize him. Dazed initially, he broke free of the assailant's mesmerizing hold. He found himself engaged in an aggressive game of dominance. Nathan and his opposition locked gazes, encircled each other, and imbued their energies against one another. Nathan knew from the attack this came from another vampire. It paled when compared with Zander's power. But he wasn't ready to face another of his kind.

"What do you want?" Nathan asked abruptly.

"Brushing aside the niceties is fine by me. I'm Carlos, and we're here to offer you a pact—membership to our group."

The silver-tongued serpent's voice rolled deep and graceful, and he dressed like the dapper devil as well. Too eloquent to trust and too dashing to ignore. His dark blue, silk-like suit accentuated his tanned skin and wavy black hair that highlighted his eyes. They glimmered in wicked brilliance and hypnotized anyone who dared stare into them, making it impossible to look away.

"What sort of pact?" Nathan asked, reluctant to trust or believe anything said to him.

"Leave this self-imposed exile and stand with us, join our kind," Carlos said.

"I prefer my solitude," Nathan responded.

"How lonely you must be." A female vampire slithered up next to Carlos, her antique white-laced dress swayed in seductive unison behind the flawless movement of her delicate pale body. Her long, flowing brunette hair framed the high cheek bones that curved down her soft, angular face. Yet, behind her beatitude lay a volatile rage flickering through her eyes. They hid an eye of a storm—lovely and deadly. "No need to suffer isolation when we welcome you into our fold."

"Trust in what Jade says. Think about how vulnerable you are on your own," Carlos said.

"You can stop your sales pitch. I've already been warned of your kind."

"Defiance misguides you, blinds you of the unbridled truth. You are under the delusion you can change what you are," Carlos admonished and continued. "A butterfly cannot change back into a caterpillar, and why would you? Mortals have evolved into something more dangerous than we could ever hope of being. Only together can we protect ourselves from them and their influence."

"Why fear humans?"

"Cautious, not fearful. We must avoid drawing mortals' attention to our existence."

"Why?"

"Humans destroy what they don't understand. It's as

natural to them as breathing." Carlos slumped as he said this and exhaled, exasperated.

"How can you pass such judgment when you're the monster who kills for blood?" Nathan asked, his head held high, indignant of Carlos's comments.

Two other vampires, both male, approached close behind their brethren. Carlos gave Nathan a cold look, his posture changed and tensed into a predatory stance, ready to pounce, "We kill to survive. It's not a choice. Humans kill with indiscretion on a larger scale than any creature on earth could ever possibly manage, so who's the monster?"

"Perhaps this isn't the right approach for someone so gifted." Jade glided around Nathan and pressed her body against his back, wrapping her arms and a leg around him. Her lips touched his ear as she whispered, "Imagine the freedom, pleasures you've denied yourself, fulfilled if only you let go of your inhibitions and give in to your deepest desires."

"And ignore morality?"

"Desire knows nothing of morals."

"Revenge, murder, nothing is taboo?"

"Bloodlust is in your nature." Her hands traveled along his body, under his shirt, and rubbed his chest. Her gentle touch captivated him, enticed his attention toward her. He glanced over his shoulder into her fierce, alluring gaze. He realized this was her effort to bewitch him.

"Never." Nathan heaved Jade off his back. She staggered, gained her footing and hissed, displaying her fangs. Unfazed by her reaction, Nathan's obstinate eyes concentrated on Carlos, "It's what sets me apart, keeps me from becoming the beast."

"Your ascetic morality cripples you. How long do you think you can last before succumbing to your nature?" Carlos asked.

Nathan dismissed the question, gave a slight bow, and said, "I'm afraid I must decline your generous offer. I don't engage in blind agreements, especially those of unscrupulous intent."

Rage fell over the vampire's face. Jade smiled, her anger subsiding, amused at such a blatant display of defiance.

"I'm willing to overlook your hasty response as an act of prudence, but if this is your final decision, then you will regret not considering the consequences of such rash words," Carlos said, as his latent anger trickled through his voice.

"Prepare for disappointment then."

"I extend my hand in unity and you slap it away like I was some beggar? You shall pay for your insolence." Carlos didn't hide his fury this time. His feral claws and sharp piercing teeth extended, ready for battle.

The three vampires in front of Nathan charged in for the attack. Their advance ceased when Zander materialized beside Nathan and created an invisible barrier. He raised his hand, palm up, and conjured a fireball that hovered and grew above it. He thrust his arm forward and three giant flaming heads with long coiling necks sprouted from the flames. The serpents snapped their burning jaws at the three vampires who slinked back in retreat. They held their arms up in defense, and growled at the evoked, blazing monster.

Nathan looked back toward Jade as she applauded and lifted her head back in euphoric laughter. She made no aggressive movement, she simply laughed throughout the attack on her fellow vampires.

"I haven't seen you in over a hundred years and you still know how to put a smile on my face," Jade wickedly grinned.

"And so Demetrius sends his lapdogs while you watch?" Zander turned to Jade and with a gesture of his hand, made the flaming beast disappear.

"All must prove themselves if they seek advancement in rank," Jade responded.

"And now that he failed his mission and contingency plan?"

"You may have left us, but you haven't forgotten." Jade turned to the vampire to the right of Carlos, "Ivan?"

Ivan reached over his shoulder and pulled out a long sword from his back and decapitated Carlos in one stroke. The headless corpse fell to the ground and Ivan impaled it, driving the blade through the heart and into the earth. He twisted the weapon and let go of the hilt as the body crumbled into ashen dust around the sword that now stood upright in the dirt.

"Why are you really here?" Zander asked.

"We need you and your apprentice for what's to come. Their society has fallen into entropy, its façade revealed. They cannot continue along this path and not expect retribution."

"There's always hope."

"Only the desperate and defeated plead for hope."

"What he wants is a war. That's all he ever wanted. His thirst for it will never be quenched, as well as his thirst for power," Zander said.

"Demetrius wanted peace, but they broke the truce long ago. Surrendering to his will is the only way to ensure the conditions of any agreement," Jade said.

"Do I look the fool?" Zander reached out, and through telekinesis, retrieved the abandoned sword into his grasp. He spun and grabbed Jade by her dress and pressed the sword's tip at her throat. "He's always ruled from a blood-stained throne. And what of his creed: 'Trust only in the hilt of your weapon, for only then will you know the truth, within the thick of battle, the purity of your actions and the measure of your worth, and if thine be just, victory will find you.'"

"Through fear, the masses obey," Jade swallowed hard.

"It's compliance through tyranny," Zander said as he lowered the blade from her neck and pushed her away.

"All who rule maintain order through force. From animals to vampires to humans, dominance reigns control. Look no further than yourself. You're a god amongst ants. Why do you resent what we are and what we are meant to be?"

"You will never understand true power, to show mercy in victory and offer peace to those who would show you no quarter if the roles reversed."

"And what of you? Will you needlessly suffer your mentor's fate?" Jade snaked around Nathan's back. Nathan said nothing, "Defiant to the end, like your mentor." She embraced him and whispered in his ear while she stared at Zander, "The war is coming and when all you hold dear is torn from you, you'll beg for death to come."

"I'll take my chances," Nathan sneered.

"I knew you would. Your silence speaks volumes." Jade walked away, commanding the others to leave with her. Nathan and Zander watched until they were out of sight.

"Now you see what I warned you of?" Zander asked.

"I do admit that panic took over reason for a moment," Nathan said.

"You felt her power. It's her gift. Even so, their group recruits by feeding off others' desperation and assurance of asylum. And within their broken vows, they enslave you. And then you realize you have forgotten who you were, what you sought help from, and wonder how they gained control over you. But then, you realize it's too late."

The vampires journeyed from the graveyard, both silent until they reached Zander's home. On the entryway stairs, a small-statured man sat and waited. His bluish-paled skin, not the blanched complexion of the dead but pallor given through heritage, augmented the color of his dark brown cotton pants and jacket. He held a wooden walking stick with a knobbed handle.

"It took you long enough. Don't tell me I missed all the fun again?" the man said as he rose up.

"Nathaniel, this is Mr. Kellan Waldron," Zander said.

"Call me Kelly. I'm not one for formalities," Kelly interrupted Zander. Out of habit, Nathan extended his hand in greeting but withdrew it. He sensed energies from the man unlike anything he had ever felt before.

"Call me Nathan. Zander apparently insists on calling me by the name my mother used when I was in trouble."

"I'm only using your proper full name for propriety's sake. I mean not to imply anything of ill intent," Zander said.

"It still concerns me when you say it like that." Nathan turned his attention back to Kelly, "What are you? You're not human or a vampire."

"True to both. I'm a wizard and I'd very much like to keep from being undead, if you don't mind," Kelly said.

"I have no intentions of doing that, I assure you." Nathan said.

"No one intends on bad things happening, but they happen. Make sure if you get the urge, I'm not your next meal."

"Nathaniel mainly feeds on psychic energy," Zander informed.

"And no touching as well then, unless he's learned how to do that without contact," Kelly said and took a step back.

"He hasn't honed that power yet," Zander said.

"That will come with practice, provided you don't practice on me," said Kelly.

"Hands to myself." Nathan folded his hands behind his back.

"I leave you now in Kellan's most capable hands."

"For what, pray tell?" Nathan asked.

"You must learn the basics, to fend off attacks. Vampires use their innate abilities against weaker foes or to measure other's power," Zander said.

"But he's not a vampire." Nathan turned to Kelly, "No offense."

"None taken."

"Kellan knows everything about mind control, things you don't realize you're capable of," Zander said before

Nathan could interrupt. "You have many questions, and they will be answered in time. You must trust me so you can prepare."

"Prepare for what?"

"A day all hope will never come but are destined to endure." Zander turned to leave.

"Wait!" Nathan caught Zander's attention. Zander turned back and saw the inundation on Nathan's face, the mortal feelings still lingered and had not faded in isolation as he had hoped—it exacerbated them. Zander knew mortal feelings made the newly-turned vulnerable, and his enemies would exploit this. Although warned, Nathan failed to see, refused to heed Zander's warning, and the epiphany felt too burdensome to carry. "What makes me so damned important?" questioned Nathan.

"You must trust me. I will explain in all due time," Zander said.

Nathan hung his head and nodded. His mental anguish outweighed his denial and he conceded under turmoil's culmination and instead asked a rhetorical question, "You're not going to answer anything, are you?"

Zander stayed silent.

"Fine then, I'll comply for now. But later on, we're going to have this same conversation, and if I don't get answers. . ." Nathan let his words hang in suspense and then fade with the tension.

"Now if you would excuse me, I must contact several people about tonight's events." Zander leaned the sword against the stair's railing and took out a cell phone from his coat pocket.

"You have a cell phone?" Nathan asked.

"What did you expect, a crystal ball?"

"Well, actually, yes."

Zander shook his head and walked up the stairs, snatching the sword on his way up. He placed it on the door frame with his phone pressed to his face and unlocked the door. He glanced back down the stairs at the pair, shook his head again as he grabbed the sword and went inside, slamming the door shut.

"Very few can get under his skin like that. Congratulations, you've found your niche," Kelly said.

"My wife used to say I had a knack for it, unintentional on my part of course." Nathan gave a devilish grin.

"The mind is a more powerful weapon than you've ever imagined. You'll see."

"I didn't know being annoying was deadly."

"Antagonizing an enemy puts them off balance, makes them react and not think." Kelly started walking down the sidewalk, "We need to get a move on before we get started."

"Where are we going?" Nathan asked, following the wizard.

"Just down the way, to get us each a pint before the pubs close."

"I don't know if I can drink anything besides blood. I don't know what it will do to me."

"Tell you what then, I'll drink both pints while you keep me company."

Chapter Five

"Close to two hundred years," Kelly said, "after a hundred, you stop keeping track. And you?"

"I was thirty-five before, you know, and it's been close to a year now so. . ."

"You're still a baby, even by human standards." Kelly spared the vampire the anguish of their discussion. Nathan seemed uncomfortable at any mention or reference indicating his mortality.

Still, Nathan had other issues gnawing at him. Everything that culminated over the past week had him skittish, on edge. The establishment's milieu he found himself in only made matters worse. The neighborhood they went through to get here didn't appeal to him while he was alive and being dead had not changed his opinion, not one bit. The dilapidated structure they entered looked as run down on the inside as it did from the outside. Smoke hung in the air so thick one could taste the ash through natural breathing. The Green Clover's ancient, battered neon sign hung in the window, flickering and buzzing louder than the old jukebox that was nestled next to the rickety, weather-worn door. A victim of ruckuses and bombardment over the years, the damaged machine belted out distorted tunes from its ripped speakers. Its coarse sound made any selection unidentifiable, and yet no one paid it any attention. The chairs and tables had seen better days as well, eroded and whittled down to nothing but nicked and splintered wood.

The bartender slammed down two more pints of dark brew next to the empty mugs in front of Kelly and Nathan. Everyone in the place received a last call round, whether they'd asked for it or not. He slammed the glass mugs on the sticky table surface, alcohol sloshing over the brims. After his rushed service, the barkeep sat down with the few remaining patrons, providing them with a flow of booze that maintained their drunken stupor. He proceeded to join them.

"Is it safe here? I feel exposed," Nathan said. He looked over his shoulder at the rest of the room, an unsettling feeling nudging at him.

"Relax. No one is paying attention, and as long as you don't frequent a place too long, you'll find yourself hidden in plain sight. It's sage advice, considering your predicament," Kelly said.

"And how long have you frequented here?"

"Too long." Kelly took a drink.

"That's comforting."

"I'm hunted too, not as adamantly as your kind, well, your kind *now*, but hunted all the same. I just happen to blend in better than you. If you act suspicious, then you will bring suspicion."

Nathan went against his inclination to peer over his shoulder and instead relaxed his body posture. He leaned back in his seat, letting his arms droop down to his lap. Nathan needed a distraction, someone to confide in, someone who understood emotional loss, someone more human. He asked, "Have you always known you were a wizard?"

"No, I didn't discover that until I came to the U.S."

"What brought you here?"

The Potato Famine drove me and many of my countrymen here."

Nathan merely nodded. Even with his diminished memories, he recalled his great grandmother's stories of her family's exodus from Ireland to avoid starvation and the blame she placed on the British for everything from the Potato Famine to World War II.

"After my parent's death, my brother and I ran away to get out of the taxes we owed on that dead piece of land we lived on. When we reached New York, it was freedom like we'd never known. We survived well enough, and although homeless, we ate better from the garbage here than what we lived on back home." Kelly took a long draft off his drink, emptying his mug. He slid the mug alongside the other empties and pulled over the other full mug in front of him, winking at Nathan.

"What happened to your brother?" Nathan asked. He'd forgotten all his worries for the moment, engrossed in Kelly's story.

"One night, two vampires found us and killed my brother. But as they attacked me, I somehow incinerated the bloodsuckers." Kelly paused. He stared into nothing, introspection swallowing any sense of time until a cacophony of laughter rose out of him, snapping him back to the now. "I'm sorry, lad. I meant no offense. It's been way over a hundred years and it still brings up all the bad."

"None taken," Nathan said.

Kelly tipped up his brew, inhaled it as if it wiped away the thought, and said, "I still to this day remember setting them ablaze. That's when Zander found me holding my dead brother, and next to me, two smoking, charred vampires. Zander took me in, and from that day, he taught me in the ways of magick, in the power of the mind."

"How did Zander teach you?"

"The same as I'm teaching you now."

"No, I mean how did you learn about wizard spells, power that's not vampire-derived?"

"You don't know?"

"Don't know what?"

"Zander told me you knew little, but I didn't realize you knew *nothing*." Kelly finished the dregs in his mug, "Before Zander turned, he was a wizard. And like him, you possess the powers of both wizard and vampire. It's in your blood lineage."

Nathan now comprehended Zander's warnings. What he considered a curse, his enemies coveted. They desired what he had and despised him for it. And if they couldn't have it, then they would destroy him.

"This is too much," Nathan said.

"That's what I thought. But you'll get used to the idea. It will come as natural as walking. Notice I didn't say breathing."

"I didn't think about that." Nathan only inhaled and exhaled while speaking. The thought of not having to breathe never occurred to him. It seemed he'd taken a great many things for granted.

"That's the point. You learn to use your powers through concentration, and then they happen without conscious thought and submit to your will."

"And what about spells that use more than thought?"

"Zander will teach you incantations and other skills such as alchemy at another time. For now, let's begin with some basics, practical magick you can use right now. Are you ready to cast a spell?"

"You're serious? Here in the bar?" Nathan asked. "Won't we bring some unwanted attention?"

"I didn't bring you here just to watch me drink, although a grand thing it is. And, if we do it right, no one will notice a thing."

"Okay, I'm listening," Nathan conceded, unable to think of a valid reason not to.

"Your first lesson is the most important of all. We will tap into both powers. They derive from the same principle—the power of the mind. After this, it's all semantics as far as I'm concerned. The finer points of magick will come easy after this basic exercise in elemental manipulation."

"I'm ready as I'll ever be," Nathan said.

"What do you know of vampires and mirrors?"

"That they don't show their reflection."

"But do you know why?"

"No."

"Their defense mechanism prevents this, so they can't get captured into something such as a mirror trap. Most of all, it's due to their unnatural presence here, among the living. All vampires have some degree of invisibility, even if they're not aware of it. Don't worry, no one of consequence has noticed," Kelly said.

"Won't I cast shadows?" Nathan asked.

"Shadows are tricky with your kind. Sometimes appearing, sometimes not, and sometimes they're used as an extension of your body if you know how to control them."

"I still don't understand, but I'll take your word for it."

"Remember you are of two different reality planes, not fully of this realm, so there's no concrete rules to some things. Your control over your powers will dictate this. Look in the mirror. You did this without thought."

Nathan looked and did not see his reflection in the mirror. He knew through vampire lore that vampires don't show their reflection in the mirror, but this was different. This was him, just invisible.

"Splendid. Don't let it go to your head though. Now I want you to imagine the light reflecting off of you. Think of it as a switch, like a fan blowing smoke around and away from you. Now turn off the switch."

He pictured his image in the mirror and concentrated. He had felt this in his mind and body before, but not like this, not this intense. He exuded his will upon his body and the pain stressed his constitution, burned his head. His mind fought the command bestowed upon it, struggled against it, and resisted its natural inclination. But then, his defenses crumbled and succumbed to his bidding. Nathan's ghostly image took form until it solidified in the mirror.

"Not bad for the first time," Kelly said. "How do you feel?"

"Tired, and I've got a headache."

"That is as expected. You'll recover. It sometimes happens when you try a new power before honing your craft. As you learn to control the flow of power, the pain will subside. The mind is not conditioned for full use yet. That will come with practice. Are you ready for the fun part?"

"Okaaay," Nathan said with trepidation, stretching out the syllables.

"Now focus on not just your reflection, but on the light around you. Deflect it instead of letting it reach your body." Kelly checked casually for onlookers.

Nathan focused on the task at hand. Slowly his mind obeyed, and his power responded as his reflection faded into nothing. His head didn't throb as severely as before, but he felt drained, mentally and physically.

"Very good." Kelly then disappeared instantly, "How do you feel?"

"You'd think I was the one drinking instead of you." Nathan looked around to see if anyone had noticed. None of the patrons reacted. They continued consuming alcohol and spouting drunken philosophy. "Can anyone hear us?"

"Only if you talk too loud. Keep that in mind when we leave. On the way out, brush your hand on someone to regenerate, but don't grab them. You'll feel better afterwards."

"Won't that kill them?"

"Maybe they'll pass out. If you grab them you might drain them enough to kill them, so don't. I will teach you how to control that ability later."

"I still think someone will notice."

"People see only what they want to. They disseminate, dismiss what they don't understand. Even flagrant acts and evidence are explained away, in fear of society's unbending judgment and repercussions of non-acceptance."

"Not all are afraid to speak out," Nathan said.

"And they are ostracized for their bravery. Relax and enjoy yourself."

"I fail to see what part of this is fun."

"The part where we walk out the door without paying."

"How many rounds has it been?" Cooper asked, stopping next to Murray at the bar. Murray called him for a ride to a hotel, so Cooper figured his partner's bad day had turned into an abject night, considering the call originated from a pub.

"Several," Murray said, his speech slurred even without the lit cigar tucked in his mouth. His torso hunched over the bar, propping his body upright on the unstable barstool. A half-empty whiskey bottle sat next to the glass in front of him, an overflowing ashtray parked to the right. Two cigar nubs smoldered in the receptacle. Murray obviously had been here for quite a while. The bartender sat with his friends a few stools down, talking and drinking. Last call had passed and only a few patrons remained. Cooper took a seat next to Murray.

"I take it that the move back home wasn't met with a warm reception," Cooper said.

"She redecorated, redecorated her way. She moved everything around. My ideas, gone, dismissed." Murray said.

"Ah, I see," Cooper said. "And so you decided to pick a fight?"

"I didn't pick a fight. I wasn't there but a minute when

she started in on me about leaving, and about our marriage, and my job." Murray poured a shot glass full, waving to the barkeep for another glass. The bartender slid a shot glass down the bar. Murray snatched it before it tumbled off. He filled it and pushed the full glass in front of Cooper. Both men slammed their drinks and sat in silence, starring at whatever sports talk show played on the screen next to the bar mirror.

"I don't know what Laura expects of me. When we were first married, I knew what to say, what to do. Now, she's a complete mystery to me. I'm tired of trying to guess what she wants, I really am." Murray took one last drag off the butt of a cigar and smashed and twisted the lit end in the ashtray.

"Everything's not as black and white as you make it out to be," Cooper said.

"I've been a cop too long to deal in the grey, my friend," Murray said, pouring two more drinks. "The lines get blurred there. In our business, if we go there, then it's way too easy to get lost in it."

"What do you mean our business isn't about working within the grey? Human nature has us crossing that line constantly. Most people wouldn't do the unspeakable things we come across if it all went into nice, neat categories of black and white. You're just more comfortable thinking that way," Cooper said.

"When you compromise your beliefs, how far will you go? And if you cross that line, how far is too far? There are no restrictions, no more lines to cross to warn you. After that, there's no going back. You never can return from that, not after tasting the forbidden fruit." Murray patted his empty pockets for a cigar.

"That's my point. That's why we do what we do, to be that line, that voice of reason that says *enough*."

"Maybe she's right, maybe I'm getting too old for this mess. I've been on the force so long. I don't know how to be anything else."

"You could do anything you set your mind to."

"Yeah, right kid. That's a young person's perspective. Tell me something, could you unlearn or even abandon all you were taught in the military?" Murray asked.

"I doubt it," Cooper had to agree.

"And what really bothers me is what bothers all old cops—the day you realize you don't have it anymore, no matter how instinctive it comes. Look in the mirror, the table in the far corner over there. Do you see it?" Murray pointed with his eyes toward the area in the mirror as he poured another round. Cooper waved off the drink. Murray kicked back his head and drank. A patron sitting at the bar, close to the exit, collapsed and fell off his stool. Someone close by picked him off the floor.

"What of it?" Cooper looked in the mirror then turned to see if he had missed something.

"Earlier, two guys were sitting at that table, an older fellow with a walking stick and another in his mid-thirties. The younger man acted rather anxious, so I kept an eye on him. And then they left, gave me the slip, and I didn't even see them get up, let alone leave." Murray poured a drink and kicked back an shot. Without another word and not knowing what to say, Cooper picked up his glass and slammed down the drink he waved off.

Jade stormed through the double doors which swung open and nearly hit the two vampires guarding the entryway, blazing into the old, abandoned munitions building. Ivan and the other accompanying vampire followed her through the living area where some of their kindred sat in the lap of debauchery, taking pleasure in blood, flesh, sadism, or various combinations of each. She came up to a freight elevator shaft and said, "Wait here."

Both vampires fell into flanking positions by the opening. Jade plunged into a free fall down the shaft until she reached the sub-basement level. She glided to a halt, spun around in midair, and floated forward. She stepped out of the pitch dark drop and made haste down the torch-lit hall to the large throne room. She entered without the guards impeding and approached the four-step dais set on the opposing end of the entrance.

On top of the raised platform someone stood next to a throne, their straight, dark hair gathered in a ponytail falling midway to the back of their midnight blue robe. The being faced the opposite direction, unabashed by anyone's approach. Jade stopped short of the inclining steps and asked, "Radomir, where is our liege?"

"He has left to tend to important matters elsewhere." Radomir turned and stepped forward, his right hand rested on his ornate dagger hilt on his belt, "I've been instructed to watch over operations in his absence."

"Where has he gone?" Jade asked.

Radomir casually descended the steps and said, "You don't know? My, oh my, have we fallen out of his graces?

It must be infuriating after all these years, after all your loyalty and sacrifice, to come so close in rank only to fall short of such yearned-for high esteem."

"You've always been impossible." Jade let her frustration come through every syllable of her words.

"And you, my dear, have always been predictable." With an animated, wicked grin that displayed his fangs, Radomir placed his hand under her chin and gently stroked her cheek. She jerked away and stepped back, "What, no forgiveness after over two hundred years? You must learn to let go."

"Your mere presence sickens me. Don't touch me again."

"The reason you're upset is that I used you first? Oh, my sweet, sweet Jade. Have you not seen the error of your ways and accepted my superiority? I'm willing to forgive your transgression and continue where we left off."

Jade didn't respond and glowered at him.

"Tsk, tsk. Unrequited love? It's almost too much for me to bear," Radomir smirked as he spoke with an insincere tone Jade knew all too well.

"Love is fleeting," Jade spat, "handed out too readily and taken back too quickly."

"Your scorn will pass in time, if you allow it to."

Again, Jade refused to answer. She knew he meant to hurt her, but she wouldn't allow her still-raw emotions to get the best of her. After a moment, when he realized she wouldn't concede to his whims, Radomir shrugged his shoulders and turned to ascend the steps, "Your loss, but as you wish."

"You never answered my question. Where is he?"

He turned back to her and said, "Yes I have. Demetrius has left me in command, and I won't answer to underlings unless our Lord deems it."

With that, Jade swallowed her anger and curtseyed, "Thank you for your audience. Please pass on to our liege that Carlos, your protégé, has been disposed of, for his failure to recruit either intended."

"Our Lord is already aware," Radomir let out in an uncaring tone.

Jade knew better though, and merely nodded.

"It must have pained you so when you received the order to dispense Carlos." Radomir saw Jade's vicious smile now as he continued, "All of that aside, I want to know if you made sure he took the sword?"

"Yes, just as our Lord anticipated."

"Excellent. You may go."

Jade stomped off but ceased when Radomir said, "And remember who answers to whom. I won't warn you again."

Without further discussion, Jade sped away. She was willing to wait for an opportunity for vengeance against the one she once loved, the one who betrayed her and claimed her rightfully earned status amongst her people.

Chapter Six

"Wake up, duty calls." Cooper shook Murray out of his drunken slumber.

Murray's head pounded from his well-earned hangover, his bloodshot eyes barely opened. The lamp glared, unsympathetic to his plight. His muscles protested, and his bones creaked and cracked as he set upright on the couch. He really missed his bed, really missed being home, the place where he should have been last night, next to her. He rubbed his face to clear out the cobwebs so he could focus on the job. Pain shot through his body as he stood up. It was going to be an agonizing working weekend, just more of what he'd had the last few days: a sleep-deprived week with no progress made.

"Patrol found another body in Dead Man's Land," Cooper, already dressed, said as he handed Murray some coffee.

"So why call us?" Murray sipped on the hot brew. It tasted horrid compared to Laura's.

"All I know is they called us specifically and they're holding somebody for us to question."

"Who?"

"They didn't say."

"All right then." Murray searched his pockets and realized he had smoked all his cigars last night, "Let's go."

Along the way, Murray stayed silent, incapable of engaging in any meaningful conversation. His mind lingered on the recent days' events. But most of all, he ached. He usually bounced back, but this time it was different. The old bones didn't want to relent, his head still pounded. God, he hated getting old. And yet, his thoughts kept returning to how he messed up with Laura and how he had compounded problems between them. No, he needed to stop this nonsense and focus on the case, on how everything connected. He brushed aside his ponderings as they came closer to the crime scene. He refused to let his emotional baggage interfere and left his personal problems in the car, tucked away under the seat, buried for another day. A preoccupied investigator doesn't catch nuances but instead allows preconceived notions and sentiments to blind him to the truth, to the facts. He wanted a cigar in the worst way.

"Oh, I don't believe this," Cooper said as he drove up to the crime scene.

Both detectives approached the taped-off alley, the alley where the blood trail had ended. Officer Barker waved them over to his cruiser.

"What do we have?" Murray asked.

"I've got someone here you might remember. Take a look." Barker gestured to the rear window. The detectives looked in and saw Kevin handcuffed in the back seat with a disposable poncho draped over him. Dried blood encrusted his entire body, including his face. Kevin had a vacant expression and didn't move, didn't flinch or show any acknowledgment of their presence. "A witness found him kneeling next to the victim."

"Let me guess, Ed saw Kevin next to the victim, and our victim is Carl," Murray said.

"He must be in shock. He hasn't said a word." Barker observed.

"I'd be scared too if I were him," Murray said. "If a big. . ."

"Whoa, that's pushing it," Cooper interrupted.

"What?" Murray's face squinted in puzzlement.

"He's thinking you were about to say something racist," Barker said.

Murray looked at Barker and laughed. Now Cooper looked baffled.

"Murray dated many women of many colors, including my aunt for a time."

"How is Joyce?" Murray asked.

"She's good," Barker said, "but she doesn't miss you. You make a lot of friends but don't know how to keep them."

"Can we get back to work now?" Cooper's discomfort on the subject bled through.

Barker turned to Murray, "It's a negative on the dogs. Nobody's having any fights since word on the street has gotten around about an animal tearing someone up."

"Bad news travels fast." Murray telegraphed a frown at Cooper.

"Don't look at me," Cooper said.

"Your girlfriend broke the story last night. Didn't she tell you?"

"We don't discuss work."

"You're seeing Sylvia Brewer?" Barker's voice went up an octave.

"Don't encourage him, Ernie," Murray said and walked past the two.

The interrogation room felt more like a walk-in closet. Three folding chairs sat strategically around the rectangular table that was butted against the room's corner opposite the door. Two chairs were positioned along the table's side where both detectives sat. Kevin occupied the chair on the end that faced the camera in the ceiling's corner. The institutional off-white, combined with the close quarters, made anyone seated there claustrophobic, distracted, preventing liars from giving a convincing story.

Kevin cleaned up at the station and put on an orange jumpsuit, the only clothing available at the station. He hadn't spoken or touched his soup and sandwich, not even his coffee. He just stared at the walls. They didn't know if he was unwilling or unable to tell them anything.

"Kevin, I can't help you if you don't help me." Cooper pulled his chair even closer to Kevin, "All I want is your side of the story."

Kevin looked down at the table, avoiding eye contact. Murray slid photos in front of him then made his way around the back of Kevin and spoke over his shoulder, "This was your friend, the one who kept you safe. It would be an extreme injustice to him if you stay silent. It's time for you to man up and tell us what happened."

Kevin turned away from the looming detectives and pushed the pictures back across the table. The detectives nodded at each other, an unspoken signal that they had made some progress; Kevin's silence was purposeful. Now the detectives had a chance of working on the witness, opening him up to them. Murray didn't figure him as the killer, but he had to know for sure. Just then, the door opened.

"Hello, Trigger Man. You didn't waste any time, putting him in a jumpsuit before the interview even began. Shameful." A Black woman in a smart brown business suit stood at the doorway, her pleasant smile and nonchalant demeanor a contrast to her verbal reprimand.

"It's the only clean thing we had, Rhonda," Murray said as he turned and faced her. Cooper did so as well.

"In any case, this interview is over. My client has been put through enough for one day, unless you plan on charging him," Rhonda said.

"We haven't charged him, but he is a potential witness that will be called on later," Murray said.

"Not without my presence. Now gentlemen, if you would excuse us, I need a word with my client." Rhonda looked and spoke to the camera, "Alone and without an audience."

"As you wish," Murray said, the red light of the camera turned off and both detectives left the room, closing the door behind them.

The men met up with Deveraux down the hall in the room where the Captain had viewed the interrogation.

"Rhonda Davis? Are you kidding me?" Murray said.

"It looks like we hooked a bigger fish than we had anticipated." Deveraux's fingers stroked his mustache.

"Who is she?" Cooper asked.

"She's a K.C. mob lawyer. I knew her when she was a public defender. A lot of low-level gangsters and drug dealers went free because of her," Murray said.

"What's with the Trigger Man reference?" Cooper

asked.

"Oh, her pet name for me? Whenever I was summoned in one of her cases, she accused me of corruption, of setting up her clients. She claimed I always conveniently found the trigger man in these shootings and implied I planted evidence. Once she even hinted that I was responsible for all of these crimes. She's one of the reasons I transferred," Murray sighed.

"She's a very savvy sort," Deveraux said.

"She's a snake oil salesman with a law degree," Murray said.

"But effective," Deveraux said. "I want to know how he got such a high society lawyer."

Cooper elbowed Murray as he looked in the open doorway. The other men turned and saw Rhonda Davis leaning in the room.

"I hope I'm not intruding," she said.

"Not at all, Ms. Davis. Can I get you anything?" Deveraux said as he stood up.

"You've always been the gentleman, Quentin. I just need a moment with Detective Murray if you don't mind."

"Certainly," Deveraux said as he and Cooper exited, closing the door behind them.

After the two men left, she said, "I need you to take this card." With her well-manicured, bright red fingernails, she extended an off-white business card to Murray.

Murray didn't even look at the card, let alone take it from her, "I think I'll pass."

"This isn't from me and isn't a request." Curious, Murray took the card and saw the address: Big Mike's downtown office. "He needs a word in private."

"I've been there. He could have simply called me."

"Not for this." Davis pointed her finger at him like she was holding a gun, "See you soon, Trigger Man."

Davis left the room, Cooper and Deveraux entered soon after.

"Apparently I've got a meeting at Big Mike's office. Well, that solves that little mystery of who hired the lawyer for the homeless kid." Murray crumpled the card and threw it in the trash bin.

"But why would he do that?" Cooper asked.

"I don't like this loose end. Tie this one up for me." Deveraux looked at both detectives.

"Will do." Murray went to leave when Deveraux put a hand on his shoulder and stopped him.

"I hope you use better judgment there. Your recent, insightful interview you gave to a certain reporter has given me pause," Deveraux said.

"Funny, I thought it went rather well," Murray said.

"I don't like what's going on here, Captain." Cooper interrupted.

"Neither do any of us. Keep an eye on our recently-released witness while Murray attends his meeting and find out how our witness is warranting Ms. Davis' service." Deveraux dropped his hand off Murray's shoulder and went to walk away but Murray had questions.

"What about Ed?" Murray asked. "Don't we need to question him?"

"It's already been done. He's only a witness at this point and subject to recall," Deveraux said.

"What?" Murray said.

"Captain, this is highly irregular," Cooper said.

"That's all I can tell you. I have my orders, and you have yours," Deveraux said.

"If someone else is working this case, I need to know right now." Murray marched up into Deveraux's face, their noses almost touching.

"Don't challenge me on this, my friend. I'm doing all I can short of pulling you off this case." Deveraux almost whispered this, then stepped back and walked away.

"You were right—politics. But why sabotage us?" Cooper asked.

Murray responded, "Let's solve this case and find out."

A bright purple electrical stream flowed from Nathan's hands in controlled destruction. The energy obeyed his slightest body twitch and mind's desire. The lightning struck and crackled against the old pallet and cascaded to the abandoned building's wall, leaving scorched marks on both surfaces and the scent of smoldering embers in the mild breeze. The more he used his power, the more he lusted after it. The energy that surged through him felt like an extension of his body, and the raw power made him desire more. He wished to stay in its grandeur forever. Despite this, he mustered enough willpower to let go, breaking the energy bolt's surge.

"Interesting." Kelly observed the billowing smoke from the burned areas, "Your innate expulsion power is lightning."

"Is that a bad thing?" Nathan asked.

"Not at all. Fire is optimal, but lightning holds great

power, even on undead. Now that we've established your reactionary abilities, we'll concentrate on other expulsion powers."

Nathan waited in elation for his next lesson. He had so many questions about where these abilities came from, but his euphoria had temporarily blinded him to the how and why. And like his bloodlust, only his passion mattered. As his display of power grew, his troubles left him. Still, he knew that after all of this, his rapture would recede and all of his worries would make their presence known again in the worst possible way.

"We'll begin with fire, then plasma energy, and then cold," Kelly said.

"What about water?" Nathan asked.

Kelly shook his head, "We can pick up on air and earth manipulation later. You don't want to mess with water."

"Why?"

"My lad, water is the last thing the undead wants to see. It's dangerous."

"Then all the more reason I want to learn about it."

"You won't let it go, will you?" Kelly sighed. "Okay, we'll take the practical approach as I explain."

Kelly cupped his hand, made a gesture, and water formed in it. He walked over to Nathan and threw the handful of water onto the doubting pupil. When he waved his hand over the wet spots on Nathan's clothing, his skin grew warm and then the heat prickled and scorched him. Nathan rubbed the areas and grunted as the burning feeling intensified. Enraged, he thumped his torso with his palms to smother the fiery sensation and tore at his dampened shirt. Kelly gathered dirt from the ground and threw it on

Nathan's tattered, soggy shirt, passed a hand over the area, and the scalding ceased.

"What did you do?" Nathan continued brushing the areas to rid him of the phantom sting still present, as well as the dirt Kelly had flung on his clothes. Nathan panted, easing the fury that rose. Like so many humans and new inductees to the unknown world around them, he feared what he didn't understand—Kelly knew he had to teach him of the dangers soon to come.

"I purified that water. Water cleanses all things, so naturally, the undead are affected by this. I'm only a wizard and look what I did to you. Imagine if a holy man or cleric doused an undead and then blessed the water," Kelly said.

"You said 'holy men,' not just priests?" Nathan asked.

"You should fear any clergyman." Kelly picked up his shillelagh from the rusted, burned-out truck shell he had propped it against.

"What about demonic worshippers?"

"Avoid them at all cost. If they take control of you, they will command you like a puppet, and there won't be anything you'll be able to do about it."

"Thanks for the tip." Nathan's sarcasm rolled off his words, his anger remaining from the water incident.

"Heed what you're told and realize the danger you face is not to be taken lightly," Kelly admonished.

"Trust me. It's sinking in. But no matter the risk, it won't stop me from finding who did this to my family."

Kelly thumped his shillelagh on the ground, "Dammit man, have you not heard a word I've said?"

"That's my son out there. The same people who took him murdered my wife. Don't tell me to forget, because I can't. And it isn't that I haven't tried. I simply can't."

Kelly lowered his head and sighed. He knew he couldn't convince Nathan otherwise or avert his attention any longer. "Have you considered that whoever did this is luring you into a trap? When we act on pure emotion, those decisions are the ones we most regret."

"I know, but I don't have a choice." Nathan's tone lowered to a sullen whisper.

"Well, if you're going to do this, I might as well do it with you. But this doesn't excuse you from your daily lessons."

"Understood." Nathan didn't dare say anything foolish or sarcastic. Finally, someone not only understood his plight, but also offered to help.

"We'll start tomorrow. There's not enough time for anything else tonight. Besides, I need a pint if I'm going to go down this path with you."

"Thank you, Kelly." Nathan's voice and posture relaxed.

"No need. If something happened to you, Zander would never let me hear the end of it." Kelly walked away, frustrated. Nathan had placed him in an impossible situation, and either choice made him the instigator. Better to lean toward caution than inflexibility.

In Murray's opinion, Big Mike's office seemed more like an upscale apartment that intimidated the uninitiated. But not Murray. This tactic didn't work on the seasoned. So why did Mike want him to come here knowing he wasn't easily intimidated? He put his thoughts aside when he walked through the threshold, marching past the sleek full bar and billiards table. He made his way around the massive desk and over toward the easel where Mike stood with his back to the door, stroking his brush on the canvas in an attempt to recreate the vase full of multi-colored carnations on the table in front of him. Mike continued without acknowledging the detective's approach, even when Murray stood next to the painting, scrutinizing every brush pass on the picture. Murray looked around the easel then back at the painting. His face wrinkled as if he smelled something putrid.

"Don't switch careers." Murray walked over to the bar and poured two glasses of scotch.

Without taking an eye off his task, Mike said, "Nobody has the guts to tell me that but you."

"You have enough people groveling at your feet to last you two lifetimes." Murray took the drinks over to the table positioned between the two plush chairs situated next to the billiards table and sat down.

"I admit it's refreshing not having to keep my persona all the time, but don't let anyone know you get away with it." Mike put the brush down and sat on the opposite chair. Grabbing his glass, he toasted his guest.

"I won't tell a soul." Both men tipped their glasses and drank in unison.

A moment passed and Murray turned to Mike, "Why did you send your bulldog and release my suspects before I fully questioned them?"

"Don't be daft or even pretend to be. Do you believe I staged all of that? You want answers, and I helped preserve them before they befell some terrible accident." Mike slouched back in his chair, holding his glass in front of him, "You're welcome, by the way." He tapped on the glass with his index finger in thought.

"How in the hell did that help me? You took away my only lead."

"Did I ever tell you about my trip to the library with my grandfather?"

"No." Murray slunk back in his chair, disgusted, but prepared to listen to another cryptic story. Mike never gave a direct answer to anything that mattered.

"When I was young, they had free shows at the library, sometimes films and other times entertainers. One day, I must have been around five, there was a marionette show, and I had the best time. And I remember afterward, I wanted to ask the marionette a question. I approached the small, curtained stage but saw the puppet master laying the marionette on a chair. And I then realized the puppet wasn't real, and if I wanted answers, I needed to ask the one pulling the strings."

"So, see who's on the other end of the strings?" Murray stood and downed the rest of his scotch.

Murray turned to leave when Big Mike said, "Don't hurry off. There's more."

"Go on." Murray stopped and faced Mike.

Big Mike stood, walked over to Murray, his drink still in hand and said, "You're probably asking yourself why I'm doing this, and the answer is, that at this juncture, it benefits us both."

"But not enough to give me a straight answer."

Mike laughed, "You wouldn't believe me if I told you.

And when you figure it all out, if you figure it out, you'll retire."

"It's that bad?"

"You might think you know what's going on here, but you haven't even scratched the truth's surface yet."

"That much dirt, huh?"

"Keep digging, my friend. All I'm offering you is a shovel. And if I were you, I wouldn't trust my superiors."

"I figured that," Murray said, crestfallen. He knew that whatever this was, it wouldn't end well.

"That's what I love about you, you see all the nuances, all the little things hidden in plain sight that others dismiss and never question. Like my painting over there. People mask their true selves in paint, but no one ever notices. Are you sure you won't work for me?" Mike tipped the glass and downed the rest of his drink with an eyebrow raised. This wasn't the first time Mike had asked him, but it was the first time he'd momentarily considered it.

"I'll see you later." Murray shook his massive hand and exited before he thought about anything but the tip he received.

Just as Murray exited Big Mike's office building, he got a call from Cooper on his cell phone. For Cooper to call this soon meant he had either hit gold or something bad had happened.

Murray answered, "Please tell me you have something we can work with."

"I'm in one of the alleys. We lost him." Cooper said.

"What? What do you mean you 'lost him?' "

"I don't understand it either. He went into the alleys again and disappeared. We had all the exits covered and he still disappeared. He's not here. We searched the whole area and he's gone."

"Okay, okay. Let's concentrate on finding him again." Murray said.

"Where would someone like that go?" Cooper asked.

"Home is where the wounded and fearful go. That's where he is, where he feels safe."

"But this is where he calls home, and he's not here."

"No, no. Remember what Carl said. He said Kevin was a stranger to the alleys."

"We don't know where he's from. His prints came up empty, like he never existed. What does that mean?" Cooper asked.

Murray had a thought, something Mike had told him: *People mask their true selves in paint, but no one ever notices.* "Look up Kevin's description in records for any distinguishing marks or tattoos."

"He's rather young for any military tattoos. Does he have scars?" Cooper said.

"I don't know. Just humor me, please." Murray said, his curt response barked into the phone.

"No need for hostility. I'm on it. What did Spinelli have to say?"

"Follow the fly into the web."

"That's it?"

"No, he confirmed our suspicions."

"I didn't want to hear that."

"I didn't either." Murray ended the call and wished for answers that he didn't want to know.

Chapter Seven

The rolling clouds projected their bleak grey curtain over the graveyard where Nathan slept in his mausoleum. The distant thunder foreshadowed the oncoming storm, waking Nathan from his slumber, his restless thoughts caught in the eye of the storm of his mind. His thoughts swept him away into the heights and misfortunes of his diminishing humanity. And the deeper he delved into this hellish existence, the further he drifted, becoming simultaneously lost within a dimming past and the surreal. Though a gradual decay laid claim to his sense of reality and his memories of days gone-by, he refused to detach himself from the world he once knew—his thoughts of her and their son.

As difficult as it seemed, Nathan pulled his mind back to the present, back to the task at hand, to the reason he slept here and hadn't given up on his desires. He needed to find those responsible for taking the last thing that mattered to him in this world and make them pay. He rose and entered the twilight of the cemetery, ready to find those responsible. Kellan had arrived earlier and awaited Nathan's emergence from his rest, his shillelagh resting on his shoulder.

"I don't know how you could stay here after sleeping in a bed again," Kelly said.

"You never volunteered to let me stay at your place."

"There's not enough room."

"That's true."

"What did you tell Zander?"

"Nothing." Nathan brushed the dust off his clothes and attempted to rub out the wrinkles, "He asks too many questions."

"Like he already doesn't know what we're up to. You're seriously underestimating everyone involved, including me by the way. You might want to listen to my counsel, especially when it comes to these things."

"I know what I'm doing," Nathan snarled.

"Apparently not from what I've witnessed." Kelly leaned in to get Nathan's full attention.

Nathan's head whipped around, his voice rose, "Are you going to help or not?"

"I never said I wouldn't. I just want you to think about what you're doing before you do it. Don't blame me if it all goes awry."

"Let's just go already," Nathan said as he stomped away.

"Impetuous. You don't even know the way."

The sun had set as they passed through the abandoned streets of Dead Man's Land. The city's dim, distant hue revealed the corroded pathway past mounds of rubble and empty, dilapidated industrial buildings. Nathan, with a good distance between Kelly and him, located where the assailant's route had also led the police: the alley where the blood trail ended. The stillness around them magnified any ambient noise. Kelly broke the silence.

"When my brother died, I tried to make sense of what happened, looked for someone to blame it all on."

Nathan stopped, turned, and said, "But you killed those responsible. You made them pay."

"No," Kelly stepped forward, "not in my mind. Don't learn the hard way like I did that vengeance is a thirst that's never quenched. The sooner you let go, the sooner you'll find peace."

"None of you understand." Nathan's voice trembled and he clenched his fists, "I can't let this go, I won't! And there's nothing you can do to stop me."

"But why, *why* torture yourself so?"

"It's the only thing I have left." Nathan went to his knees, his head slumped, "It's the only thing I remember, the only thing good. Everything else has been nothing but a nightmare. I wish I would have died that night. The more I remember about my death, the more I forget about my life, and I can't do that. I refuse to forget."

"Death is merely a change. Don't fear or hate it." Kelly squatted down, "There's no going back, no return for those like us. And even if you could, you wouldn't be the same."

Nathan looked at Kelly, "Change? I died, Kelly. I don't think you could possibly imagine what I've been through or know what was taken from me."

"I know all too well. That night, when my powers manifested, my world, my life before that, died with my brother. I've never been the same since. And when I accepted that, it all made sense. You're not surrendering your life. You've only changed."

"Tell that to my son."

"And then what? You can't be there for him. You're not human."

"But I can save him."

"Although I know your attempt at redemption is folly, I promised you that we'd do this together, and I won't break my promise. But know this—if all goes well and we somehow rescue your child, you have to let him go all the same. He cannot know of your existence. It's too dangerous for both of you."

Nathan didn't answer but contemplated Kelly's words. He had never considered the aftermath of success. His station would not change. No one from his former life could know about his life now. It would tear their life apart knowing what he knew: the world around them was a lie, and that another world existed within the confines of their naïve perception of what was real.

Suddenly, Nathan caught a whiff of an unfamiliar, overpowering stench rushing through the air. The putrid aerosol gathered into a concentrated odor thick enough to choke on. Its rank fragrance, not of the undead but of animal origin, slammed into him as if he had been throttled with a bat. Nathan dry heaved and bent forward, struggling to gain control of his faculties. Kelly, alerted by the force thrown over the area, looked around for their stalker.

Were-rats.

Kelly snuck toward a nearby mound of rubble where three rats scurried about. He took a hold of his shillelagh by the shaft and extended out the knotted end to the ground like a golf club and said, "Get ready."

Kelly swung his weapon and hurled one rat into the air.

As the rat sailed back, it morphed and grew in size into a half-man, half-rat and hit the wall of a building, slumping to the ground, only to spring up as quickly as it had hit the wall.

The two other rats, who had finished morphing, dashed toward Nathan, growing as they moved, and their speed almost rivaled his. Nathan managed to gain his composure just in time and hovered back and up in the air, shooting streaming lightning bolts out of his hands at each rat. He hit one, it flung back upon impact from the electrical force and rolled away and convulsed. The second rat dodged the attack and leapt forward and up, swinging his claws as if swimming in the air. Nathan moved to the side and countered with his own unnatural claws, but the rat's claw scored a hit on his forearm as well and sent both of them tumbling to the pavement. Their descent wasn't kind to either of them as they spun and plunged to the ground, both taking a moment to recuperate from the impact. Nathan attempted to get up, but between the fall and his gaping wound, he didn't know which injury to favor. Out of sheer will and survival instinct, he exerted himself to move, but the rat recovered faster and pinned Nathan under his body, swinging his claws and landing blows on the vampire below him. Nathan put up his arms in defense. His injured limb throbbed in protest to his actions and landed a hand on the rat's jaw, an effort to keep it from biting. It hissed as it struck and snapped its razor-sharp teeth, pressing its attack. As Nathan held the were-rat at bay, the rat's expression changed from anger to terrified, their roles reversed as the rat attempted to flee Nathan's now ironclad grip. The were-rat's energy poured into Nathan, draining the being's life force as if he were drinking his blood. He felt invigorated and the pain in his arm subsided. A dark feeling of lust grew with his power. The rat struggled until he slumped over and twitched in death throes.

When Nathan heard the commotion in the background, he threw the drained rat's body aside and rolled up into a standing position. And with an instinctive reflex, a power he didn't know how he'd come about, he turned into a mist, like a wraith, as another rat leapt through him and crash-landed into a crooked signpost behind him. He saw Kelly who was fighting off five other attacking rats, wielding his shillelagh in one hand and shooting fire from the other. Nathan sensed other rats forming a perimeter around them, and he surged over to assist Kelly. He concentrated, just as Kelly had shown him at the bar, and changed back to a corporeal state. He bull-rushed a rat, taking it down with a body block. They stood back to back, fighting off the were-rats. Suddenly, in unison, their enemies quit their assault and stepped back, keeping the two surrounded.

"You're not welcome here," the leader hissed.

"We're only passing through," Nathan said.

"We weren't speaking to you, vampire," the rat leader said.

Nathan turned to Kelly and their expressions said it all—Nathan's look was quizzical while Kelly's expression feigned passive acknowledgment that he knew what they were doing was wrong. The rats' hisses escalated at Kelly's dismissive manner.

"Wait a minute. Can't we work something out?" Nathan asked.

"Forget it. It's not worth it," Kelly said.

"Let the vampire speak since you have abstained, wizard. Let us parlay," the rat leader said.

"What do you want?" Nathan asked.

"They want information for passage, that's how they took control of this town," Kelly said.

"Silence, wizard! You had your chance," the rat leader said.

"Maybe they know what we're looking for," Nathan said to Kelly.

"They can't be trusted—they're rats," Kelly responded.

"I grow weary of you, wizard. If you do not parlay with us, then you are in violation of the terms set between us and the other ruling bodies. What say you now?"

"I refuse to parlay with an underling who holds no sway. Bring your leader here for negotiations or let us pass," Kelly said.

"Agreed." Nathan let his doubt creep through with his slow response.

"You leave me no choice then. Kill them," commanded the rat leader.

As the rats rushed in, Kelly reached out with his power and knocked two rats out of commission. Nathan went into hand-to-hand combat and disabled three other attackers, despite his own injuries. Kelly conjured a wall of flame around them and yelled at Nathan, "Use your spells to fight!"

Nathan extended his uninjured hand as lightning sparked from it, building in intensity and strength

He let out a scream while crackling energy streamed and forked out, electrocuting four other rats that convulsed in pain and dropped to the ground.

Both seized the opportunity to escape, turned into their wraith forms and flew away, leaving the rats to curse them as they left. Nathan hated those vile creatures, and now that he knew their scent, he had no problem with taking them out as long as he wasn't outnumbered. Physically, he craved the next time he fed from them. Their life force enhanced his vampiric powers and soothed his desire for blood. Yet, he felt lower than ever. The answers to this mystery seemed impossible to get to, guarded by those set to destroy him. He wondered if he'd ever solve his wife's murder or find his child, and even questioned his own motivations after Kelly's interjection on the matter. Should he let go and leave vengeance behind? No, he couldn't, not after hearing her voice, not after she asked about their son. That's why he was doing this, for the boy. But for now, he didn't have any leads to follow or have safe passage through enemy territory. He would need to involve Zander, someone not keen on saving the living and for some unexplained reason, was dead set against doing what Nathan perceived as necessary. "All in due time" wasn't good enough for Nathan and he feared his son had little time left.

They arrived at the graveyard, and without a word, Nathan stomped into the mausoleum, slamming the door shut. He hopped up on his concrete slab as ire percolated and tempted to boil over. Despite Nathan's actions, Kelly entered. Nathan lay on the slab and refused to turn his head to acknowledge Kelly's presence in what he now considered his home.

"So, you've decided to procure your residence here instead of going back to the comforts of Zander's house. How quaint," Kelly said.

"I didn't invite you in."

"I'm not a vampire. I go where I please." Kelly leaned his shillelagh on the wall next to the door, came over to the tomb, and sat on the slab next to Nathan.

"So I've noticed." Nathan turned the opposite direction.

"Let's have a look at your wounds, shall we?" Kelly grabbed Nathan's arm and Nathan jerked his arm away. The pain arrived once more and radiated all through his extremity.

"What's the matter with you? You handled yourself well back there. Why so glum?" Kelly asked.

Nathan spun around and whipped his legs into a sitting position, almost knocking Kelly over, and said, "What's the matter? Why didn't you warn me about that little welcoming committee we ran into? How's about that?"

"I did try to warn you, but you wouldn't listen. You dive in without knowing what you're getting yourself into. You took off, hell bent on answers. Now you know why we don't rush into places like that."

Nathan went to argue, but admitted to himself that it was indeed his fault, and said, "You still should have told me." Nathan begrudgingly held out his arm and lifted his shirt with the other. Kelly didn't point out that he was right, and looked at the wound on his arm and the gash on his torso's side. His injuries, though not fatal, had compromised his defenses. He swore to never forget this harsh lesson in combat: never lower your defenses, even during your attack.

"They will heal overnight if you rest. I can't heal these instantly," Kelly said.

"Why not?" Nathan asked.

"They're wounds from a lycanthrope and that takes more time to heal. And besides, you're an undead. I only heal the living."

"I thought you knew necromancy and could manipulate the undead?"

"I don't practice in that. It's too dangerous. I don't dare reanimate anything. I have the knowledge, but such abilities can bloat one's ego and you forget to respect the dangers of magick."

"What are the dangers?"

"Your intended can turn against you, or become a slave to you, or you simply think you can wield the power of a god and falsely believe one can control the nature of life and death, which isn't so. No, I leave temptation alone." Kelly stood up and went over and picked up his shillelagh, "Get some rest."

As Kelly left, he said, "And Nathan, we need to improve your skills and mix your magical powers with your vampiric abilities. They do you no good if you forget to use them in battle."

"Point taken," Nathan said, holding his arm which throbbed in unspeakable agony. He hadn't hurt like this since he was ten and wrecked his bike. He flipped over the handlebars, broke his arm and bruised his ribs. His injuries brought back such a painful memory, and yet he couldn't help but smile, for this piece of insignificant memory brought with it another detail of a life that seemed so long ago but concurrently, like it happened yesterday.

Nathan sunk back into the darkness of the crypt. Two sunrises came and went, though he only rested enough to heal. His mind raced, unwilling to give in to deep slumber the first night. His thought dwelled on the past until his body couldn't fight off the deprivation of sleep.

Murray sat in the passenger's seat and stared out the side window where beading rain water contorted visibility beyond the glass. He looked out into the nothing where his thoughts strayed, and he wondered about something that had never crossed his mind until recently: *Why haven't I retired?* He searched for reasons and reflected on this, but the answer went beyond logic. He narrowed it down to pure stubbornness, not wanting to lose, and he refused to let go over some self-imposed image born from pride. He justified to himself that his credibility was at stake, and he didn't want to be one of those burnt-out cops that had no driving force. Still, he drudged on, but couldn't justify it any longer. The bitter truth tasted of crow and defeat. He spat it out in defiance.

He didn't want to admit it, but he liked being a cop and all that came with it. But at what cost? The last thing he wanted to become was what he detested: apathetic. And in spite of all his hatred toward those who felt they were privileged, whose complacent nature superseded common sense, he admitted he did enjoy his station in society as someone who mattered and the occasional fringe benefits that came with the job.

He wondered when he'd started to lie to himself, how long had passion's flames turned to dying embers. Cooper's optimism clashed with jaded age. If only life hadn't rid him of naivety. This left a sour taste of mortality in his mouth.

As they passed Beshkno's city limits, Cooper said, "I don't like not informing the sheriff's department about this."

"No," Murray snapped out of his introspective moment, "if we did that, then we'd involve Deveraux and our department and I'm not going to let them know anything unless we've got something concrete. Until then, we go dark."

"Oh, I agree. I don't like going into a situation where I may need back up and it's not available, is all I'm saying." Cooper moved his head forward and peered through the drenched windshield and slowed down.

"It's the next turn," Murray said. "I don't like it either, but sometimes you don't have a choice."

Cooper drove on until he arrived at the correct turn and steered into the winding gravel road. He continued on, passing farmland and the occasional home along the way. Soon after, they pulled into a gravel parking lot on the roadside where several motorcycles were parked. The old, wooden building resembled more of a log cabin than a business. Cooper entered the parking area next to an unlit sign that read "White Fang Country Club—members only."

Cooper switched off the ignition and put the keys in his pocket. Murray leaned his seat back and lit a cigar. Cooper almost got out the car but noticed Murray had settled in. Cooper waited a moment, but saw Murray wasn't in a hurry to get inside and find Kevin who had run off and disappeared. They didn't want their only potential witness or suspect falling off the face of the earth before they solved this case, a case no one wanted solved except the two men sitting in this car. Though Murray acted as if he had no worries about finding their witness, and this confused Cooper.

"Don't we look conspicuous sitting out here?" Cooper questioned.

"That's the point," Murray said.

"I thought we were coming to take the kid in."

"He's here, and they'll hide him. He has no charges pending, and we don't have a search warrant." Murray didn't even have his eyes open when he responded, his cigar dangled from his mouth.

"So why did you have me ask Sylvia to track these guys down if taking Kevin in isn't a part of the plan?" Cooper removed the cigar that teetered and drooped from Murray's pursed lips, drawing his partner's attention toward the task at hand.

Murray peeked over at Cooper with the one eye he had opened, snatched his cigar back from Cooper's grasp and relit it, "We go in, question the upstanding citizen's brigade in their establishment, and then leave them guessing our next move. Kevin gets spooked and comes back to us under his own volition, if all goes well."

"If all goes well? Murray, has it ever occurred to you that this guy might run away out of our reach?" Cooper asked.

"He won't." Murray puffed on his cigar and blew

smoke rings, then continued, "He's too scared to go it alone. One doesn't tend to stick around when a major crisis happens unless they have nowhere else to go, and he has nowhere to go. Follow me?"

Cooper slouched back in his seat, "That's still a hell of a risk you're taking. You assume a lot."

"When you encroach on someone's sanctuary, they either burrow in and hide or panic and run." Murray flicked ash off into the plastic container he used as an ashtray.

"What if he skips town?"

"Okay, let's say he does. He's homeless, has no money. If these guys move him too far away, someone will notice, and these are the type of guys that don't want that. Not now anyway. And you know as well as I do that he'll get picked up eventually if he goes somewhere else. I doubt it comes to that, so trust me on this."

"Oh, that's an encouraging thought."

"Have I ever been wrong?" Murray put out his cigar and left it balancing on the edge of the makeshift ashtray. Cooper rolled his eyes.

"Are you ready?" Murray asked.

"I've been waiting on you." Cooper slammed the car door shut.

Murray opened his door and climbed out, "Just leave the questioning to me."

"You've got it. The floor is all yours." Cooper bowed and let Murray step in front of him and he followed along as they passed through the motorcycle maze, up the steps to the front entryway.

The doorman said, "Members only."

"Fletcher is expecting us," Murray said.

"You have a lot of nerve showing your face around here."

"What do you think, Cooper? Should we make this friendly visit into a not-so-friendly visit?" Murray asked.

"I could invite the Sherriff's Department along. I can call them if you like," Cooper said.

The doorman grunted, "Go in."

The weathered and rustic wooden walls and cathedral ceiling's condition inside matched the outside of the structure. Filth and stale beer ingrained the floorboards. Rickety tables and chairs were scattered about in no chronological order. Only the pool tables to the left of the entrance reflected anything modern within the establishment. The attending members wore jean or leather jackets, an emblem on the back depicting a full moon with a huge wolf fang piercing the celestial body. 'White Fang" was written on the bottom of the moon, in line with the moon's curve.

"Just looks like your normal watering hole," Cooper said.

"It does hold a certain charm, doesn't it?" Murray replied with a smile.

The members ceased their various activities and watched the two detectives enter and step up to the bar, ordering beers. The onlookers gathered and surrounded the detectives as the bartender glanced over Murray's shoulder to someone who stood behind them with his arms folded across his chest. The man nodded approval, and the bartender uncapped two bottles and slid them toward their unwelcomed guests. A patron sat next to them and gawked at Murray with an unkind expression on his face, projecting anger and disgust. His attempt to make the two feel uncomfortable failed. Defiantly, the veteran detective turned and blew cigar smoke in the intimidator's face and then burped. Laughter erupted from behind them as the man backed away, infuriated. The man who allowed them to be served claimed the stool next to Murray, his back and shoulders leaning against the bar's edge and said, "Well, look who stepped into my lair."

"Fletcher, it's been a long time." Murray continued drinking his beer and smoking without giving him any eye contact, "About how long?"

"Six years. I got out almost a year ago. I wasted away in a cell for nearly five years and now my turf decays, thanks to you. Spinelli exploited the situation and lay claim to the spoils of a war he never had to fight, a pure coincidence to be sure." Fletcher spat out the last words as if they were meant to cut deep. Murray didn't react to this verbal pressure.

"You can't blame that one on me." Murray turned to Fletcher, "I got the other charges dropped. You got charged by the Feds for conceal and carry. As far as your turf's concerned, better it remain in ruins than another urban battlefield. You going away for a spell probably saved many lives, including your own."

"I'm sure you tell yourself that before you go to sleep at night, isn't that right boys?" Fletcher yelled out the last part to the entire place. They answered in a stir of indistinct, rabble rousing cadence, like a lynch mob that responds when prompted. Cooper's eyes went to Murray who ignored his telling stare.

"Who says I can sleep, that is, without a little liquid

help." Murray held out his empty bottle and signaled for another. The bartender looked to Fletcher, who again nodded allowance. Murray thanked the man behind the bar as he snatched up the recently-opened bottle. Murray's gratitude was acknowledged with a dismissive grunt, "And by the way, you forget that you were losing that war anyway, so don't ask me for penance over your sins." Murray tipped up his newly-opened bottle and took in a huge swig.

Fletcher's palpable rage emanated in his eyes, "What do you want? Big Mike sent you to check up on me? I haven't entered his territory, so tell him to back off."

"I'm not here on Mike's account. I didn't even know you'd gotten out. I just learned about your little club house this evening. I'm looking for a youngster named Kevin. Happen to know where he went?" Murray asked.

"Never heard of him," Fletcher deadpanned.

"Well, that's funny. He has your paint on his arm."

"What do you want from him, in case he stops by?" Fletcher rose from the stool and walked around in back of the detectives, stalking them like a beast waiting for his cage to open, ready to pounce.

"Oh, come now. Let's not mince words. You know why I'm looking for him," Murray said as he and Cooper turned and stood up. "It's not safe for him to run off like he did."

"I take it you came here out of the goodness of your heart. No arrest warrant?" Fletcher asked with a grin that went ear to ear.

"They'll kill him if they find them."

Fletcher stepped in close to Murray, "Not while I'm

around. So, you have no warrant, no back up, and you're out of your jurisdiction. How gullible are you? Do you think I'm just going to let you walk away without me getting my retribution?"

Murray glanced over at Cooper and back at Fletcher, he let the beer bottle slide through his hand until he had it by the neck, concealed behind his back, "I'm no fool. I just don't give a damn."

Before anyone could react, Murray busted the beer bottle over Fletcher's head. It shattered and sent Fletcher riling as he bent down and to the side upon its impact. Murray and Cooper started punching the group that closed around them, but they were quickly subdued. They went to the floor where they were kicked and beaten until Fletcher stopped everyone. The crowd picked up the bloodied men and Fletcher said, "Next time you come here without a warrant, I'll bury you."

The group threw the two out the door onto the wet, gravel parking lot where they landed hard. It took a moment for the detectives to move from the ground where they lay in pain. Murray managed to crawl on all fours when Cooper threw gravel at him. Murray put up a hand to protect himself as he made his way off the rocky surface and said, "What was that for?"

"What in the hell did us getting our asses kicked accomplish?" Cooper yelled as he unsteadily got off the ground.

"Quit your whining. We got the job done." Murray patted his pockets for a cigar despite the rainfall. He found his remaining cigar in his pocket, soaked and mangled. He cast it aside, frustrated.

"I fail to see what that accomplished other than showing somebody you've arrested before that they can bully you." Cooper brushed off his sopping clothes.

Murray walked over to a cycle familiar to him, its reddened gas tank with purple flames glistened in the rain. He pulled out his revolver, shot both tires, and put two holes in the gas tank. The cycle toppled as people armed with bats and chains rushed out of the building onto the wooden deck in response to the commotion. Murray stood there, his revolver at his side, and stared at Fletcher who had made his way to the front of the crowd, signaling for everyone to remain where they were. Murray turned away and walked to the car.

"Are you out of your mind?" Cooper got in front of Murray.

"Don't ever question me in front of people, especially people like this, ever again," Murray spoke through clenched jaws, his anger latently guised, He walked around Cooper and without breaking his stride or looking, shot out the driver's side window. He went over to the passenger's side door and opened it as if nothing had occurred and slid into his seat.

"Great! Just great!" Cooper brushed out the glass from his seat with his jacket balled up around his hand, "I get to leave with glass in my kicked ass and mud on my face."

Cooper spun his wheels on the gravel and took off down the road.

"This guy is trouble, isn't he?" the man who had tried

to intimidate the detectives said in Fletcher's ear while the rest of the crowd proceeded inside.

"He's relentless." Fletcher watched the headlights disappear into the night.

"If he knows. . . "

"Then everyone else will, if they don't already," Fletcher sighed.

"What do we do about Kevin?"

"Have you found where he's hiding?"

"He's somewhere in the city again. Probably went back to the alleys. I say we let him burn. He should have stayed with us. He's caused enough damage."

"It wasn't his fault." Fletcher paused for a long moment and said, "We'll find him and protect him."

"What about the truce? If we harbor him, then we risk all."

"The damage is already done. Our hand is being forced here. We have no choice. We stick together and protect our own," Fletcher said.

"I'll tell the others to prepare," the man said.

"And tell them we're not coming back here." Fletcher looked into his eyes with conviction, "No retreat."

"That'll be a hard sell."

"We don't have a choice. Besides, subservience doesn't befit us anyway. We should have done this long ago."

"You only did what you thought was right, what kept us safe."

"Did I, or did I delay the inevitable?"

Ivan stormed into the underground courtroom with his sword drawn. The audience, now silent, parted for his entrance. Unannounced entry violated decorum unless there was a crisis, and this act seemed brazen even for such a warrior. The six foot, blond-haired Enforcer flourished a distinct battle scar along his left cheek as a badge of honor., It had historic meaning for the warrior that few knew, not to say he unwillingly kept this secretive if one pried, but few to none dared to pose the question. Ivan kneeled at the steps of the dais and lowered his head with his sword propped up in front of him. Amused, Radomir turned from his colleagues to address the warrior.

"What a pleasant surprise." Radomir gestured for Ivan to rise, "I don't recall summoning you. So, pray tell, what brings you before me, Enforcer?"

The coterie laughed at Radomir's quip as Ivan stood, his head still bowed and his blade held firm in his hand, "I've come to rightfully claim my place in the stead of the one who has fallen."

"You refer to the one that failed. The one you executed and mean to replace?"

"That I am." Ivan raised his chin up high. His grimace emanated a warrior's rage, ready for the challenge.

Radomir brushed away the crowd surrounding the suitor, "How am I to believe your conviction, that your dedication and pursuit of rank hasn't been devised by Commander Jade in order to spy on me?"

The adoring throng parted even wider from the warrior. The guards flanked the vampire and closed in, their hands readied on their hilts. Prudence kept them at enough distance as to not incite a confrontation but they prepared to cut Ivan down at the slightest deception or at the mere will of their liege. He hadn't shown himself as a threat but was armed in the High Commander's presence, so prudence dictated caution.

"I desire advancement, and my superior has lost favor. I hope for redemption from my superior's failure."

"Spoken like a true warrior. But again, how to prove your conviction?"

"I request consideration only after a trial by combat."

"Granted." The guards stood down as Radomir summoned two vampires from the assembly, one an Enforcer named Baldar who strutted forward, his blade resting over his shoulder, his arrogance matching that of the one who summoned him. The other, Miro, glided over, his black and red robes fluttering behind him. He posed, his hands crackling with energy in a boastful power display. "These are the other suitors," said Radomir. "I thought it would be a treat to see two competing for station, but three is a dream come true. The last one standing earns their rightful place at my side. You may begin."

Miro acted first and vaulted energy bolts from his hands at the other opponents. Baldar jumped to the safety of the low ground, barely dodging the sudden aerial barrage, and rolled toward the partial cover of the dais. Ivan sidestepped the volley and rushed in for a counterattack. The errant projectiles slammed into some unexpected onlookers, rendering them incapacitated, or worse.

Before Miro launched another foray or reacted in any other fashion, the encroaching adversary closed the distance and spun as he maneuvered past, his long sword trailing in his path, and lobbed the intended's head off. As his enemy's cranium fell unceremoniously, Ivan's spinning assault ended with his blade impaled through the decapitated body's chest from behind, piercing the heart that exploded within upon impact. Ivan pulled the blade from the slumped corpse that quickly decayed upon contact with the floor. He whipped his blade around in an arch, his weapon brandished, and readied against the next combatant.

Baldar raised himself from his prone position on the ground, paced slowly in the direction of his rival with his sword dangling loose in his hand, slapping the blade on his leg, studying his opposition with haughty expectations of a quick kill. And yet, the assailant's theatrical flair amused him.

"Lovely pirouette, but this isn't the ballet." Baldar pressed an aggressive series of wild side swings that caught Ivan off guard and drove him backwards. Ivan blocked the first wave of the ferocious assault and Baldar broke off his attack. He didn't want to get too aggressive and expose himself to a counter move. Both fighters tested each other's strengths and weaknesses with brief clashes of their blades. Both sought an upper hand and exploited their vulnerability.

Embraced in a seemingly never-ending power struggle, the warriors broke from their ironclad hold and stepped away, encircling one another, and studied and scrutinized their challenger's form and technique. The adversaries collected themselves and bided for the next opportune moment to strike, trying to anticipate the other's subsequent move.

Unable to discern his enemy's fighting style, Ivan set

into a defensive position, poised to counter but letting Baldar take the offensive, baiting him in, hoping to find an opening. But his rival's assertive melee forced Ivan into an all-out defense that left him unable to counterstrike. The attacks came from every conceivable angle, flawless and seemingly without end.

But after several frays, Ivan perceived an attack pattern in the foe's arcing, whirlwind form that consisted of circular motions that, when followed with precision, made one succession of attacks seem relentless. Its method had an overt flaw. The beginning stance telegraphed the attack pattern and relied on unerring execution of the form. Hence, with such an inflexible style, if one disrupted the attack's fluid movement, one rendered the pattern useless.

Once Ivan discovered this, he found his adversary's onslaught predictable and manipulated the skirmish with ease. "You're right," Ivan mocked. "This isn't the ballet, it's a waltz. Now I'll take the lead."

Ivan took the aggressor's turn this time and leveled his blade downward two-handed in a swift, mighty blow. His nemesis blocked the strike at the last second at the cost of sure footing. Baldar lost his balance and fell back to the ground. He managed to land into a crouched position and rose up, enraged.

"No need to curtsey," Ivan said, "the dance isn't over." He had his opponent frustrated and venomous, and Ivan wanted to keep him that way; not thinking and only reacting. He permitted Baldar a straight charge at him, drawing him into a false sense of control as he parried and countered, just enough to keep him at bay with false hope while he waited for the perfect opening: the killing blow.

When Baldar overextended a wild downward swing, Ivan pushed his final retaliation. "I believe the music's crescendo is approaching." Ivan didn't want to just kill Baldar, he wanted to make an example out of him, to degrade him in order to prove his worth to his new commander. He parried the swing, whirled around Baldar, and with his back to his opponent, made a blind side stroke. And in that moment, before the sword's edge burrowed through flesh, Baldar's eyes went wide open as he realized defeat had come to claim him when Ivan's blade encircled through the intended target's neck.

Again, Ivan had decapitated his enemy and the body drooped to the ground. Ivan clawed his way through, underneath the ribcage, and ripped the fallen's heart out, holding it up in the air triumphantly. Deafening applause roared throughout the room as the audience clamored around the victor to congratulate him, especially his new commander who stepped down to greet the winner on the killing floor, kicking Baldar's head out of the way as he stepped toward Ivan.

"Bravo!" Radomir said. "All hail Ivan the Terrible."

The crowd responded in laughter and cheers while Ivan presented the heart to Radomir who took the trophy and bit into it, holding the organ up in victorious fashion.

As the victor's celebration thrived, a vampire slipped away from the rest of his cohorts. Making his way into a hallway off the throne room, he approached the being sunken down in the darkness and said, "It is done."

"Excellent." Jade stepped out from her darkened cover with a derisive smile and thought, *All is set in motion. The time for him to give back what he has taken has come.*

Chapter Eight

Nathan and Kelly weren't surprised with Zander's requested audience with them held true when they arrived at Zander's home. Zander stood, his arms cradled behind his back. Two guests sat on the couch. The three ceased their debate when Nathan and Kelly stepped through the door. The tension filled the room. Nathan smelled the all too familiar scent of were-rat from the small, thin man with beady eyes. Next to him sat a much larger man. Despite being only human, he possessed an aura of authority.

"Please join us." Zander grabbed two chairs from their spot at the dining room table and placed them alongside him and facing the two guests on the couch. Kelly settled in to one of the chairs while Nathan remained standing. He peered at the were-rat, his fixed gazed turned into a staring contest with the beast who openly displayed his aversion for the vampire through his own defiant glare.

Zander turned to Nathan, "Remember, you are all guests in my home."

"This one smells of rat." Nathan said, making made his disgust known.

"Let the man introduce himself before you go and judge him," Kelly said.

"And act civil," Zander said.

Nathan took his cue, put his apprehension aside, and

sat down. He didn't like pandering to his new-found enemy one bit. Though he conceded, he hadn't changed his opinion nor quelled his fury, but his intuition told him of the meeting's importance. Hence, he swallowed his pride while he clenched his teeth, displayed his fangs, and complied. He knew he had to bend to their whims, a price he promised to pay if it led to his son and those responsible for all of this. Nobody present here trusted the rats either, but necessity dictated this course. They needed to gain access to the rat's territory for answers.

"Do you smell that?" the were-rat said to the man sitting next to him. "It smells like something died in here."

Nathan sprang from his chair and hissed at the were-rat, ready to lash out at his antagonizer. Zander held his arm in front of Nathan to prevent any rash hostility. The rat smiled in defiance while the other man patted him on the shoulder and laughed, "Pardon my brother's wicked sense of humor. I assure you he didn't intend to disrespect anyone here, especially after the unfortunate misunderstanding that occurred yesterday."

Zander directed his gaze at Nathan, who in turn nodded a non-verbal assurance that he wouldn't pursue the transgression even though it took great self-restraint to stand down. Zander lowered his arm and said, "You must forgive Nathan for any trespasses as well. He still possesses lingering mortal emotions that he hasn't yet purged. It's something our kind must endure and takes time."

"No harm, no foul," the big man said.

"Well then, I'm sure we'll resolve this matter quickly," Zander replied.

Nathan dropped down to his chair but didn't settle

117

back into it. Rather, he dangled on the edge of his seat, prepared to bounce upright at a moment's notice.

"Excellent!" said the large man as he turned his attention toward Nathan. "I'm Michael Spinelli. Most call me Big Mike, so please, feel free to do the same. This fiery little runt next to me is my brother, Angelo."

Angelo didn't acknowledge them or offer any form of greeting whatsoever. In fact, he seemed aloof, like he wasn't paying attention to anyone. But under close scrutiny, you would notice his nuances of awareness, that he watched every reaction to everything spoken or implied and communicated this with his brother through non-verbal means. And like all heightened beings, his senses were in tune to catch the subtlest of hints and actions; a useful tool for someone of stature.

"I know who you are. You're splattered all over the news, rubbing shoulders with politicians, being treated like royalty. But the truth is, you're nothing but a mobster," Nathan said.

Angelo's head snapped between Nathan and his brother, a blatant reaction he didn't normally show, and waited for the signal to act on such brazen insolence. Big Mike's eyes went cold, "I'm that and more. I own half this city legitimately, and all of it otherwise. With that in mind, next time you boys go wandering through my territory, get clearance before someone makes a fatal error in judgment and someone gets hurt, or worse."

"Will you allow us safe passage?" Kelly asked.

"That is precisely what we were discussing before you joined us," Zander interjected to bring some levity and calm matters. "That is, under certain agreements set here. I believe they are acceptable given that certain past transgressions have been resolved. Agreed?"

"Seeing that our interests are the same, how could I say no?" Big Mike's eyes brightened and his demeanor returned to the jovial persona he displayed in public. He stood to leave. Even so, his eyes never left Nathan.

"Your generosity knows no bounds." Zander bowed to both men as they rose and exited. Both guests nodded as they left.

Zander stood over Nathan, his arms crossed, and glared at him. Nathan leaned back, defiant, and rolled his eyes that skimmed over Zander and darted his gaze away as if he could not care less.

"What did that cost us?" Kelly asked.

"Dearly, I'm afraid." Zander continued staring at Nathan as he responded to Kelly, but his reply seemed more for his defiant novice than him. "Whatever information we gather we pass on to them before we act, and they allow us safe passage through their territory."

"That's madness," Kelly said.

"I didn't have any choice." Zander turned toward Kelly, "There's more happening here than you know."

"I'm perfectly aware of what's transpiring. Don't treat me as someone who doesn't." Kelly raised his voice, something Nathan never had witnessed before.

Fair enough," Zander nodded in acknowledgment. "Regardless of what I feel, I've been designated to resolve this dispute for all parties' interests."

Nathan shot a glare up at Zander and let his sarcasm roll from his lips, "Well, their needs conflict with mine, and I refuse to twiddle my thumbs and wait for their approval."

"Your impetuous decision caused this. Any leverage I had turned into irrelevant fodder once your rash actions came to light. If you had come to me I could have secured safe passage through the proper channels and avoided all of this. Your mortal pride got the best of you and you just couldn't wait that long, could you?" Zander's fury thundered through his admonishment, and he hoped Nathan understood the implications of his deeds.

Nathan stood and waved his finger in Zander's face, "You're damn right I couldn't wait. I'm not bending to anyone's whim, especially one coming from a rat."

Nathan stormed out and said as he went through the door, "And neither should you." When he reached outside, he took to the air and left as a thunderclap of power boomed, the aftershock forcing the door shut.

"You told me you'd keep him under control." Zander strolled over to the cold, unlit fireplace and stared into the sod-covered bricks as he stroked his chin.

Kelly walked toward the fireplace, "His temperance will settle in time, although I can't disagree with him. And since I subscribed to his deeds, I'm also to blame."

"I'm sure he left you no choice. Without you, he would have been killed. He's reckless." Zander whipped a glance over his shoulder, "Emotions still cloud his judgment."

"But his reasons are sounder than you're willing to admit. Keeping him in the dark this long has been a mistake and almost cost us our lives," Kelly sighed. "We shouldn't have let the rats take the city. They're burrowed in too deep now, not without a fight."

"I'm well aware of that," Zander turned and faced Kelly. "The Dark Temptress herself said that the Council agreed yet the Assembly voted differently. I pleaded my case, but she informed me that the rats had already made their move and convinced the humans and the others not to interfere. Before we knew what was coming, checkmate. In retrospect, our inaction cost us more than defeat would have."

Kelly said nothing. He grasped what occurred and their position at the time. But now their past gaffes had come to haunt them, and they had to deal with the collateral damage. Most other vampires and lycanthropes abandoned the city after the rats gained control. And when Big Mike and his brother rose to power, it complicated things further; Mike was human and Angelo was a were-rat with ties to organized crime, and they used this influence to make the rats untouchable. With Angelo as Rat King and his brother in charge of the city, there was nothing that anyone could do about it.

"We can ill afford another open war, not in this day and age. The Dark Temptress wants me to quell this situation before it gets out of hand, by any means possible." Zander paced as he said this aloud, speaking more to himself than Kelly.

"So we allow the rats to build their power structure and do nothing?"

"We wait out the storm and rush in when all is calm, when apathy sets in. It's what vampires do."

"And our passiveness will be our downfall. We can't afford to sit idle this time. We must act."

Zander turned back to the fireplace, "You sound like Nathan, an impetuous human."

"Perhaps that's why we've lost so much over time,

pondering our existence while it's being chipped away by those we consider inferior, who are willing to delve into the fray without fear of the future. Perhaps we stand a better chance fighting instead of posturing," Kelly said.

"You don't believe I haven't considered these scenarios? That I blindly disagree with you? No Kellan, I believe we are making a grave mistake with our inaction."

"Then why argue?" Kelly asked.

Zander sighed, "If I approve openly, then our kind is held responsible," he turned to Kelly, his hands cradled in one another behind his back. "But if I object. . ."

Kelly interrupted, "You're using him as bait." He slowly walked closer to Zander, nose to nose and tilted his head, "And you figure, he's expendable."

As Kelly marched out and slammed the front door shut, Zander replied, "Precisely."

"I told you we'd catch a break." Cooper whipped around the sharp corner into the old, narrow street, and headed toward the crime scene, or rather, across the street from the crime scene.

"How reliable is the witness?" Murray thumped on his legs with his fingers to sate the gnawing sensation that the addicted endure when deprived of their cravings. And right about now, with such a persistent itch, he yearned for the soothing burn on his lips that only smoke inhaled deep within could scratch. He couldn't light up a stogie before questioning a potential witness in their own home.

In all his years, Murray had never experienced such an

emotional rollercoaster ride, and this sense of helplessness made matters worse. From second-guessing himself on the job and allowing his relationship problems to convolute, not only were these issues foreign to him, but were dangerous trends that got people killed in his line of work. And with that, his fierce determination took hold, and his patience had worn thin. He wanted to get this over with and see if the witnesses' story held up or led to another dead end.

"Did our witness have a memory lapse until it hit the news or what?" Murray asked.

"She claims she saw something on TV that reminded her of something," Cooper said.

"Great, an armchair detective is exactly what we need about now."

"Don't be so pessimistic. Besides, Barker says she's a sweet old lady."

Murray sighed, "Wow. Thanks. Now I feel all better. We'll have this whole case wrapped up in no time." Dejected, Murray leaned back in his seat and pulled a cigar out of his pocket.

"What's your problem?"

"Have you ever interviewed anyone elderly?" Murray struck a match on the car's dash.

"I talk to you on a daily basis, don't I?"

"Yeah, yeah, laugh it up. You won't find it so funny when we get in there." Murray lit his cigar and inhaled. At this point, he didn't care who he offended, the witness or the captain. He decided that at least he wouldn't be completely miserable if he lit up, regulations be damned.

"What crawled up your ass today? Or are you just old

and cranky?" Cooper pulled in front of the witnesses' house and parked street-side.

Murray ignored the gouging remark, "I hope she's not a widow, they're the worst. They tend to talk about everything except what you're there for."

"Why is that?" Cooper couldn't follow Murray's rationale.

"They're lonely, so they stretch out the conversation to avoid the end." Murray blew out a puff of smoke that choked up Cooper who rolled down the window. "And their recollection isn't what it used to be, so they claim, and their eyesight, and their hearing; not a reliable witness in my book."

"That book of yours has a pretty dusty cover," Cooper said.

"Watch it, smart ass," Murray replied as both men got out of the car.

They went up the sloped yard on the cobble stone walkway to the house when Cooper said, "My grandfather was ninety-four when he died, and his mind was as sharp as anyone's."

"Just out of morbid curiosity, what did he die from?"

"He got drunk on a family skiing trip. Went down a mountain he had no business going down, even sober, and hit a tree. We were told he died instantly, probably didn't feel a thing."

"Remind me to never go on vacation with you."

The weathered steps creaked in defiance as the

detectives ascended onto the unevenly sloped porch. A path, worn to the wood and devoid of the dark-gray, flaking paint that clung on to the rest of the floor, led from the steps straight to the door. Cooper pressed the yellowed, plastic intercom button situated next to the splintered, wooden screen door.

"Who is it?" a graveled from age but pleasant voice sounded from the speaker.

"Police, ma'am," Cooper said.

"Please ma'am what?" the voice asked.

Cooper grunted, and then, with apprehension, looked at Murray, whose silent laughter deafened any utterance given.

"It's Detective Murray. Officer Barker told us you were expecting us."

"Oh yes, dear," she said. "I'll be right there."

After a while, some time that seemed longer than it really was, the door locks disengaged and the solid wooden monolith of a door swung inward. The elderly woman's frail, petite frame leaned on her cane and greeted them, smiling, "Come in, come in. I just made some warm tea."

She wrapped the shawl draped over her shoulders, shaking, while the detectives opened the screen door and entered. The hinges and hydraulics that hadn't been lubricated in years sung out as she closed the massive door behind them. She led the men down the hallway until they reached her living area opposite the ascending stairway. The hard wood floors continued, but most of the floor was covered by an area rug centered in the room. The living area consisted of antique furniture, a television in the far corner, and walls that teemed with knick-knacks. Along with her accumulation of odds and ends, dust collected on most surfaces and permeated the air so much that one could taste the particles, making the room reek like a forgotten library.

The detectives seated themselves on the couch that aligned a coffee table. She nestled into her easy chair at the end. The chair's Florentine-patterned upholstery and wooden legs matched that of the chair and the other wooden furniture in the room. Placed on the end of the table in front of her, a tea set on a tray waited for them, the steam rising from the pitcher's spout.

"There's nothing like a warm drink on a cool day. It makes the bones ache less," she said as she poured hot liquid into three porcelain cups on dainty saucers and offered them to her guests. Cooper thanked her, the warm cup clattered on the saucer as he grabbed it. He sat the saucer with the cup still on it on the table and put his tablet on his lap, reviving the device to take notes. Murray also placed his saucer on the table but held his cup like a bowl and drank the scalding beverage, despite his hatred for hot tea. To him, there was only one way to drink tea, and that was iced. Although, in this case, he would make do. The dust coated everything from the walls to the flat surfaces and saturated the air, making his mouth feel barren of moisture. Anything that rid the dryness was most welcome. He never thought he'd desire a helping of Cooper's cheap brew, which only made him miss the special coffee at home even more, and the woman who made it.

"Now, Mrs. Nagle," Cooper began, "Officer Barker said you had some information for us concerning your neighbor's case."

"Oh, Ernie's grown into a fine young man. His mother and I were in the church choir together."

"Yes, he's a fine officer." Cooper only got that much out before she interjected again.

"He used to ride his Big Wheel up and down, up and down the sidewalk all day long. He had such energy."

"Mrs. Nagle," Cooper said.

"Don't be so formal. Call me Martha, or Marty. Friends call me Marty."

Murray sat by in silent amusement, save his eyes, and sipped on his tea, watching his partner's frustration mount. Cooper couldn't hide his befuddled expression if he wanted to but managed to pull it back in and stay on task.

"Okay Marty, you reported you saw someone with Mrs. Brooks the day before the incident?" Cooper asked.

"No dear, that afternoon."

"Did you happen to see this person around the block that day or recently?" Murray showed Marty a picture of Kevin. He handed her the photo for a closer look. She reached for her glasses that dangled from her neck and put them on. She viewed the photo carefully and said, "I haven't seen this young man around here during the day. At night, I cannot tell you. I'm usually in bed early. Is he related to this in some way?"

Cooper took the photo and handed it back to Murray and said, "No, ma'am. Just checking on a possible lead. Now back to my original question. At what time did you see Mrs. Brooks and this other person, if you recall?"

"Sometime after four I believe. Yes, it was right after four." Marty sipped her tea and brushed the wrinkles out of her skirt. "I went to collect the mail when I saw the other woman."

"Can you describe what she looked like?" Cooper stayed poised, ready to dictate the description.

"I can tell you exactly who it was, although I didn't realize who at the time."

Intrigued, the detectives paused and glanced at each other. Either this was the luckiest break one could catch or a total waste of time.

"The five o'clock news came on the other day, and that's when I remembered where I'd seen her before."

"What lady?" Cooper leaned in as he spoke.

"The Indian doctor, or Native American, or however it's said now, from the clinic. She's got such flowing, gorgeous hair."

Murray leaned back, convinced this lead was bogus, his doubt bled through his voice, "Dr. Half Moon?"

"Yes," Marty said, "I remembered her name having something to do with the sky."

"So, where did you see them together?" Murray's stern curtness took Marty by surprise. Startled, she set down her tea quickly, almost spilling the rest of the cup.

"They were in front of Rachael's house. Like I said, I went out to the mailbox and saw them going in the house." Marty stood and went over to the opposing wall where a picture of her husband hung. "The poor dear. I remember when my husband died. It was the saddest day of my life." She touched the picture as she finished. Murray rolled his eyes and Cooper dismissed him with a disgusted glance.

She turned and said, "She's too young to have gone through all of that, only to meet the same fate."

"And that's why your statement is important to us,"

Cooper said.

"Just a moment, if you don't mind," Murray said. "How did you see who it was if their back was to you?" Murray asked.

"They didn't have their back to me the whole time. They stopped on the porch for a moment and talked while Rachael hunted for her keys in her purse." Marty's indignant reply seeped through her decorum.

"So when they turned, did you see them from the front, or only the side and back?"

"I saw a brief glimpse of her from the front." Marty seemed more flustered, her answers shooting out more quickly as Murray pressed her.

"What else makes you believe this was the woman she was with? Can you describe anything else about her?" Murray asked.

"She had a lab coat on and carried a big bag with flowers on it," Marty said indignantly. Her posture and tone changed as she looked directly at Murray and said, "You think I'm making this up, don't you?"

"No one is implying that. We have to be sure," Cooper intervened to no avail.

"This is about my age, if I'm still competent, isn't it?"

Their brief silence said it all, the truth exposed without an utterance. Cooper felt instant guilt by association. Murray held steadfast to his belief and gave Marty nothing in return.

"Come with me." She marched into the dining room and both men followed. She went past the dining table to the buffet covered in pictures and pointed at a picture of a young woman posing in a flowing ballroom dress, "Do you see that young woman there. That youngster never would have imagined needing a cane, or growing too old and frail to dance. And that everything she ever held dear or loved would be taken from her. In her mind, she's still that young lady dancing."

She turned around, silent tears forming along the edges of her wrinkled eyes and said, "Just because I'm old doesn't mean I'm incompetent or blind. I know what I saw. How dare you insinuate such a thing. Didn't your mother teach you any manners? And to think, you did this to a lady, in her own home. Shame on you!"

Cooper went to speak but she shushed him before he could respond. She glared at Murray and said, "You should be the last one to judge. In a few years, you may be right where I'm standing. Now gentlemen, if you don't mind."

Marty headed to the door and the detectives followed quietly. As they made their way down the stairs, Cooper said, "I don't know about you, but right now I feel like an asshole."

"Yup." Murray could barely respond. Marty had hit too close to home for him to debate. But that's how his luck had run lately: when it came to women, he had it all wrong.

Chapter Nine

Zander and Kelly entered the crypt and found Nathan reclining on a stone slab, his favorite spot. Their entry didn't produce a response from Nathan who remained unfazed by their presence, even as they advanced toward him. Zander stood over Nathan, expressionless. Kelly remained behind and said nothing. Nathan turned his head slowly toward his uninvited guests, but anger burned through his eyes, and then he looked away.

"You could use a change of clothes and a shower," Zander said.

Nathan said nothing and brushed off his sleeves.

Zander continued, "I must tell you something, something you've waited a long time to hear. Although you're enraged, I believe you are ready to face some truths. And you may hate me for them."

"I hate you now." Nathan continued to look in the opposing direction, refusing to allow his eyes to drift in Zander's way.

"Then I can't do any more damage than I already have," Zander said, and sat down on the slab next to Nathan.

"Go on then, if it pleases you. Just don't expect any warmer of a reception than you're receiving now," Nathan said.

"I know what you seek."

Nathan turned toward Zander and said, "You don't have the slightest idea what I want, nor do you care."

"I have the answers you seek, but do I care? What I'm about to tell you will answer that. Do you remember the night—how did you put it—your mortal life ended?"

Suspicious, Nathan said, "Vaguely."

"The night you died I was there. You were the victim of Desmond, a Seditionist vampire. He had been on a killing spree, and when I tracked him down, he had just snatched you from the streets."

"Back up a moment," Nathan shook his head, attempting to make sense of all of this while trying to remember what happened, hoping all his questions would be resolved. "Why were you following him?"

"I have certain duties, believe it or not. Tracking down rogue vampires is one of them."

"Who made you the city watchdog?"

"We've digressed too far. That's a discussion for another day."

"It's always later with you, isn't it?"

"Let's focus on the subject at hand," Zander said. "You may admonish me at another time."

Nathan paused, "By all means. I wouldn't want to keep you from engaging me in this fabricated story of yours. After what you have put me through, I don't know if I can believe a word of this."

Without reacting, Zander continued, "He flew up and carried you to a nearby rooftop and began to take your life. By the time I arrived, he had bled you to the edge of death and had engaged some other humans who had the misfortune of seeing this event occur."

"Did you kill Desmond?" Nathan sat up, his interest peaked. For whatever reason, whether for vengeance sake or some other unknown factor, his doubt began to wane.

"Unfortunately. I tried to take him to face justice, but his brood would rather die in combat. You've met his kindred."

"So did he. . ." Nathan's question died off, and the realization crashed into him like a wrecking ball. His doubt had melted away, and he saw in Zander's eyes the truth in it.

"I sensed your power and couldn't let it die with you. Other humans came before I could act, and so that night I waited until you reached the morgue. When the opportunity arose, I assisted you in your transformation," Zander said.

Nathan stood and walked to the other end of the crypt, "You should have let me die."

"And if I had done that, then who knows what fate would have come to you, or any of us, including your son." Zander said.

Nathan charged at Zander, but Kelly blocked Nathan and said, "What's done is done. Let it go. It turned out to be a good thing."

"A good thing?" Nathan yelled. "He made me into a monster."

Kelly stepped back.

Zander explained, "It was necessary. Little did you know that you weren't entirely human, did you? Is that my fault too? Or did you prefer to die in ignorant bliss, just another victim the world would never know?" Zander's words cut deep.

"Why did you abandon me then? Why keep this from me?" Nathan paced about.

"I believed you would discover some of these things on your own. And I wanted to see if some of your powers would manifest naturally, without training." Zander stood and brushed the wrinkles from his suit. "It is rather dusty in here."

"I could have died, been destroyed, or worse." Nathan frowned while his shoulders and back slumped.

"I have seen my miscalculations and hope to rectify them. That is why I'm here," Zander said.

"No. You don't get to clear your conscience that easily." Nathan clenched his fists, holding on to the rage that filled him and pleaded to come out.

"What would you have of me? I cannot change what has passed."

"But you can change what is to come. You owe me." Nathan pointed a finger at Zander.

"In that I have already agreed to assist you. Fail or succeed, I cannot guarantee you will like the results. No matter the outcome, you will never forgive me, of that I am certain." Zander then turned and left.

"I'll come back later for training." Kelly's somber tone echoed in the tomb as he followed Zander.

Nathan thought for a moment. He never considered his son might already be dead or that he could not be saved. No, he had to be alive somewhere. Call it fate, intuition, or baseless hope; his son had to be alive. As the night became day, Nathan settled back to his stone slab and fell into another deep sleep.

"This way," the man in the White Fang sleeveless jean jacket waved, signaling his brethren to gather at the alley's four-way juncture of Dead Man's Land. The other six members, four males and two females, reached the indicated location. They traced their course through the putrid, confined space, a faint scent guiding them to their intended path.

"Oliver," a dark-haired female said, "the trail's gone cold. It's impossible to track here."

Oliver stood and rubbed his closely buzzed hair, frustrated. The muscles in his six-foot stature tightened, his compact upper torso making him look as wide as he was tall. They had entered deep into familiar enemy territory, but had lost their way to their objective. If they stayed, they had only blind luck to go on. If they left, they might not get another chance at this without being discovered. Either choice wasn't ideal.

And then an odor crossed them, all of them, from all four directions.

"Dammit, they led us right into an ambush." Oliver searched the darkened alleyways for the closing enemy stalking them. The group formed a tight, defensive circle, awaiting the inevitable attack. Glowing eyes shone in the black veiled paths, shrieking and hisses followed as were-rats stepped out from the shadows, their numbers at least doubled to that of the encircled.

A guttural voice sounded from one of the were-rats, "You shouldn't have come back. Although I'll admit, some of the boys had hoped you'd show up eventually."

"We're here to claim what is rightfully ours," Oliver said.

"Something or *someone*, perhaps?" the rat leader said, his overconfidence seeping through. "Predictable. No matter. Whatever you believe is yours is ours now. That is, if what you're saying is even the truth."

The rats gathered in a tight formation surrounding the trespassers, displaying their intimidating dominance over them with a show of force. Though outnumbered, Oliver's group stood defiant, unimpressed. In fact, their desire to fight outweighed their extraction plan and their bestial power radiated within them from their already changing forms. Oliver's eyes gleamed in anticipation, like that of a beast tethered far too long.

"Let us show you what happens when one stands in our way," Oliver said.

Oliver's group growled and morphed into their werewolf forms and pounced into the fray with teeth and claws. The were-rats began to scurry and take the defensive, but soon gained confidence through their numbers and struck at their rivals in unison. Although outmatched in strength, the were-rats started to gain the upper hand through sheer numbers and soon overwhelmed some of the werewolves. Oliver had five on him, having killed three already. He realized that more had come in reinforcement and joined the skirmish. His fury intensified as he viewed two of his fallen comrades around him, the dark-haired woman, her tresses now covering her fallen form, lay motionless on the ground. He howled into the sky in pain as his wrath engulfed his cognition and all that remained was vengeance. He began to fight without mercy, without benevolence. He clawed through the carnage toward the fallen woman. All who stood in his way were put aside in ruthless ferocity; bodies of the fallen flanked his path to her. He picked her up and carried her away amongst the clash as more combatants, werewolves who answered the call to their distress, rushed into the battle. The rats, seeing their position was overrun, scattered, abandoning their territory.

The limousine pulled in parallel along the curb where Radomir, Ivan, and another guard named Rowland waited in front of the Gomorrah night club. Music pounded from inside and patrons clamored behind a velvet-roped line that stretched down the entire front of the sidewalk. Two men in black suits exited from the front of the vehicle, approached the three and said to Radomir, "Only you."

"I don't like it," Ivan said as his hand gripped the short sword secured down his back, his jacket concealing the hidden blade.

"Don't fret," Radomir motioned to his guards to stand down. "Humans are stupid, but not that stupid."

One of the guards signaled for Radomir to lift his arms so he could be searched.

"Really?" Radomir tilted his head, "I'm a vampire. My teeth aren't in my pockets." Radomir winked at his brethren, who couldn't help but laugh.

The guard searching him looked at the other guard, who merely shrugged in uncertainty. The guards stood down and stepped aside. The vehicle's door swung open and Radomir looked inside vehicle before entering, only to step back when he peered in. Ivan stepped in front of Radomir, pulled out a dagger and said, "As you were saying about stupidity?"

"I admit my error in judgment," Radomir said.

Rowland pulled his handgun at the two men in black who pulled theirs as well. Some of the crowd behind them dispersed while others moved out of alignment of the drawn weapons and remained to watch, some ran away and hid or fled. The door man kept a level head and didn't react or abandon his post.

"Easy now," a voice from inside the limousine said. The two men lowered their weapons and Rowland did the same.

"What are they doing here?" Radomir pointed toward the inside of the vehicle.

"They're your clients," the voice said.

"I really don't like this now," Ivan said.

"Neither do I," Radomir said, passing by Ivan. "Wait here."

Radomir stepped into the limousine and the two men holstered their handguns and got into the automobile. The pulse of the music and clamor of patrons entering and exiting the club faded as they pulled away and headed into the streets and cruised through the heart of the city.

"Meeting you in front of the club is a bit conspicuous, don't you think?" the bald man who sat next to Radomir said. The man's black suit seemed to blend in with the leather upholstery of the seats. Three other men were positioned on the opposing seats. One of the men wore a grey suit and had brownish-blond hair that receded at his temples. The other men wore red suits with silver cross pendants on their lapels. Both had similar looks: olive skin and dark hair, except one had a groomed, thin beard and the other clean shaven. Their demeanor seemed stilted, fixed on their passenger.

"I prefer a throng over seclusion given the parties attending this meeting," Radomir said.

"Good point," the bald man said.

"I hope not to banter any longer than I have to. It's trifling and a waste of time. Shall we proceed?" Radomir viewed his surroundings, as if aloof to those present.

"Okaaayyyy," the man stretched out his response and glanced at the others, "Do you have the package?"

"Not currently. We've run into a little snag, as they say."

"What happened?"

"Someone beat us to it, but we've tracked down those responsible and shall retrieve it soon."

"That's unacceptable," the man leaned back, his frustration showing. "You guaranteed delivery, and now you tell me you not only don't possess it, but someone else has it?"

"I assure you all is well and under control, a mere hindrance."

"Then why are we hearing this from you instead of him?"

"Perhaps our Lord knew not to step into the viper's nest while the serpent is aware of intruders. But who am I to question his will?"

"Or your ulterior motives haven't played out yet, like instigating a war between the wolves and the rats."

Radomir said nothing in response, but his smile spoke volumes.

"Very well," the man said, "we will defer. But if you lose control of the situation and can't deliver soon, then I'll consider our contract nullified and hand the reigns over to these gentlemen," the man gestured to the men in red. "And that may get messy, as in collateral damage messy. Not to mention, you won't receive support in the Assembly, something you desperately need. You would be wise to remember that."

"Don't attempt your petty threats on me. I could end your pathetic life any time I please." Radomir bared his fangs as he said this.

The men in red drew silver-edged daggers and held them to the vampire's throat.

"I've endured the last of your idle threats," the bald man said. Radomir quelled his rage and smiled in a mischievous manner. The two men withdrew their weapons. "As you can tell, I cannot stave off their temperament for long. If you or Demetrius play games with us, then you might want to consider that the playground already has too many bullies in it. Treachery isn't wise. Are we clear?"

"Savvy. I will convey your concerns to our Lord as soon as possible."

The limousine decelerated and pulled up to the curb where Ivan and Rowland awaited their return. Ivan didn't hesitate and opened the door himself. Radomir exited without looking back or acknowledging the men whom he rode with. Ivan slammed the door shut and the vehicle drove off.

"I take that it didn't go well," Ivan said.

"Human dullards! They think they can threaten me with trivial words and empty promises? I wouldn't even have to deal with these sheep if Carlos hadn't failed to procure the child."

"Good riddance as far as I'm concerned," Rowland said. "Carlos was reckless, unreliable."

"Well stated. But now I have to retrieve the child before this egregious error comes to light and I find myself paying the consequences for his ineptitude," Radomir replied, "Come, let us ease our troubles with a drink of young blood."

The three vampires walked up to the ropes, and without a word, the doorman pulled the velvet barriers aside and they entered the club unhindered.

As the limousine pulled away, the bald man turned to the others and said, "I thought I explained that you're to refrain from intrusion into the proceedings until either the deal is finalized or I sanction such actions."

"I believe I speak for all present when I say that dealing with such creatures is pointless. They have no intentions of honoring the agreement," the man in grey said.

"That's exactly why they're here," the bald man looked in the direction of the other two men in red, "and consequently, why you're here as well. Whether the vampires deliver or not, we're to take out this brood's leaders. They've caused enough trouble in almost every country they've been in."

"Speaking of their penchant to cause chaos wherever they go, what happens if they manage to instigate a war here?"

"I doubt that Demetrius is even privy to Radomir's plans. This group's mantra is to conquer and gain power through any means necessary, and it's usually accomplished through subterfuge. So I don't see it as a viable scenario, yet it's not an unforeseen one. There's a course of action in place for instances such as these." He poured himself a drink from the minibar.

"Please elaborate." The man in grey followed and poured himself a drink as well.

"We take them out, as many as we can. It's best if we wipe them all out. Any threat of war in the United States is met with extreme prejudice. Not one wolf, rat, or vampire is spared. We do that, and we will squelch any type of conceived uprising from any other group in this country." He sipped from his drink and raised his glass, smiling.

"I only see one flaw in your plan: Spinelli. I don't think they will respond kindly to the government taking out any of their leaders," the man in grey said as he rubbed his chin.

"We'll compensate for their loss such as we've done before. Hell, with any luck, they may save us the trouble and take out their own if they stir up enough attention. Wrap up an inexpensive gift of self-preservation in fancy paper and they'll dismiss any action we commit against their own. It goes both ways." The bald man laughed at the irony of his last statement and tipped his glass to consume the rest of the drink.

"What if someone, let's say a third party, ensures a war occurs?" the man in grey said.

"Whoa, that's a rather delicate scenario you're presenting." The bald man pulled down his glass and gestured with an open, outreached hand. "Manipulating a war between two recognized entities of the Assembly is way beyond our authority. We could be charged with treason for even discussing this."

"Only if we fail," the bearded man in red spoke with a thick Italian accent.

"And what will your government do if they discover you abandoned your mission in order to start a war?" the bald man asked.

"The war for us began long before you or your country ever existed," the clean-shaven man in red spoke in the same thick accent. "Our ultimate mission is to win by any means possible."

"I believe our governments only care about the results of a war. Who and why won't matter, as long as humans come out the victors," the man in grey said.

The deafening silence that followed hung in the air as the men gave knowing looks at each other. The bald man put down his glass and took a gum pack out of his inner coat pocket, opened it, and wedged a single piece into his mouth, saying, "Then it's decided."

Humanity of all types, young and old, employed and destitute, stirred about or planted themselves in plastic-formed seats supported by flimsy legs in the waiting room just beyond the clinic's entryway. Murray and Cooper stepped over to the left of the locked-down double doors and approached the rectangular opening along the back wall, blocked off for the most part with thick Plexiglass, save for the bottom opening to pass paperwork back and forth between either side of the wall. The middle-aged nurse behind the glass busied herself shuffling papers and gnawed on her gum while she screened phone calls. She held up a finger upon the detective's approach, signaling for them to wait as she conducted business. Murray had no patience for this treatment and pressed his badge to the window, signaling to the nurse for her to hang up the phone. She immediately told the other party she would call them back and put down the receiver.

"May I help you?" the nurse failed to mask her disdain.

"We need to speak with Dr. Holly Half Moon." Murray said.

"She's seeing patients, and as you can tell," the nurse gestured toward the lobby, "she's very busy today. Perhaps I can schedule you in at another time?"

"This is time sensitive. We won't take but a minute of her time," Cooper said.

"She's in with a patient now, and I don't know how long it will be until she's through with them." The nurse seemed hesitant to comply.

"Don't worry about that. Just buzz us in and we'll catch her between patients." Cooper said.

"I'm not sure I can legally do that, patient confidentiality and all."

"How's this for legal? I get on the phone and get a search warrant, we shut the clinic down for at least a day, and you get to explain to everyone in this lobby why they don't get treated today."

The nurse glared through the glass, said nothing, and buzzed them in.

The detectives came through the door as Cooper asked, "Which way?"

"Down that hall." The nurse pointed them to the hallway that headed straight toward the back of the building and then turned away.

"Oh, one more thing," Murray said. The nurse turned back to him and crossed her arms. "Does Dr. Half Moon own a bag or a purse?"

"Yes."

"What does it look like?"

"It's a big, flowered bag. Are we through?" The nurse shifted her weight to one hip.

"Thank you for your cooperation," Murray said as he and Cooper proceeded down the hall toward the curtained area where they walked along and waited until they caught the doctor going from one curtained area to the next.

"Dr. Half Moon?" Cooper showed his badge hanging from the lanyard around his neck. The woman almost passed by before stopping.

"Yes?" The woman peered over her shoulder, her long hair hiding part of her strong but feminine cheekbone and jawline.

"We have a few questions. . ."

"Gentlemen, please," she interrupted, "I will speak with you after I take care of this one last thing, I promise."

The detectives nodded in agreement, but she had already disappeared. They found two chairs and sat in the hall. They waited half an hour before she reappeared.

"Thank you for your patience," Dr. Half Moon said. "What can I help you with?"

"I'm Detective Murray and this is Detective Cooper. We'd like to discuss Rachael Brooks with you."

She looked from detective to detective, shrugging her shoulders, "Yes?"

"Would you care to elaborate on that visit? If you weren't aware by now, you were the last reported person to see her alive. You do remember that visit, don't you?" Murray asked, smirking. Her evasive behavior told him everything, and he hadn't asked her anything remotely pertinent yet.

"She contacted me about a class project for her students about health." Dr. Half Moon's eyes shifted away from them to a cart in the hallway full of medical supplies. "She wanted to coordinate a time when I could come to the school and speak to her students during that week."

"At what time did this happen?" Cooper asked.

"I don't remember, around four or five." She approached the rollaway cart, gathering supplies from the shelves. "It was a very brief meeting. Essentially, I told her I'd have to see when it came closer to the time and work something out from there."

"How long did this meeting last?"

"Less than an hour, I'm guessing."

"Why bother meeting at her home then? You could have discussed that anywhere, or on the phone, for that matter." Murray said.

"I don't know what to tell you, detective. She invited me over, and I was free at that time, so I obliged her."

"Did she discuss anything else with you?" Cooper asked.

"Her pregnancy, briefly." Dr. Half Moon fidgeted with the supplies cradled in her arms.

"Is there anything else that you can remember? No matter how trivial you may think it is. It's very important."

"Look, detective," she stepped backward down the hallway, "I understand you're only trying to solve this terrible crime, and I hope you catch who did this, but I'm afraid I have nothing more to tell you."

"Call us if you remember anything." Cooper pulled a card out of his pocket.

"Leave it with the nurse at the front and I'll pick it up later."

Murray and Cooper watched as she scampered down the hall and disappeared. Simultaneously, the detectives looked at each other, their thoughts attuned to one another.

"Did you buy any of that?" Murray wore an incredulous expression, not bothering to hide his disbelief.

"She didn't even bother to feign a reaction when we told her she was the last person known to see her alive."

"The guilty or those afraid for their lives usually won't admit what they know until pressed, leaving out anything that makes them culpable or will get them killed."

"And which do you think she is: guilty or afraid?"

Murray put a cigar in his mouth, "We shall see."

Cooper typed notes into his tablet, "Either way, she has to know we're onto her. You'd think someone who earned a doctorate degree would have more sense than that."

Murray walked away, "They don't teach you how to lie effectively in medical school. That's saved for lawyers and journalists."

Cooper began laughing and stopped, his mood changing when he grasped the meaning. He threw his arms up, followed Murray, and asked, "What's with you and all the backhanded comments?"

Chapter Ten

"I demand retribution." Oliver leaned over the rickety table, his knuckles whitened on the semi-flat surface as he leered at Fletcher.

"Not yet. We can't go in there with a full-frontal assault. If we do, they'll mow us down before we ever reach those responsible." Fletcher sat still, unflinching, in the dilapidated chair while Oliver bared his clenched teeth and let out a low growl from his throat. Oliver's display did nothing to shake Fletcher's resolution. The others stood back and let the leaders engage in their feud without interference so they could state their stance in the matter.

Fletcher didn't make an example out of his second-in-command, although he thought he should have, but he understood what happens when the fear of loss takes hold of someone. Oliver's wife, Julia, had sustained some serious injuries in the fight, which had resulted in the wolves claiming part of their territory back. But their victory came at a heavy cost. Two of their pack had died and Julia teetered on the edge of death.

"That's not good enough!" Oliver tossed the table to the side. It hit the wall and decimated the already compromised sheet rock along with the table that splintered into pieces. "You drag the pack back into a war and after the first confrontation you relent."

Fletcher crossed his arms and said, "Are you suggesting that I've grown weak?"

"No." Oliver's expression changed. He stepped back, expecting his alpha leader to attack him.

"That I'm not strong enough to lead the pack?" Fletcher didn't move. He glowered at him with dominion and intimidation until his second-in-command submitted. Oliver lowered his head and backed away.

"You will have your revenge, but we do it my way," Fletcher said as he stood and approached Oliver. "I understand how you feel. We all feel your pain. We can't let our rage blind us. We keep a clear head, stick to a plan. That's how we'll win this."

Oliver's rage bled through in his voice, "I don't care about winning. I just want them dead."

"I know, brother. But you have to trust me."

"I always have." Oliver looked up. "That's why I've never challenged you."

"One day you must, but not today. Now go to your wife. She needs you."

"He can't go alone. They're out in force, looking for him. And word on the streets is he killed Vito, one of their lieutenants, and they're out for blood," Phil said in his guttural voice. Fletcher's enforcer had a short but wide stature, not wide from obesity, but wide as in pure compact yet undefined muscle. His dark, curly hair and unkempt beard made him look like some mangy dog kept on a leash, waiting to be released in a fight pit. The deep claw marks along his throat told the story of his voice.

"You escort him," Fletcher said.

"Do you want anyone else to accompany us?"

"If they can take you two out, then twenty more people wouldn't make a difference."

The group had a long overdue laugh at that remark, something they definitely needed more of in these grim times. Fletcher strived to keep everyone's spirits elevated, knowing their pack's psyche remained frail and uncertain from the decision to challenge the mob and rats. They had taken back only part of their turf, but Big Mike would counter, and so they waited for the backlash to come. More so, Fletcher knew their next move would determine their fate. This conflict had come to their doorstep and knocked. He committed the pack to respond in kind, whether the choice seemed wise or not. What's worse, one of their own remained unaccounted for, hiding from everyone, a young pup scared and alone. Finding him took precedence, even over the war. The pack always protects its own. No matter the cost.

Nathan's translucent body hovered in the vacant surroundings of utter blackness and left him adrift in the void. The nothingness dissipated his senses, muffled them in the stark color around him. Though his tension mounted, he refused to fall victim to his fear which only fed his self-oppressed misery, festering in his mind like it had on his prior journey here. He squelched the rising trepidation with the knowledge of what lay beyond the sable curtain.

He had some recollection of this place yet he couldn't remember how he escaped. Only that his body had been propelled out of the dark and into the light. He screamed into the pitch black hoping to trigger whatever set him in motion beforehand. Nothing happened. His voice echoed and faded, the darkened chasm swallowing all from his lips. When this happened, he realized it wasn't his body that moved through this seemingly empty space. His *mind* pushed him forward. He concentrated on the image of a light. That visual brought about the memory of a glimmering beacon that appeared the first time he traveled through this dimension, or whatever this place was.

Without the slightest fear or hesitation, he drove himself forward. A rip in the fabric tore apart, gaped open, and an unknown force flung him through. He landed on his side, the impact feeling the not-so-forgiving dusty ground. Nathan sat up and saw stairs leading toward giant double doors of an ominous grey building. His destination.

He entered through the massive doors where he noticed an entity in a grey, hooded cloak sitting at an opulent wooden table faceted with intricate carvings of religious symbols and angelic beings. The table sat in the middle of the oval room. Nathan felt something familiar about the room but couldn't definitively recall any of it.

The hooded figure gestured for his guest to sit in the chair on the opposing side. Nathan did as prompted, his nerves tingling within him. He folded his hands and put them on the tabletop, as to not fidget.

"If you don't mind my saying so, this all seems odd and yet familiar to me." Nathan couldn't help but interject aloud, his anxiety and curiosity teeming to the brim.

The hooded entity remained quiet.

Nathan continued after the uncomfortable silence, "It's like something from a dream you vaguely remember but can't articulate. Do you know what I mean?"

"It's unusual for someone to travel so far a second time, let alone remember much about their trip," the entity said.

"We've met before?"

"Yes we have, but you must have remembered something about your last trek here. No one comes to this desolate place on their own accord."

"I don't know for certain of the where or why of it all."

"And yet here you are. Look into your heart and don't second guess yourself. Why are you here?"

Nathan's thoughts went to the only thing he could remember about this place, the reason he came: Rachael.

"I sense you need something of me, something I won't be able to provide," the hooded entity said, reiterating his question but knowing the answer before Nathan could ask.

"I want to be with Rachael." Nathan hung his head, his voice sounded meek. He felt ashamed and desperate for asking.

"That is an impossible request. It's not your time."

"But I don't want to go back. I can't go back." Nathan raised his head, the words swelling in his throat.

"I don't determine anyone's time."

"Then who does?"

"You will know when the time comes."

Nathan stood and banged his fist on the table. "I don't want to live like this!"

The entity didn't react. "Nobody gets to choose the circumstances in which they live. They can change their station, but not all can or will."

"Then I've been damned before I've ever been given a

chance." Nathan slumped into his chair. The hooded entity rose and floated toward him. Nathan sunk as deep and low into his seat as he could and looked upon the approaching figure with dread.

"What makes you certain you're damned?" the entity asked.

"I'm a vampire." Nathan's confusion superseded his worries.

The entity leaned down to Nathan and said, "Do you really believe that?"

"I guess. Most people do."

The entity straightened up, "You assume too much. Death isn't the end or a new beginning. It's a perpetual state of one's existence, like when one goes from boyhood into manhood. Don't you believe that it's what looms in our hearts and deeds that defines us?"

"Honestly, I don't know what to believe anymore. I feel so lost."

"Don't fret. It goes beyond your comprehension. You're not meant to understand, not yet. Look into your heart. Don't give in to the destructive path. Safe journey, my friend."

"Wait. Will I ever make it back here?"

"Perhaps," the entity reached out its skeletal hand and touched Nathan's shoulder. "One way or the other, you will know."

And then all around him faded into darkness.

Radomir parted and stepped through the entryway

curtains of the regal chamber. An audience had gathered within and awaited his presence. Ornate tapestries containing their vampiric families' insignia decorated the normally-bare walls, only donning the room during special events. Golden candleholders sat perfectly spaced between each tapestry, illuminating the wall's badge of glory. A red carpet ran from the entryway and stretched along the middle of the room, leading up the dais and to the throne where Demetrius sat. One giant hand rested on the hilt of his sheathed, long sword and his other arm propped upright on his knee with his chin anchored against his fist.

Despite the lavish décor, the room felt as cold as the earth on the first freeze of the year, when the air and icy rain hits the skin. The congregation's presence took him aback, but he feigned his surprise and turned the situation into an expected reception for someone of his station. As a result of this self-induced ego boost, Radomir strutted down the red carpet as the crowd cleared the path. He approached the dais with his two guards that marched phalanx behind him and reached the steps. He lowered his head and knelt before his master.

"Rise," said Demetrius, whose darkened-brown hair and circle beard intensified his furrowed brow. He cast an unflinching gaze down on his first-in-command.

Radomir got up and straightened his stance, his muscles tightened every time he bowed to anyone, but he didn't dare challenge his liege or show any shred of defiance, despite the shouting objections within. Instead, he tilted his head to the side and downward, peering behind him. The crowd had moved and left an encircled, empty space where only Ivan and Rowland now stood. He breathed a sigh of relief. With his personal guard behind him, he had a chance to escape if need be. His lord's mood seemed tense, but he could only guess why such ire radiated from his master's eyes.

"My lord, what a pleasant surprise. I didn't expect your return so soon." Radomir did what he did best and deflected any wrath he faced with warm tidings.

"Really." Demetrius let his quiet rage fill the silence in the chamber. "Why then, pray tell, did you summon me?"

"There must be some mistake. I didn't call upon you." Radomir failed at hiding the puzzlement on his face and in his voice. He realized this as soon as he uttered his response and then sought to veil his true thoughts and intent for the rest of the conversation. This could prove fatal if he didn't get a grip of the situation. Whatever he had done, he needed to be prepared for and appease his lord's concerns or else the swing of a sword would silence any objections he had.

"Oh no, you are the one mistaken," Demetrius stood. His stature towered over most on ground level, let alone while on a platform. He stepped down the stairs and then paced around Radomir as they conversed. "Your hail came in whispers from the shadows, the scent of betrayal on the night breeze. Do you care to explain such allegations?"

"Whoever provided you these false ruminations, they..."

"I don't believe they have," Demetrius interrupted. He cradled his hands behind his back and continued circling Radomir. "In my absence, I directed you to uphold certain parameters while you ruled in my stead. Your blatant disregard of this may have endangered my plans had I not acted immediately."

"I never intended. . ."

Demetrius took Radomir by the throat and pulled him close to his face, his fangs protruding, and said in an almost-hiss of a voice, "No one ever does, and I expected as much out of you as any other coward who dares to cross death and expects to live!"

Demetrius released his grip and threw Radomir to the ground. He turned to the onlookers that gathered into the shrunken circle around them and addressed the crowd as if no transgression had occurred, "Let us convene sometime after we sort out this unfortunate incident."

Radomir stood and nursed his throat while the crowd dispersed, all except for the high-ranking members of the War Council and the Enforcers, which meant Rowland dispersed with the rest of the congregation. But Ivan remained, his guard's presence no longer ensuring his protection. He was, in fact, likely more endangered than before. Regardless of Ivan's station, as an Enforcer he ultimately answered to and obeyed their Council's bidding. Radomir considered fleeing and then dismissed the notion as fast as he had concocted the idea. If he attempted any resistance, he would forfeit any possible leniency and would seal his fate. No, his best chance of survival depended on his honed skills as a negotiator. He claimed his position within their brood through his aptitude in politics and believed he could weather through this setback. He didn't know who had betrayed him or figured out his plans, but he had a pretty good idea who it was. He planned to keep all in secret until the right moment, knowing the probability of keeping such things in the dark were slim.

He had hypothesized this dire scenario, so in a sense, everything had happened as he had predicted. But for now, he needed to persuade and ensure his liege that this wasn't a power play. More so, he needed to salvage the rest of his plans before all came to ruin.

Besides Radomir and the councilors, the assembly vacated and the vast chamber seemed to shrink as an unsettling quiet fell over the room while the tension mounted. The silence broke under their lord's footsteps as he ascended the stairs, trepidation hanging in the air. No one spoke until their liege nestled into his throne and placed an assuring hand on the pommel of his sword.

Ancelot, the chief officer of the War Council and ancient member of their brood, addressed the others about why they were gathered, the severity of the crime committed, and their responsibility as representatives of their kind to speak candidly while they debated the judgment of the accused and the proper punishment for the offense. Radomir had endured this embellishment at prior hearings and took no stock in it. Ancelot had never gained further status within their power structure due to his unbending ways and lack of status amongst his kind. He was considered an insufferable blowhard that didn't retain their brood's respect. Demetrius tolerated his ranting out of tradition's sake.

When Ancelot finished, which came as a long-awaited relief to all involved, Radomir had the right to ask questions pertaining to the accusations and to defend his position before the members openly discussed their opinions. Afterward, Demetrius would render judgment of the accused. Based on the council's history of pleas, to gain favor Radomir only needed to perform his dance for what he considered a kangaroo court and sway those who opposed him that his intended actions were meant to benefit their brood. He'd done this many times before. He'd just never gambled with such high stakes.

Radomir felt a breeze entwined with power encroach from behind. Her predictable theatrical display revealing her presence, Jade came forth, gliding just above the floor and landing next to the accused. This didn't deter Radomir in the least, nor disrupt his focus. Besides, he figured she would beg until she was granted permission to act as the accuser.

Radomir decided to play along as a ruse and make Jade overconfident, her greatest weakness, "My Lord, I take it that she is the prosecutor?"

"Is she not a high-ranking member of the council?" Demetrius asked in response.

"I believe her biased emotional state is compromised and I will get an unfair trial." Radomir said this to Demetrius but looked directly into Jade's face. He predicted this chide would give her a false sense of security and feed her overconfidence, playing right into his hands.

"I will take your opinion into consideration," Demetrius said with dismissive brevity. "Proceed."

"My Lord, Council members," Jade began, her words laced with boastful assurance, just as Radomir predicted. "How long are we going to endure this member's long history of defiance? Once again, he stands before us, accused of the same crimes. His actions defy and endanger our leader's wishes and plans, which impacts and endangers all of us. When will we, as protectors and leaders of our brood, correct this defiant recklessness? If this continues, severe damage will come to claim its debt. We must take decisive action and make an example to those who believe they can challenge our laws without consequence."

"I concur," Ancelot said.

"As do I," Viggo, another longstanding council member, chimed in and the weight of his opinion mattered more than Ancelot or even Jade. His soft, round face and curly hair made him look deceptively pleasant, which matched the gentle inflection in his speech. But his political savvy made him a dangerous adversary.

"Since when has past judgment defined guilt, especially when the aforementioned were deemed innocent of the crimes?" Radomir asked.

"He does bring up a valid point," Horace said. Jade glared at the devil's advocate of the council.

Jade decided to change tactics. She refused to let him get away with this again. "I will concede to the point. Let us concentrate on the current accusation then. Why did you disobey our Lord's directive?"

"I never deviated from his directive, although I saw an opportunity to expand on it and take liberties with the situation that only benefited our interests," Radomir said.

"It's more like you took advantage of the situation to benefit your interests."

"From your point of view, perhaps it seems that way, but this was never my intent."

"Perhaps the accused could enlighten us of his intended plans so we may have a better understanding of what transpired?" Viggo interjected before the debate between the scorned former lovers degraded into drawn-out banter that wasted the time of all involved.

"When our Lord ordered me to recover the child, I saw an opportunity to take the unborn and lay blame elsewhere than leave questions," Radomir said.

"But you failed to recover the child as instructed," Jade replied.

"Someone had beaten us there and taken the child. I decided to stick to my plan and have the young wolf under my control dispatch the woman and still leave blame on the wolves. Any investigation, whether human or otherwise, would deflect blame from our involvement."

"How are you controlling the young wolf?" Ancelot asked. "The wolves have rebelled and refused our call to aid for over a century."

"I've acquired an amulet that allows control over lesser lycanthropes and they remember little to nothing afterward," Radomir said.

"If the wolves discover your indiscretion, they will declare war on our kind. And to what end?" Ancelot asked.

"An attack in rat territory breaks the uneasy truce, and a war between rats and wolves creates attrition on both sides, weakening them. When the time is right, we take control of this city," Radomir said.

"And what of our deal with the humans? Were they as forgiving as our Lord over your failure to obtain their anticipated prize?" Viggo asked.

"I've assured them of recovery, and they have promised support and agreed to no entanglements in our affairs," Radomir said.

"Pending recovery?" Ancelot asked.

"Yes." Radomir became smugger with each response.

"If all fails, then what?" Ancelot didn't feel assured.

"Then the results remain the same as if I followed my original orders," Radomir shot his answer back curtly.

"Very clever," Viggo said cheerfully.

"I believe so," Radomir smirked.

"Although," Viggo's voice dropped an octave, to an unusually deep, deadpan tone, "you haven't explained how you're going to find and take back what is ours."

"Don't fret, we know who took the child, and we are tracking their movements. Eventually, they will lead us to the infant," Radomir said.

"You're leaving much to chance," Jade said.

"As I stated, this wouldn't be any different whether I implemented my plan or not. I don't believe you're seeing our advantage," Radomir said.

"Then, please, clarify this embarrassing situation for us," Jade jabbed.

"The focus has been shed elsewhere. The distraction has kept our mission covert." Radomir threw up his hands as if he were speaking to a simpleton.

"That's a comforting thought," Jade stepped up to Radomir and looked directly into his face. "And yet word came to our Lord from afar. I don't believe you're operating in as much guile as you want us to believe."

"Patience, my dear," Radomir almost spat the words at her, "all will be well in the end."

"My patience has worn thin with every passing scheme you make," Jade said.

"As has mine." Ancelot hissed these words.

Radomir turned and growled at Ancelot, "You've no

patience or ambition and live in the days of what-was, you mindless fop."

"That's rich, coming from such a dapper don," Jade said, laughing.

"Enough!" Demetrius stood. His voice boomed and echoed throughout the room. The force of the concussion of sound pounding against their chest hit them as a reminder of who held sway and power here. All went quiet and then his servants bowed to their master in submission.

Moments later, Jade spoke, "I believe the council has made its case. We are prepared for our final statements, starting with the accused."

Demetrius nodded for the proceedings to continue.

Radomir stood at the bottom of the dais and turned as he addressed everyone as he spoke, "My Lord, fellow council members, I have made my point very plain. My actions have not defied, nor endangered us in any way. What has transpired would have happened regardless of any transgressions I might have committed in the act of attempting to obtain more for us. All is well, and we find ourselves in a position to take this city as ours. So, I ask you, what have I done wrong?" Some Enforcers nodded in agreement, as if to subscribe to the point.

"He has made promises he can't guarantee, made the consequences for such failure that much more probable and severe. Most of all, he openly disregarded your instructions. He should be punished for such contempt," Jade said, incredulous that anyone would listen to such blatant lies.

"I concur with the prosecutor. He should be punished," Ancelot said.

"As do I. The risk isn't worth the reward, and he did so without consent or counsel," Viggo said.

"I believe the opportunity warranted the calculated risk. Since when did mediocrity suffice within our ranks?" Horace said.

"I have heard your arguments and have weighed them. I feel prosecution is premature at this point. Radomir has not succeeded or failed in his endeavors as of yet, so judgment will stem from the results of said mission. Radomir will resume his operation under the scrutiny of fate. Whether this brings him glory or ruin will hinge on his doing or undoing." Demetrius said.

"My Lord," Jade went two steps up the dais, stopped and said, "as soon as the opportunity arises, he will betray you and us all. He can't be trusted."

"Of that, I have no doubt," Demetrius said. "But he was assigned the task, and he holds rank above all except me. I will hear no more of this. My decision stands."

Jade turned to Radomir, the scorn plastered on her face made Radomir smile that much more. He gained victory and had gotten under her skin to where it openly showed. He couldn't have asked for a better outcome.

"I thank you all." Radomir turned to Demetrius, "Now if you will excuse me, I have important matters to attend to."

Demetrius excused him with a nod. Radomir bowed and walked away, winking up at Jade on the dais as he turned and passed her. Ivan fell in behind him but nodded to Jade as he accompanied Radomir. She stood there, seething, as the others dispersed from the meeting. After the room emptied, she turned to Demetrius and asked,

"May I speak freely?"

"You may," Demetrius said as he remained seated on his throne.

Jade glided up in front of the throne and asked, "How could you let him get away with that after I brought you news of what's transpired? He is in league with the humans, and they will betray him and us all, now that he failed them."

"That depends on whether we find the child before they do. And I believe you underestimate Radomir and his tactics. He's untrustworthy, I grant you that, but he also brings results, in which gained him his rank."

"You know as well as I do that he brought you those results only because I made it possible."

"And yet he claimed the glory."

"The rank was mine."

"But you didn't challenge it."

Jade stopped for a moment as an epiphany came to her, "You knew, but gave him glory. Why?"

"Your weakness made it possible for him to claim glory and leave you powerless. Your love for him clouded your judgment. I cannot have a first in command that would let such a flaw impair their resolve."

Jade leaned into Demetrius's face and said with an edged, seductive whisper, "It's a decision you will rue."

"Where was the woman who stands before me now on that day?"

Murray and Cooper took a table on the far end of the

room and faced the doorway. The Green Clover had only a few patrons scattered throughout the room, but none seated in their immediate vicinity. Murray held up three fingers to the bartender, who acknowledged him with a nod and spoke something indistinguishable to his fellow coworker. The other bartender, one Murray hadn't seen before, brought over three empty glasses, a glass full of ice, and a full bottle of Bushmills that they had opened for one of their favorite patrons, or that's what Murray liked to think. Murray grabbed a glass and chucked in two ice cubes.

"Jeez, come here much?" Cooper asked.

"More often than I care to," Murray poured his whiskey to the brim. "But lately, not as often as I need."

"Looks like you're aiming to catch up," Cooper said. Murray failed to respond. He tipped his glass and the sound of high-quality alcohol drowned out the cynicism and made him immune to such verbal assaults.

A brief moment went by, and Cooper glanced around and said, "I feel conspicuous here. Isn't this a little too public?"

"This is the perfect meeting place," Murray lit a cigar and blew out the match, "hidden in plain sight."

A few minutes later, a gust of air followed a woman through the door and blew her brunette, loose-curled hair from her hairclips. The strands dangled in her face, and she brushed the wind-blown hairs out of her sight and straightened her brown overcoat. Light blue scrubs and black low-heeled shoes peeked out from underneath. She grasped her purse straps close and tight to her body. Her steps clopped on the wooden flooring as she scuttled over to them and took a seat in an opposing chair at the table.

"That's my girl," Murray said out of the side of his mouth to Cooper, "the one that got away, Dr. Iris Herrick."

"Mother warned me of the pitfalls of men like you," Iris said.

"And what kind is that?" Murray asked.

"The kind that are never home. Too big of a headache to go along with the heartache." Iris straightened out her coat and hair.

This hit too close to home for Murray. His initial reaction was to deny such allegations. Yet, his thoughts led to a conclusion he didn't want to face: he saw the wisdom in her rationale. His thoughts snapped back to the here and now as Iris thumped her purse down on the tabletop and pulled out a file.

"Ouch," Cooper said, "I like you already."

"She is a feisty one." Murray poured a glass, added two ice cubes, and slid it her way.

"It's a little early for me, but you might want to drink up after reading this." Iris passed the file to Murray, "I'm afraid I've left you with more questions than answers."

Murray opened the file and thumbed through each page, passing each sheet for Cooper to examine.

"This was all I could get before the Feds came and took all the evidence, including Mrs. Brook's body," Iris said.

"Did they give a reason?" Cooper asked.

"They never do," Murray said. "They just give you the paperwork and that's all she wrote, although I've never seen them confiscate a body before."

"What's odd is, right before you called, Deveraux called me a half an hour prior and told me to gather all of the evidence for them and comply without question. He's never given me fair warning like that before." Iris reconsidered the drink offered to her, laughed and grabbed it, and took a sip, "Agent Fisher, I've worked with him on other cases. But the other three, I've never seen before."

"So I take it you didn't get the opportunity to speak to the other three?" Cooper asked.

"Agent Fisher did all the talking. But I got the names of the men in red," Iris reached over and pulled out a change of property custody requisition with two signatures.

Murray took the paper and read aloud, "Agent Martes and Agent Loreto."

"The third party, I couldn't even venture to guess." Iris said.

Iris looked over at Murray whose brow furrowed and jaws clenched.

"Murray, I know that look. What's wrong?" Iris asked.

"The other man is with Interpol," Murray sighed.

"How do you know that?" Cooper asked.

"It happened to me before on another case. Same thing, in the exact same manner, which means we're running out of time. I wonder why foreign agents have any investment in a local murder?" Murray shook his head. "It's as confusing as these results, or lack of."

"The blood work had to be repeated, but hasn't come back. Probably never will."

"Why repeat the labs?"

"Initially, we got unidentifiable results back and believed the sample had been contaminated. But after reviewing the hair fiber results as well, I think there's a reason the results were found inconclusive."

"Why then? I'm not following."

"We're looking at either someone who's crossbred something into a canine or something else with a canine. Whatever it is, it's huge."

"How big?" Cooper asked.

"The paw print left behind in comparison to its size left us to estimate that its body size is two to three times bigger than the largest Mastiff," Iris said.

"Impossible. You've got the measurements wrong," Murray said.

"Science doesn't lie," Iris said.

"But it's misinterpreted plenty," Murray's tone was curt. "Is there anything in here that isn't science fiction?"

Iris snatched the file from him, turned some pages, and handed him the open file, "We determined she had Valium with a Droperidol and Fentanyl cocktail in her bloodstream. This mixture isn't something you medicate yourself with. My best guess: someone sedated her."

"Why dope her then?" Murray asked.

"For surgery," Iris said. "Look at the next page."

"Well, well," Murray turned the page, "somebody was in a hurry."

"The hemostats were confiscated, but not before I tested the substance in its grips. It's definitely a piece of an umbilical cord that had been cut by a sharpened object. No fingerprints though. I don't know if the baby survived but we didn't find anybody else's blood at the scene," Iris said.

"But why go to such great lengths to retrieve a baby and then cover it up in such a manner that gets attention from other government agencies?" Cooper asked.

"At least we know who to ask first," Murray said.

Chapter Eleven

The old man never stood a chance. When he disengaged the deadbolt and turned the knob to answer the knock at his door, Agent Martes barged his way in and impaled a sleek, silver-bladed dagger into his victim's torso before the door finished swinging open. The old man's eyes went wide, and the pain stifled his scream into a muffled grunt. Martes recited a prayer of forgiveness while he pushed the man backward and guided his victim into the apartment with the weapon's handle embedded hilt deep in the man.

Right behind Martes, Agent Loreto stormed through with steadfast intent, placed one of the two black duffle bags slung over his shoulder on the ground next to the doorframe, and slammed the door shut. He took over for Martes, who removed his dagger and wiped the blood off on the man's shirt, sheathing the blade in one seamless, flourished motion before he stepped away. Meanwhile, Loreto slid the other duffle bag to the floor, opened it, pulled out a large width roll of plastic, and began wrapping the man with cellophane before their victim could fully collapse to the ground.

When Loreto had almost completed the task, with only the head left to encase, the old man tilted his neck up and moved his lips. Loreto leaned in close enough to feel the gurgling gasps of air from the man's mouth on his cheek.

His breath labored, the old man whispered, "Do not fear those who kill the body but cannot kill the soul."

Loreto sat upright and while he finished wrapping the man's head, replied, "Rather fear him who can destroy both soul and body in Hell."

He completed mummifying the man and recited a prayer of last rites while their victim gave his last breaths against the plastic cocoon. Loreto reinforced the body wrap with heavy industrial tape so blood and stench wouldn't seep through.

With the strategic position of the apartment in coordination with their target, and despite the terrible act they had committed, their directives came first. And their directives stipulated they eliminate all loose ends to maintain anonymity, despite any collateral damage accumulated along the way. They truly believed any sins they made were for the greater good.

Meanwhile, Martes shut off the lights and unplugged the phone. He pulled the shades to all the windows but one and applied dark see-through mesh, save for an incised slit where he could access the partially-open window. He unslung the case he had on his back onto a nearby table, unlatched the case's clamps, and opened it. He removed pieces of a Ruger Mini-14 from the case and assembled the weapon in quick, flawless precision. He unfolded the stock, screwed on the suppressor, and snapped the scope into place. He inserted a thirty round magazine, loaded with 5.56 x 45 mm cartridges with silver tipped bullets, and chambered a round. He set up a tripod near the window and placed the weapon on it, adjusting the scope from his fourth-floor vantage point to the target's projected position across and diagonal to the street.

Loreto guarded the door and reported over his hidden earpiece that they were in position. Both remained quiet, stationed in place until their target arrived.

The intelligence they had gathered indicated their target would arrive at the warehouse across from and twenty feet to the right of the apartment building around dusk. They couldn't have asked for a better time to engage in stealth from a distance with the shade of the building as their cover and the light of day in their enemy's line of sight. The perfect ambush. They had silver bullets needed to take down the target, but they only wanted to take down the leader, not the accompanying entourage. It was imperative to their plan that the remaining members of the group survive the attack. Kill the leader, and an imminent power struggle would take place. If their splintered forces and fragmented loyalties held in disarray long enough, they would suffer irreparable damage.

When dusk settled over the street below, the entourage pulled along the front of the Bigsby Foods warehouse. Four men, two from each sedan, exited and searched the surrounding area before the other four remaining men stepped out of their vehicles. It didn't take Martes long to find the leader and place his crosshairs on him, although the scope also lingered around the group and found their inside man who would confirm the target.

Six men formed a circular barrier around the small-framed man who stood out from the others while the seventh walked side by side with the target. When the group reached the door, Peter Calvillo, the inside man, glanced over his shoulder and nodded. Martes then said,

"Target confirmed."

Martes filled his lungs to capacity, held it while his crosshairs steadied on the back of the intended's head. There was no margin for error with this mission. The risk for exposure would unravel a multitude of plans for all involved. He had to hit his target and squeeze off a second shot into the target's torso to guarantee the kill. Martes pursed his lips and blew out. Midway through his exhale he squeezed off two shots, then a third at the end of his breath. The first found the square back of the head which dropped his target, and the second managed to find its way in the target's back as he fell. The third was a target of opportunity. Peter's demise soon followed with a shot to the head. He slumped to the ground never to get up again. Dead men tell no tales.

The two agents didn't hesitate after the visual confirmation. Loreto exposed the device in the bag next to the door and hit the toggle switch to activate, setting the delay on it, just long enough for their extraction. Martes broke down his weapon and tripod faster than it took to assemble, stuck the pieces into his case, placed a similar rifle next to the window and said, "Target down." The two men took the stairs to the roof where they grappled over to the next building's roof and then rappelled down to the escape vehicle.

A short time later, the four men broke into the apartment and triggered the motion sensor, activating the explosive which engulfed the entire apartment. No one who entered the apartment survived the blast.

The barricades set around the crime scene for a block's radius caused traffic congestion. Murray drove at a snail's pace, creeping along for about a car length and then braking. Smoke from the fire blighted the sun, its unnatural shade didn't help with visibility either and made the traffic flow that much slower. Within the grey, the scalded scent of ground zero made its presence known.

"Just when we get a lead, this happens." Cooper thumbed through the videos, pictures, and comments being posted.

"Disasters supersede cases." Murray glanced over at Cooper's phone while he drove through the congestion of traffic. "Why in the hell are you on social media?"

"Social media can keep me up to date in real time."

Murray scoffed. He took one hand off the wheel and pulled out a cigar and box of matches and placed the cigar in his mouth.

"I don't understand your apprehension toward technology. Laura works in the field." Cooper looked at Murray in exasperation.

Murray looked out into the near motionless traffic, lit the cigar, and blew out the match, "I believe nothing can replace one to one interaction. You can't ask a screen a question or see an anonymous source's reactions, any subtle tics, when asked questions. And don't get me started on relying on their written beliefs, stories, or opinions as fact. How do you follow up with an absentee, unknown witness?"

Cooper rolled his eyes, "They're not anonymous. You can find their profile easily and track them down. It's a tool."

"Well, while you search for a twelve year old and his profile, I prefer to interview real people."

"You're impossible sometimes," Cooper said.

"Sometimes? Thanks for the compliment." Murray put out his cigar, placing it in his pocket for later, when they came into view of their destination. "That doesn't look good."

Prior to their arrival, Barker sent a cryptic message on where to meet, stressing discretion. Normally, Murray took subtlety with blatant disregard but conceded since Barker wouldn't have framed such instructions unless out of necessity. And when they saw the destruction firsthand, the implicit ramifications became clear.

Within the barrier, the fire department had almost finished their battle against the flames in the apartment building. Remnants of smoke rose out of a gaping hole where a window used to be on one of the upper floors. It snaked up along the brick exterior and dispersed into the air above. Debris covered the street below where onlookers and evacuated residents scurried about, their panic and despair adding to the already chaotic situation as the police struggled to bring order to the area. There were attempting to preserve the crime scene of the building and the one across the street and diagonal to the smoldering building.

The yellow tape in front of the door of the warehouse flapped in the breeze from the whirlwind of people rushing about. The white sheets laid over the bodies lifted then settled, exposing the sprawled corpses on the ground. The barrier failed to keep the roving masses at bay.

Meanwhile, onlookers from other surrounding buildings captured the happenings before police could quell the panic spread through social media. The public held witness to the carnage and had already made their opinions known. A clear, unintended message conveyed to the public demonstrated the lack of control the city had of their domain and the police couldn't pick up the pieces fast enough. Any effort to soothe the public's concerns faltered before they tried. All they could do now was quell the disorder so it wouldn't spread throughout the city.

"This reminds me of my first tour." Cooper said as he and Murray walked half-blind toward the cordoned off gate. Murray used his hand and arms to shield his eyes from the dust, Cooper wore sunglasses.

"No matter the time or place, war zones are the same," Murray said.

"I thought you never served," Cooper said.

"Gangs sometimes get a hold of grenades."

Silence passed over them as they viewed the aftermath before they proceeded. The human condition evokes an urge, no matter who you are or where you come from, and you can't help but gawk at horror.

"It's going to take months for us to sift through this." Cooper wiped dust off his sunglasses while they approached the carnage.

"I think that's what someone was counting on."

Murray lowered his hand and squinted when he reached the sight of Barker and yelled out, "I never like being told something so cliché as 'I have to see for myself,' but I believe this justifies that statement."

"It's worse than it looks," Barker said.

"Well, you're full of good news," Cooper said.

"Give us the rundown," Murray said.

Barker looked around before he spoke, "To the public, they're already trying to bury this as some kind of freak accident. Hell, they're even trying to tell us that. But my source says different and he wanted me to pass on the real story to you. He said you'd know what to do with it."

"I usually don't pry, but who's the source?"

"Philips." Barker pointed his thumb over his shoulder toward the large detective who paced about the scene near the warehouse. "He was lead until the Feds came and took over jurisdiction."

"Strange, I'd never thought he'd give me the satisfaction of admitting being stuck." Murray found this perplexing. If Philips passed this information on to him, then things must be bad. All in all, if someone in the department hits a wall in a case, your fellow officers will take up the mantle for you. But for Philips to trust him with this case showed how much he thought of him as an officer. And despite their mutual dislike, they were both after the same thing—justice. "What's the big secret?" Murray questioned.

"From what Philips gathered, the explosion covered up the real crime, an assassination. There's eight fatalities in the building, five from the apartment blown to kingdom come, three from other neighboring apartments, and several wounded in and around the building."

"What evidence did they find at the scene?" Cooper asked.

"Hellens from the Bomb Squad found pieces of the motion trigger in the apartment and Ross found the remnants of a scoped rifle on the streets."

"Are those the shooter's victims?" Murray said.

"And there's the rub." Barker lowered his head and shook it.

Murray's voice went deeper in tone and his volume decreased, "I take it the bodies have been identified."

Barker peered at Murray, "Angelo Spinelli and Peter Calvillo. Angelo took one to the back of the head and through the back and into his heart, Calvillo to the side of the head. Four of the bodies upstairs haven't been officially confirmed yet, but word is they're members of Angelo's crew."

Murray lowered his chin to his chest and rested his hands on the side of his waist and exhaled. Cooper wrote in his tablet, a dour expression slid down his face. Cooper glanced up and then nudged Murray with his elbow and pointed with his eyes, "Well, look who's here."

Murray leaned out from behind Barker. Next to the wrecked building, the detectives saw Deveraux who surveyed the area and directed the ground operations.

Murray ducked back behind his human shield. "What the hell is he doing here?"

"Like you said, all hands on deck." Cooper held his tablet up to obscure his face and turned around.

"Now you know why I warned you. He responded before we had the scene contained." Barker glanced over his shoulder. "I've never seen him in the field. What's going on?"

"I wish I knew. He hasn't shown up to a scene since he got his cushy promotion. Time's running out." Murray narrowed his eyes to peer down the street. "Where is she?"

Cooper glanced at his phone texts, "She's almost here. Traffic's bad and they're having difficulty maneuvering through it." Cooper looked up, "There she is."

"It's about time." Murray marched toward the oncoming news van pulling up.

Cooper fell in line to catch up and yelled out, "Don't call it in yet, Barker."

"You'd better hurry," Barker said.

The Action 9 News van doors flung open, and Sylvia Brewer darted out, microphone in hand while the cameraman pounced out of the side door, his camera already focused on the wreckage. Brewer slowed her pace, a latent disdain came over her face when she saw Murray. She rolled her attention to Cooper and her face brightened, not in the rehearsed way she did on remotes, but in an intimate way lovers do. She greeted him with hello, and it meant so much more. Cooper broke his usual demeanor with a response that matched. Murray now understood, he understood love beyond reason. His thoughts came back to the moment at hand when Brewer said, "He isn't going to jerk me around again, is he?"

"No, no. This is all his idea," Cooper said.

Brewer raised an eyebrow and the corner of her mouth slanted down, her expression bled through thick with silent disbelief.

"You wanted an exclusive, well here it is." Murray gestured his palms out to his sides.

Brewer glanced past them, "It looks as though someone doesn't want you to."

In the distance, Deveraux approached in a hastened walk, waving an arm as he spoke on the radio. His voice came over Barker's shoulder microphone, "Tell Murray not to say anything. This is an ongoing investigation."

"Copy that." Barker stared at them as he responded.

Murray glanced over his shoulder and turned back to Brewer, "Time's up, Brewer. It's your choice."

Without a word, Brewer positioned herself next to Murray with the disaster as their background and raised her microphone. The cameraman pointed his camera toward the two for the interview.

"This is Sylvia Brewer with Action 9 News, and I'm here on the Southwest end of 48th and Wesley where first responders are attending to a reported explosion from the Bender apartment buildings. I'm here with Detective George Murray to help us sort out what's happened." Brewer turned toward Murray, "Detective, was there an explosion as reported and does the department know what caused the explosion?"

"All I can report at this time is there was an explosion in the building, and as far as the cause, I cannot comment on an ongoing investigation," Murray said.

"Are there any reports of fatalities from the explosion?"

"There are fatalities, and we are not releasing any names right now. The families have a right to be informed first, wouldn't you agree?" Murray couldn't help but let an undercurrent of sarcasm roll out at the end of his response.

Brewer ignored Murray's quip, "Is there any further threat of explosions in the area?"

"No, the threat has been contained and the fire department is working on making sure it's safe to continue the investigation."

"There are reports of fatalities in front of the Bigsby Foods building. Can you confirm this and is it a cause or related to the explosion?"

"That crime scene is being investigated separately at this time."

"So, the explosion didn't cause this?"

"No, that much we do know."

"Can you comment on what caused the explosion?"

"I cannot comment any further on an ongoing investigation, other than to say that this is being looked at as a homicide."

"Are the explosion and the homicide related?"

"As I said before, I can't comment on an ongoing investigation, especially before relatives and loved ones are contacted."

"Thank you, detective." Brewer spun back to the camera and signed off.

"Give me one good reason why I shouldn't kill you right now." Jimmy Calvillo stomped across Gomorrah's dance floor and into the dimly-lit lounge area with six of his crew. Vengeance poured out of his eyes, his sorrowful loss mutated into bloodlust. His men wielded shotguns that contained shells with silver buckshot, rounds deadly to any creature, whether mortal or immortal. They pumped rounds into their barrels, the snap of their weapons being cocked echoed into the high ceilings. What held back his wrath was a nagging need to resolve the single question dangling in the back of his mind: *Why did they kill my brother?* Usually he wouldn't think about it, he would simply get on with the killing. But this was different. This was family, and he would get his answers one way or the other.

Jimmy came up and towered over the vampire nestled on the half-circular, black leather couch. Radomir slouched back, almost in a supine position. Jimmy's threats and posturing unfazed him, as if he expected such a reaction. The Enforcers hadn't responded or moved either. Despite Radomir's instructions, Ivan had a contingency plan in place and maneuvered Enforcers in the above level, ready to pounce on the invaders from all angles. Ivan had fought in too many wars and had seen too many ambushes to not take the proper retaliatory precautions. An attack by the rats here would be a suicide run, but not unheard of. Ivan didn't discount this and was prepared.

Jimmy looked down at the vampire who slowly raised his head and met his gaze, "I don't know if you're that brave, or if you're arrogant enough to think I wouldn't come here and exact revenge for my family. Whatever the case, you're going to talk, asshole, and tell me why my brother is dead."

Jimmy and the others morphed into their half were-rat form, baring teeth and claws. The rat's power radiated and spread outward and rolled toward the dead's negative energy field like a tidal wave. And like water that slams into stone upon the shore, the energy collided and ceased the current's momentum, dispersing the concentration of force into a harmless ripple.

"Oh my, can't make up your mind on whether to shoot me or maul me?" Radomir remained motionless.

"Sir?" Ivan's singular utterance took on a twofold meaning: it cautioned his master and asked what actions he wanted him to take. He stood nearby, prepared for battle.

"I think I'll riddle blondie over there with buckshot and then rip your limbs off one by one until you beg for me to end your pain-filled existence." Jimmy's guttural threat wasn't an empty one nor lost on Ivan. He'd seen the rats pull someone apart and devour the victim's appendages while they watched firsthand. Ivan's rage rose and brimmed over, his fangs and claws jutted out as he hissed at the rats. An army of vampires soon appeared from every direction. They had the rats surrounded as well, from the catwalk above. Automatic weapons with laser sights covered the rat's heads and hearts in red. The rats froze and saw what throwing caution to the wind had brought them.

"Now everyone, relax." Radomir's even keel, lackadaisical voice didn't match what could possibly transpire around him. This was so out of character of him, it unnerved everyone, vampires included. Ivan had seen Radomir keep his composure in the face of danger before, but this was different. This arrogance teetered on either the edge of passive aggressive taunting, blind belligerence, or pure denial. He acted as if his plans were without consequences for missteps of judgment or execution. Not too bright.

"Mr. Calvillo, please have a seat." Radomir gestured to the opposing seat before addressing Jimmy's entourage, "Would you gentlemen care for a drink at the bar? On the house, of course."

The rats looked at each other, uncertain of what action to take next. Jimmy turned back to his human form and motioned for his crew to stand down with a singular nod. They lowered their weapons and took their human form again. Two vampires escorted the group to the bar while the other vampires faded out of sight, save for Ivan who hadn't kept but two steps from intercepting any threat that came his superior's way. Jimmy took the seat offered to him and, without prompting, a drink was placed on the round table between the two seated creatures. Jimmy took a sip from his drink, "That's good stuff."

"We only serve the best here," Radomir said as he rose into a still-slouched but upright position.

"I know. We supply you." Jimmy looked up at Ivan, as if to ask why he was still standing there while they discussed business, and then stared at Radomir.

"He rarely leaves my side. He's loyal."

"You sure about that?"

"He's not only my guard but also an Enforcer. They're honor bound, follow the code of old. I wouldn't dare question a knight's honor unless I intended to provoke him into a trial by combat."

"Well, I'm here for my family's honor." Jimmy pointed at Radomir, "And you are going to tell me what happened to my brother."

Radomir sat up straight, "First of all, let me offer you my condolences."

Jimmy smiled. Radomir's statement was so brazen, Jimmy couldn't help but praise the sheer audacity. He sprang up and jutted out his hands, "Oh! This fucking guy over here. You've got some big fucking balls saying that."

"It wasn't meant to offend you. I truly mean it. I apologize if you took offense."

Jimmy calmed down and sat, "Let me take a breath here." He tipped his glass and gulped down the rest of his drink. Another was delivered. He brushed off the wrinkles in his clothes and sat down again, "I accept your apology. I'm sorry too. I get a little worked up sometimes."

Radomir waited a moment before he continued, "I never sanctioned your brother's death."

"Do you really expect me to believe that bullshit?" Jimmy's demeanor switched back to intense displeasure that radiated from his eyes as they darted back and forth between the two vampires, searching for any nuances of deception. Ivan stood vigilant, the attentive soldier, his face neutral. He had practiced and trained to do this back when he was human and it had served him well ever since. Ivan's eyes feigned ignorance of any such plot, but he had been in the room when Radomir ordered the hit on Peter Calvillo, only as a secondary target, although his elimination was highly suggested.

Radomir stretched out his arms, "It's true. I gain nothing from his death."

"But. . ."

"I believe you could benefit from this terrible set of circumstances, and I would like to offer my assistance in this matter."

Jimmy took a drink, his eyes never broke contact. He lowered his glass to the table in a slow, deliberate manner as contemplation set in on his face. His silent attention spoke volumes, and Radomir knew he had hooked him. He needed to finish reeling him in, but only with caution and precision. He couldn't allow too much slack or pull too tight. He had to play the long game, use the enemies' weakness against him and exploit it. Temptation begins with convincing the prey that they are the predator. And if all went as planned, he would add another powerful asset into the fold.

"Still not convinced?" Radomir asked.

Jimmy rubbed his chin and leaned back, sizing him up.

After a moment, Radomir said, "Let me make a proposition. If I can't convince you by the end of our negotiations here, then you may conduct yourself in any way you see fit."

"Let me make a counter proposal," Jimmy leaned forward, unholstered his 1911 Series .45 Caliber handgun and placed it on the table in front of him, "if I don't buy what you're selling, I'm putting one in your head."

Without looking back, Radomir raised his hand as a silent command to stand down, and Ivan eased his grip on his short sword concealed on his back. "Agreed."

Jimmy nodded.

"I made a deal with the Inquisitors."

"You did what?" Jimmy's eyes opened wide and he stiffened up in his seat.

"They have no interest in us. They want what everyone wants—the child."

"I trust them less than I trust you." Jimmy slammed his drink down, held up his glass and said, "Keep these coming! Lord knows I need it now."

Another drink came over except this time Jimmy snatched it out of the server's hand before it touched the table.

"Subterfuge," Radomir said, "but we'll get to that later. Here's something to think about. Far be it from me to tell you how to run things, but has anybody had a meeting since the King's death?"

"No."

"The Spinellis have been a thorn in all of our sides since Angelo took the crown as King. If that's not bad enough, he lets Big Mike dictate the ruling policies of your kind. Now that the King is dead, how is it that a human still controls your kingdom?"

Radomir knew he had struck a chord when Jimmy looked away in silent contemplation. He downed the drink, slammed down the glass, and took a breath. Radomir wagered this had been discussed but no one wanted to step forward for the challenge before they were ready. Big Mike might be human, but he held power that went beyond the city. To challenge him meant possible annihilation for anyone involved in a coup if they lost. Radomir had to goad him into taking the risk. Worst case scenario for Radomir would be the thinning of his enemies in an inner conflict. He had to convince Jimmy that this was in the rat's best interest, while he would take all of the credit or blame for their actions while he would sit back, reaping the benefits and watching the rats tear each other apart.

"You should take the crown. We all know Peter would have most likely inherited the title. Your ascension makes perfect sense."

"Not everyone will agree." Jimmy rubbed his forehead with his finger and thumb, "There'll be a challenger."

"We'll support your claim. Big Mike can't do anything about it. He's not a rat. When the others see your power base, anyone with a notion to oppose you will shrink away. And when you claim the crown, you can supplant Spinelli."

"He'll want our heads on a platter."

"Not if you control over half his gang. And if so, there's an answer for that. All we ask for is something simple in return."

"Ah, the cost of doing business is finally revealed. How much?"

"Money holds no interest for us. When you live several lifetimes, wealth becomes an unnecessary pursuit."

"Something of power then, I take it."

"The child."

"I see." Jimmy's deadpan response said many things: his disapproval, his doubt, his trepidation of cost. But the lure of status, of power, excited him. His desire to rule made it too perfect to pass up. He could always turncoat on Radomir once the deed was done. Besides, Radomir probably had a plan to double cross him anyway.

"I don't see you reaching for your weapon, so I assume we have an accord." Radomir leaned back, satisfied.

Arrogant son of a bitch! Jimmy thought. He picked up his pistol and pointed it at Radomir's head, "If you try to pull anything stupid," Jimmy pulled the trigger, dry fired it. Radomir couldn't help but to wince a little. Ivan had his sword out and at the aggressor's throat. He backed down when Radomir waved him off.

"Savvy." Radomir stood and outstretched his hand for a handshake. Jimmy snubbed the olive branch extended to him as he got up and walked away without as much as an acknowledgment of the gesture. His men soon followed suit and exited right behind their boss. Radomir laughed and lounged back on the couch.

"I take it that went as expected." Ivan normally didn't comment on such matters.

"Like clockwork. Rats and humans are so much alike, so predictable. They'll tear one another apart before we even have to lift a finger."

"And how do the Inquisitors factor into this? You know they will betray us."

"Of that I have no doubt." Radomir sprang up, "I have accounted for their treachery. All will be well soon, my friend."

"Let me know when this is to transpire. I can't protect you if I don't know what's coming for us."

"I have faith in you." Radomir walked toward the bar.

"But you don't trust me."

Radomir continued walking, "Mistrust is one's greatest tool if they seek to rise above their station."

"I will always serve you, but don't question my loyalty. I'm an Enforcer, a sworn guardian to our kind."

Radomir stopped and looked over his shoulder, "Your pledge is to our leader and his bidding. Until I retain that power, I will keep my own council. Is that understood?"

Ivan had to retain himself from baring his teeth, "Yes, sir."

"Marvelous." Radomir spun around and held out his arms in a flair of showmanship, "That was rather an unpleasant exchange between us. It's never happened before. Let's not do it again."

"You're right, sir. I don't know why I did that. It won't happen again."

"No need to apologize. You're a strong, like-minded vampire always thinking ahead, who's never satisfied or trusts that all will go well." Radomir came up to Ivan and placed his hand on the back of his neck, "When we take control of all of this, you will be right beside me, and together we shall take our kind places they hadn't even dreamed of."

Radomir patted him on the side of the head and left the room. Ivan watched him leave, and thought, *If Jade has anything to say about it, you won't.*

Nathan marched toward their training yard hidden amongst the industrial complexes and shipping ports where Kelly masked the area in an invisible protective dome of magic. When he phased through the shielding, he found Kelly there accompanied by a woman with brunette hair and snow white skin that clashed with her bright lips. She donned dark brown leather fatigues with bladed weapons strapped on multiply-placed harnesses and holsters on her body along with a sidearm slung from her hip. She busied herself with her training, throwing out punches, elbows, knees, and kicks in succession at an unseen assailant.

When Nathan fully came through the viscous wall, she halted her drills, whipping her head toward him and peeked through her long, wavy hair that hung like a curtain in front of her delicately-curved face. And when those eyes met his through the luscious locks, it sent a chill up his spine. At first, he thought he'd let his psychic guard down and that her unnatural power bled through and affected him. He shielded against any further invasion into his mind, but alas found his defense worthless to the burning sensation flooding within him. This wasn't any vampire control or magical spell, although he had sensed her vampiric aura prior to his entry into the protective barrier. Still, he couldn't keep his eyes off her. He hadn't been taken aback by anyone since his wife. He shook his head slightly before turning his attention toward Kelly. The woman darted her head aside and made her way to the wizard whose eyes raced back and forth between the two vampires. He smiled, "You took your time. I didn't know whether to expect you today or not."

Nathan had difficulty keeping his eyes on Kelly as he approached, "Where's Zander?"

"He's attending to things, things you're not privy to."

"He said he'd help me."

"And he is. There's a whole world in which you have no knowledge or access to. He is securing these issues before they become problematic."

Nathan said nothing. He couldn't argue with a valid point. He would need exposure to it sooner rather than later though.

Kelly bowed to the woman, "May I present Winter. She is an Enforcer for the Dark Temptress. She is here to assist in your training."

"Back up—who's the Dark Temptress?" Nathan asked.

"You weren't exaggerating," Winter said to Kelly, "Zander really didn't tell him anything."

Kelly looked back to Nathan, "The Dark Temptress is the head of the Council, the bodying leadership for vampires. Imagine the council as governors and she is the president."

"So what are Enforcers?"

"They're a mix of a knight and a musketeer, if you will, for the vampire leaders."

"I see, I guess."

"We can discuss politics and their structure later."

Winter stepped forward, "Zander has requested that I train you in hand-to-hand combat, and from what I've been told, you definitely need my training." Winter nudged him with her fist on his prior injury. It wasn't a full force hit, but her contact came hard enough for him to feel it in not such a pleasant way, as he stumbled back a step. He quickly gained his balance and stood up straight again as if he wasn't affected by her touch.

Nathan couldn't help but grab at his arm where she trumped him, "I don't know what you heard, but I handled myself pretty well last time I got in a scuffle. And why would I need to know hand-to-hand combat? I have powers."

Winter's voice stiffened to a commanding tone as she marched toward him, sizing him up, "A group of rats almost overtook you, and you barely tapped into your abilities. If you rely on instinctive reflex to get you through, you'll lose. Plus, the fight went from weapons and powers to hand-to hand-combat anyway. It always does."

"I didn't have any weapons."

"The results would have been the same. Let me show you." Winter fetched a duffle bag and pulled out holsters for weapons and strapped them on Nathan. He held out his arms and let her put them on, half of him wanting to believe this was an elaborate ploy to win an argument, the other half knowing she was serious. This last thought concerned him the most. She took a silver edged dagger, a silver-bladed sword, and a 9 mm Glock 19 and placed them in their appropriate sheath and holster, "So now, you're armed, you have your powers, and all you have to do is defeat me. If you do that then I'll concede and you won't have to train."

"Oh come on, you're joking, right?"

"If you beat me, I will do your bidding. If I win, you will do exactly what I tell you to do, when I say, and how I say. Agreed?"

"I don't want to hurt you."

"You won't," Winter said this with a smirk. Nathan couldn't help but laugh. "Let's begin with the handgun. Point it at me."

"Okay then. Nathan took out the pistol and aimed, only for Winter to disarm him by stripping the gun out of his hand. Before he could react, he found the gun pointed at him. She twirled the pistol and handed it back to him, handgrip first.

"Nice trick." He snatched the weapon out from her hand with a dour slump of his mouth.

"I won't take it away from you this time." She stepped back a few feet.

"Is this loaded?"

"With silver bullets, so be careful not to shoot yourself."

He pointed the weapon at her and then immediately lowered the muzzle downward, "This is stupid."

"Nathan, you told me you would do exactly what I told you. Are you a liar?"

"I didn't think trying to kill you would be part of the bargain."

"How are you going to learn to do it for real if you can't practice doing it?"

Nathan shook his head, not able to raise the pistol up.

She glowered at him, "Then you leave the fate of your

child to those who took him."

He shook his head and whispered, "Don't do this."

"I wonder if he's still alive or not."

He clenched his teeth and bared his fangs, "Don't you dare."

"Or if they feasted on him, like his mother."

Nathan yelled and pointed the weapon at her, pulling the trigger until he ran out of bullets. Winter moved in a blur, dodging each projectile as it whizzed by and hit the outlining protective barrier. Bullets fragmented into harmless splinters against the invisible shielding. Nathan pulled out his sword in a rage and swung it erratically at his intended target, only for the blade to cut through wind, sending him chasing her in an unbalanced stupor of rage. She kicked his legs out from under him and left him tumbling, his sword sliding away in his collision with the ground.

Nathan sprang up on his hands and knees, pulled out the dagger and crawled after Winter, his animal-like hisses and grunts took Kelly aback who yelled, "That's enough!"

Nathan heard nothing but the pulse of rage pounding in his ear. He scampered at her as he swung the blade without regard to even his own safety as he cut his arm committing a flailing attack. She knocked the weapon from his hand and picked it up in a defensive position. He grunted and then leapt from his haunches, claws first, at her. Winter kept a defensive stance, readied for a counterstrike with the dagger, or, if necessary, a killing blow. Kelly intercepted Nathan's projected strike midair with a hard gust of wind that propelled him ten feet. He landed hard on his back, stunned by the gust that flattened him into a prone position.

Kelly raced over to the now helpless attacker before he could recover, he waved his hand in a circle motion that drained the enraged vampire of his anger like one would draw out poison from an open wound until the catalyst of the situation dwindled down to nothing. Nathan arose from the ground into a seated position. His head and body throbbed from the painful lesson of letting anger turn into a bloodlust of rage. He wouldn't let that happen again. He rubbed his head to rid himself of the tingling.

"Apologies, but your enemies will use your emotions against you to keep you unbalanced and exploit your weakness." Winter held out her hand to assist him up. He grabbed her arm and stood, making sure he didn't sap any energy from her.

"I've told you words are powerful weapons, as powerful as a fist," Kelly said.

"I get it." Nathan brushed himself off, "You both have made your point."

"Now that you have seen the error of your ways, can we begin to train?" Winter asked.

"We made a deal." Nathan slumped in defeat, his hands rested on his hips as he looked into the dirt and then at Winter.

"That you did, but do you intend to keep your word?" Winter raised her fists up and took a readied stance.

They spent the rest of the night training in basics of hand-to-hand combat. She taught him how to block attacks, properly fall, and avoid vulnerable situations. He also learned how to strike and counterstrike while incorporating magical attacks and parries. But most of all, he learned how not to let his emotions distract or get the best of him. The only instances where he lost focus was when his mind and eyes wandered over Winter, and every time he did, Kelly or Winter made sure he paid for it in spades. When their training was completed for the night, Nathan asked Winter, "When is our next session?"

"Don't get too riled up there, newbie." Winter patted him hard on the chest as she walked away, "My other duties take precedence, so don't count on me to come back around anytime soon. In the meantime, practice."

"I can't wait for you to toss me around like a ragdoll again."

And with that, Winter looked over her shoulder, gave the slightest grin, and disappeared from sight into the mist. Nathan watched until she faded from sight. Kelly came up to him and said, "Don't get too attached to the warriors. They're committed to their station."

"What do you mean?"

"I'm old but not that old. You could barely keep your eyes off her."

"I don't have time for that. She's a means to an end." Nathan stepped up close to Kelly, "Besides, I didn't ask for any help, especially from some bad-assed femme fatale who spent the night flipping me around like I was nothing."

"Hmm," Kelly walked away, "I didn't realize you had no interest. That's too bad. I think she took a liking to you."

"Really?" Nathan chased after Kelly to catch up with him, "It isn't that she's not attractive it's just. . ."

"Oh, of course not." Kelly interrupted Nathan, "Heaven knows you wouldn't want to let any joy into your self-deprived existence."

"I'm being serious here." Nathan grabbed Kelly's arm,

and both stopped, "Even if I wanted to, I have too many things going on right now before I could even consider that."

"Nathan, your wife, she's gone. It's okay to move on. Haven't you ever considered she wouldn't want you to torture yourself like this?"

"And what if don't want to move on. Who says I want or need to?"

"You keep on telling yourself that." Kelly left Nathan behind to contemplate these harsh truths as Nathan stood there, refuting Kelly in his mind and denying the undeniable.

At the peak of darkness Big Mike stood next to the SUV parked in the middle of the rock quarry just on the edge of the city. Flood lights illuminated the site and cast shadows from the mounds of rock that seemed to reach the height of a small mountain towering over the property fences and the surrounding landscape and trees. Inside the quarry, heavy machinery congested the pathways leading to the metal camper located in the epicenter of the quarry. Big Mike waited there for his guests. A mild breeze whipped through the caverned path, sending rock dust into the air, filling the nasal passages of everyone on site. All parties involved chose the site for a reason other than privacy: the dust dulled the effectiveness of inhuman senses. The playing field would be fair. Noodles leaned on the vehicle as he waited, keeping in communication with the men scattered at their posts in and around the area.

Noodles held the earpiece in his ear, "He's coming through." He reached into the vehicle, pulled out a large brown suitcase, and came over next to Big Mike. He placed the case on the gravel pavement then took his station. He skimmed the surroundings for any intrusion to this pivotal meeting, a meeting that could determine the survival of their crew.

The light-silver Cadillac pulled up close in front of them, its high beams flashed into the two men's eyes. The reflection bounced off the sunglasses they had donned to protect their eyes from the stirred up dust devils, a hazard especially on cold fall nights like this one.

Three men with automatic weapons exited the vehicle, two flanking the vehicle as lookouts, while a third marched back and forth along the passenger side gaving one last look around before opening the back-passenger door. An elderly, portly man dressed in a tailored tan suit complete with matching vest and shoes, adorned in accessories of gold from cuff links and chains to the gold and diamond studded ring occupying his pinky finger, exited the car in a nonchalant manner. And despite the gold-rimmed, dark-brown tinted glasses he wore, he raised his hand in front of his eyes as the wind increased for a moment, bringing up more dust. It subsided as quickly as it rose. He approached Big Mike, and with every step he made, a crunching sound from the rock surface resonated from the footprints in the shifting surface. Big Mike stepped forward as both men embraced in a hug, kissed each other on the cheek, and patted each other's back hard.

"Uncle Frank," Big Mike stepped back and signaled with his hand to Noodles, "you look as solid as an ox."

Noodles brought the large suitcase and handed it to Uncle Frank's guard who took the case to the car, opened it, checked the inside, and once he was sure it was safe, nodded at Uncle Frank who waved in approval to place it in the Cadillac's trunk.

"Tell that to my doctor." Uncle Frank's voice had a raspy quality, sounding like he ran out of breath at the end of his sentences. A lifetime of smoking cigars didn't help matters either. "We're all sorry for your loss. Your father is beside himself with grief."

"Thank you, Uncle. Tell him I'll call him after I take care of some business."

Frank wrapped his large, aged paw around his nephew's shoulders like he was gripping a softball and steered them down the gravel paved road for a walk while they had their conversation. Their guards followed at a distance, just far enough not to eavesdrop. With Noodle's abilities, he could listen in if he concentrated enough, even under their surroundings, but he didn't want to pry in family business. Sometimes not knowing is better.

"I take it that business is the reason you brought me here?"

"It is."

"That tribute bag, it's bigger than usual. Does that have something to do with it?"

"It's compensation."

"For what?"

"I have a request."

"That's unusual. What do you want?" Uncle Frank put his hands in his pants pocket.

"I'm asking permission to take someone out."

"You want to sanction a hit?"

"It's more complicated than that." Big Mike stopped and faced his Uncle, "These people are connected, and they have somebody on the inside of my crew. I need to take care of things."

"You want to clip someone in the family?"

Mike's voice took on a quality of subtle rage. "These bastards killed my brother and now want to take what's mine? That's not happening."

"What do you need?" Uncle Frank asked.

Big Mike anticipated this question, a benign question that had fatal consequences if answered wrong, "I need you to look the other way while I conduct business my way."

Uncle Frank paused in thought, and then nodded, "Agreed."

Both men shook hands and headed back to the car. Uncle Frank and Big Mike parted with a hug and kiss on the cheek. When Uncle Frank departed, Noodles got on his earpiece and gave him a status report.

"All clear, boss," Noodles said.

"Did they have the place surrounded?" Big Mike almost laughed as he asked, knowing the answer already.

"Oh yeah. They had a bunch of men in the tree line, a small army. What was this about?"

"They know who snuffed Angie."

"Really? So why the army?"

"They wanted to hear whether I would take care of our problem or not. If I didn't, they'd take me out."

"Do we really earn that much for them?"

"Not without me but explain that to the bosses. There's too much at stake here for them to lose it to somebody outside of the family." Big Mike leaned on the SUV and crossed his arms.

"If they know all of this, then why not help out?"

Mike shrugged, "It's a good business decision for whoever wants me to fail. It's a built-in business structure," Mike rubbed his chin while he stared in the air and then drew his attention back at Noodles. "But we're not going to let them take away what we earned."

"You got it." Noodles turned to open the car door but stopped when Big Mike didn't follow.

"Come here." Mike waved him over.

Noodles went over to Mike, puzzled. Mike stood up and put his hands on Noodle's shoulders and leaned in.

"You're more than a Capo. You're my cousin, my family. And so, I have a favor to ask you. But you have to keep this conversation between you and me."

"Fuhgeddaboudit. I'll take it to the grave. Name it."

Big Mike and Noodles had a lengthy conversation, and at the conclusion, Noodles gave the signal over the earpiece to head out. As they drove back to town, Mike got on the phone and called someone, "We're proceeding. Pass on the message."

He hung up and then sat back and rubbed the bridge of his nose. Noodles looked at Mike in the rearview mirror and asked, "Why warn him?"

"Because he's the closest thing I have to a friend outside of the family."

"Do you trust him like that?"

"I trust him to do the right thing."

"But he's a cop."

"One thing doesn't have anything to do with the other."

Chapter Twelve

Detectives and uniformed officers scrambled around to preserve order on the Homicide Unit, creating a deafening wall of clamor that hit Murray and Cooper when the elevator doors opened. Fletcher and most of the members of White Fang were brought in from a raid of their headquarters within the city, save for a few that escaped. As for the lot brought in, most didn't cooperate on any level. Some resisted only verbally, others became physically aggressive, tossing over desks and chairs. The very unruly ones struggled against the officers who attempted to hold them at bay while trying to process and question the group. The police figured there would be resistance, but not to this extent. This was nothing short of chaos.

The two detectives went to step out of the elevator when, from out of nowhere, Philips stepped in front of them, blocking the room's view from inside the elevator. The only person Murray could see from his vantage point was Fletcher who sat handcuffed at Philip's empty desk. Both men's eyes met, and they nodded an unspoken understanding between one another. This was nothing more than a shakedown and both acknowledged it as such.

"Step back." Philips' voice came out stern and low, trying to avoid unwanted attention. Murray and Cooper complied without hesitation. They didn't have many of the details of this predicament, but they could guess. Normally, Murray would challenge and berate Philips and his agenda, but circumstances dictated otherwise, and no one there had conflicting ideals about it.

Philips stepped in and pressed the ground floor button. The doors closed and Philips said, "Deveraux is looking for you two, and the Feds are in his office with him."

"What in the world is going on? This can't just be a reprimand for talking to the press." Cooper, who usually kept his composure, leaned against the back elevator wall and sighed at the ceiling.

Murray spoke over his shoulder and kept his eyes fixed on Philips, "Like I said before: politics. Oh yeah, it's supposed to look that way, bringing us in for a slap on the wrist, but there's more to it."

"Whatever's going on, whatever they think you know, they're damned sure going to keep it contained." Philips let the disgust show on his face.

"I won't let that happen." Murray's soft and yet tense inflection said it all.

"I hoped you'd say that." Philips handed Murray a file, "Here's everything I have on this. I hope it sheds some light on what you have. Nothing makes sense here. Maybe you have the missing puzzle piece?"

Murray hesitated, not out of mistrust but out of concern. Philips risked reprimand for simply warning him about the captain's intent. No, this meant more than that. He jeopardized his career doing this.

"I shouldn't take that." Murray stared at him and hoped he'd see reason. But he already knew he wouldn't.

"Just take it." Philips shoved the file into Murray's chest, "What are they going to do to me on my last day?"

"What?" Cooper stood straight, his astonishment superseded his chagrin.

"Since when?" Murray's voice went up an octave.

"Since an hour ago. I go sign the papers after I help with the zoo upstairs," Philips said.

Murray had seen that look before, the look of a downtrodden man ready to give in just to be rid of what ailed him. "Did they pressure you?"

"No, it's nothing of the sort." Philips seemed older to Murray as the big man said this, more hunched, not as imposing, more vulnerable, "I'm done with all of this. And trust me, you will be too."

"I don't know what to say. Thank you." Murray truly experienced a loss for words. He felt grateful for the help Philips gave, sorry for giving this man such a hard time over the years, and regretful since he never gave him a chance or the praise he deserved. The man who he considered his bitter rival had come through for him, while some others he believed were his friends, had impeded him. And what Philips had said about being done with it all had hit closer to home than even he wanted to admit.

"Don't get too sentimental on me." Philips stepped aside as the elevator dinged and doors slid open, "You're still an asshole."

Murray smiled and exited without rebuttal, finally letting Philips have the last word. As Murray and Cooper walked away, Philips yelled out, "Hey guys!"

Murray spun around. Cooper reacted a bit slower and had stepped a bit further but then caught on and turned.

Silence passed for a brief moment between them until Philips said, "Kick their ass."

The elevator doors closed and Murray said to the long-gone detective, "You got it, partner."

As soon as the two exited the precinct, a voice called out and grabbed their attention, "Oh detectives!"

Murray stopped and rolled his eyes. Cooper spun around to see who beckoned them, but Murray didn't turn around. He didn't need to. He already knew. With his back still to her he said, "Yes, Ms. Davis."

Rhonda Davis approached the two, briefcase in hand, "Good day to you, Detective Cooper." She glanced over at Murray, "Didn't your mother teach you it was rude to not look at someone when they're speaking to you?"

Murray turned slowly, "Yes she did. Hence, my back."

Davis ignored the spur, "I take it Philips delivered the message so you didn't get ambushed by the powers that be?"

Murray and Cooper kept their trained, cool demeanor, and didn't let their eyes or body betray their thoughts, though their lack of immediate response let the seasoned lawyer know the answer.

"So, I can assume he didn't mention his reason for his retirement from the force?" Davis asked.

Again, silence and stares from the men. Davis continued, "He has procured employment as personal security for Mr. Spinelli."

"It seemed to have slipped his mind." Murray kept a calm outer appearance but raged inside. Everything he thought about Philips a minute ago went out the window with the lies he fed him. Murray admonished himself for thinking Philips could have changed his ways, letting moral decency supplant the opportunist tendencies he'd displayed over the years. He had a knack of never enduring the karmic impact of his misdeeds, drifting through life guileless. Some people always seem to get a pass, no matter what.

"As long as you received the message, it'll do." Davis always followed such statements with a smile. Murray caught on to this long ago, like it was her nervous, devious tick preceding her leaping on someone with the rabid ferocity of an infected dog. To Murray, her teeth might as well have fangs.

Murray dispensed with the pleasantries, "What do you really want? What's your end game here?"

"Take it easy, Murray." Cooper attempted to intervene. Davis stood vigilant with a smile still plastered on her face, her gaze bouncing back and forth between the two. Murray went to say something even he thought was stupid, but stopped just short of spouting it out, letting it pass as a fleeting thought. Besides, arguing with someone whose job consisted of debating on a daily basis would be a fruitless endeavor. He had to hand it to her; her veins had ice pumping through them. She never got rattled by any barrage of insults he'd ever thrown her way. She was the only woman who didn't cave to his verbal badgering, a feat not easily accomplished. Just ask any of the women Murray had dated or divorced. This line of questioning would get them nowhere, and he knew it, but he couldn't help himself.

"Now that's the Trigger Man I know and love." Her grin went wider than usual. Murray clenched his teeth and balled up his fists until his knuckles went white. She had hit the right nerve. Latently guised body language and pretense went aside, along with his patience.

"Enough already!" Cooper had reached his tolerance level for this charade between them. Neither had seen this kind of reaction out of him before. Normally, he composed himself in an even-keel manner one would expect from a former MP. This outburst got their attention.

"You're absolutely right, detective. Please forgive my behavior." Davis extended her hand as a gesture of peace. Cooper shook her hand and then nudged his head to Murray to do the same. Murray slumped in defeat and gave a half-hearted shake. He learned from his other failures with women to never deny an olive branch extended to you.

"Now, if you will answer some questions for us?" Cooper asked.

"Anything for you, detective." Davis went back to her routine of smiling after responding.

"Why warn us about Deveraux and the Feds?" Murray kicked back into detective mode.

"They want you off the case," Davis said.

"And why does it concern Spinelli in any way?"

"It's bad for business. He told me he would speak to you about it sometime soon, after his brother's funeral."

"That tells me nothing."

"I realize these matters can be quite infuriating. All I can tell you is to continue your investigation. Perhaps you'll want to revisit Dr. Half Moon."

"We already established the connection, but not the reason." Murray said.

Cooper glowered at him, more amazed than angry.

"What?" Murray answered Cooper's silent protest. "She already knows."

"You'll preferably want to visit after clinic hours. You might find it an enlightening experience." Davis turned to Murray, stepped forward and leaned toward him, "I'd hurry if I were you. If you recall the last time foreign agents came here, things went sideways very quickly. We don't want a repeat of that incident."

"I remember." Murray's face morphed to an expression of stone, the type of stern look that makes people uncomfortable.

"I'm a little out of the loop here. I need some information please." Cooper waved his hands around, impatient.

"People vanished from existence, and anyone who continued to question or raised a fuss about their situation was warned that if they chose to rattle their sabers, they would meet the fate of the missing." Davis didn't smile this time and stepped back, returning to her usual self, "Now if you'd excuse me, my employer would like me to procure the release of some innocent men from custody."

"Why would Spinelli want to spring a biker gang?" Cooper's curiosity had gotten the better of him. He couldn't help but tell Davis things he wouldn't under normal circumstances. It wasn't her skills, it was something undefined, a charismatic way about her that compelled people to open up to her and tell their most inner truths.

"They're innocent of the crimes they're attempting to accuse them of," Davis said.

"On what charge?" Murray asked.

"Terrorism. These guys weren't anywhere close to the

scene and had no access to military grade explosives.
Spinelli isn't going to let anyone come here and burn those
men for something they didn't do."

Murray and Cooper couldn't argue with that.

"Those are ridiculous charges." Murray normally
wouldn't say this to a lawyer, but this was simply unjust.
"They have to know they won't stick."

"And that's why they'll be out of this door within the
hour. Good day to you, gentlemen." Davis headed toward
the door.

As she exited, Cooper said, "Why do I feel like we're
the only ones who don't know what's going on here?"

Murray pulled out a cigar and put it in his mouth, "It's
more than a feeling, kid. Let's remedy that."

"So, we catch up with Dr. Half Moon tonight, question
her, and finally get some straight answers?" Cooper asked.

"You sound like you've got some place to go." Murray
struck a match and lit his cigar.

"I've got a lunch date in a while. You need me for
anything?"

Murray waved him off as he puffed away, "Nope. And
tell Miss Scarlett hello for me."

Cooper shook his head and left.

Kelly stood in the middle of their training area,
awaiting Nathan's arrival. When he stepped through the
invisible domed barrier, he discovered a company of three
gathered here. Zander and Winter's presence meant
something was amiss, something of great importance had

or would soon occur. This took him aback. He had hoped for this time to come, but now that it had, he doubted his abilities, had second thoughts on rushing into such dangerous territories. He was sure Kelly would find this as growth, progress in his training. But it didn't look that way, at least from his perspective.

"Fancy meeting you all here. I wasn't expecting company." Nathan's attempt at levity faltered, the subtle quiver in his voice betrayed his deception. All shared the same grave expression and demeanor which didn't waver.

"The time has come, lad." Kelly held his chin up high to show his pride for him, and yet, behind his eyes the same fear ran through them. Kelly might have been a wizard with many more years of living, but part of him was more human than Nathan could ever be. So his efforts to guise his true thoughts and feelings were more evident than the other vampires he encountered, a symptom of more exposure to the mortal world.

"What's going on?" Nathan's temperament soon joined theirs as he took on the same sternness to his face.

"We've been summoned." Although sheathed, Zander carried the same sword he took from the vampire's burnt corpse. Nathan recognized the hilt and that the ornate sheath's styled décor and writings matched the blade. He figured the sheath and sword had been crafted as pair entities, except it didn't explain how or why they had been parted from each other for who knew what amount of time. Perhaps he'd ask Zander. Now wasn't the time for trivial inquiries.

"By?"

"The Dark Temptress." Zander gestured to Winter,

"She is here to escort us."

"May I offer a suggestion?" Winter stepped forward. She wore her normal battle attire, except she came more heavily armed with various bladed weapons strapped to the cross harnesses on her torso and belt. A long sword hung from the right side of her belt and a Glock on her left, indicating she was left-handed. That didn't seem correct. Whenever he practiced, she fought with her right side as the dominate side. Then it hit him. She had been practicing with him with her weak side. How emasculating.

"Go ahead." Nathan squinted with just the side of his face, "I take it this won't be just a suggestion, or is this more of a scolding?"

Winter tightened her vocal pitch to an intensity he hadn't seen from a woman since he pissed off his wife, "Your disrespect will not be tolerated in the presence of Her Majesty. Treat her with the decorum of royalty or you may face fatal consequences."

"From you?" Nathan's chest went heavy, the severity hit him and he felt flushed as the warmth of terror fell over him. If he were still human, he would have passed out.

"If she orders it, then yes, I will land the killing stroke." Winter turned her gaze ever slightly, unnoticeable if only one hadn't observed the nuance.

"I'm sorry." Nathan's head slumped down and he rubbed his forehead.

Winter looked at him as if to say something but walked back behind Zander. Nathan watched her until he noticed Zander and Kelly staring at him. Zander showed nothing, his stoic posture said everything he needed to know. Kelly grimaced in disapproval, nodding his head. Still, both stayed silent, their inaction said enough.

Nathan nodded his head in shame, "On my best behavior then."

Nathan spotted Winter from in between the two, arms crossed with her eyebrow raised, she overtly displayed her disbelief with a frown. Kelly discerned Nathan's focal point of attention and turned his head. Winter had changed her stance by then and stood in vigil like the soldier she was. He studied Nathan again who changed his posture as well, but he fidgeted around and couldn't stand still. Kelly smiled and this eased his student back to some normalcy.

"Where are we going?" Nathan asked.

"Not here," Zander cut him off. "We can speak of it when we get there."

"Okay," Nathan said, annunciating the single word to express his disapproval in the way he was being treated but not blatant enough to incur the other's wrath. "How long is our trip or are we teleporting?"

Zander ignored the tone directed toward him, "Not far and no."

Zander waved his hand in a circular motion and opened a hole through the fabric of space to their destination, such as the folding of space to reach another planet, except occurring within the realm of earth.

"Wow, I have to learn to do that," Nathan's eyes went wide open. "Why not teleport there?"

"Where we're going has incantations that protect against such spells," Kelly said.

"Quickly now." Zander motioned for them to step through.

All four stepped through the portal, into an

underground cavern. As soon as the group crossed the threshold, the circular pathway shrank until it closed behind them. Nathan eyed the surroundings, taking in its haunting glamor. This wasn't a typical rough and dank grotto. The vast underground lair had been finished and shaped with smooth walls, ceilings, and flooring with uniformed, rounded pillars etched in ornate symbols and lettering of a language foreign to him. Decorative designs and emblems with lettering of similar fashion aligned the borders of the ceiling and covered the various surfaces. The floors matched the borders in comparable designs, save for the size of the emblems that were bigger. And unlike the rest of the cavern, the flooring was made of marble slabs engraved with similar markings as the rest.

The cavern glowed in a bluish hue from an undefined light source as if the walls and the air itself lit the adorned paths. Nathan gazed at the surfaces and studied the décor more intently. He couldn't decipher any of the emblems or the language written along the borders, but he couldn't pull himself away from viewing it, mesmerized even though he could not comprehend it. He touched the contours and grooves of the writing, tracing the lettering with his fingers as it filled him with a desire to let the power he shared with the flow of energy connect to and through him to its source.

His surroundings faded into a bluish hue of light in a tunnel, nudging him toward an unseen destiny, with only a promise of more of the same elation that poured into him. It drew him further, though he never sought to fight the urge to go deeper into the tunnel. The vim seized his mind, connecting the man to the epicenter, its call to become one compelled him. And when he reached out to the heart of the source, something ripped him from the cord that coaxed him to its origin and flung him back to his body. When he came to, he found himself on the floor, shaken from his violent departure from another world. Kelly had a hold of his arm, kneeling there, and Zander standing next to him with a grip on Kelly's hand. Both let go when Nathan awoke. Winter stood back observing the phenomenon while she watched over them, without interference.

"Are you mad?" Kelly shouted.

Nathan shook his head, still half dazed, "What, what happened?"

"You bonded with the power emanating from Her Majesty's palace." Zander reached out with telekinesis and picked Nathan up. And despite the assistance, Nathan's legs wobbled before gaining their bearings and finding the strength to stand upright on his own.

"How did I do that?" Nathan asked.

"Direct contact. It appears your vampiric and conjured powers work in unison." Zander looked thoughtful.

"You're saying that as if you didn't know." Nathan felt the all too familiar warmth of fear come over him.

Zander held his hands behind his back and paced, "I believe your innate abilities crave other sources to hone on to, to siphon off of as well as connect to."

"The truth is, we don't know the limits to your power," Kelly said.

"I see." Nathan paused and tried to process what they had said. "What if I can't control it, or give in, or can't break free?"

"If you can't, you may either get hopelessly lost *or* take in all of its power. The question is: will your corporeal body harness or implode or dissipate?" Zander continued to pace.

Nathan shuttered at the thought.

"We'll keep on training, learning how to control your urges, and then concentrate on how to control and manipulate them." Kelly reassured the obviously shaken pupil.

Nathan had so many other questions and doubts but stayed silent. The problem remained uncharted territory to even his masters and so he endeavored to try being patient. *Easier said than done.*

Zander and Kelly departed on their prior terminus, leaving Nathan behind. He remained in a stupor, transfixed on the further implications of the link between him and the energy he came in contact with. He stared at the ceiling's emblems that seemed to call to him in a wordless beckoning he couldn't articulate. Winter nudged him with her shoulder, breaking off the communion he shared with the words and symbols that spoke to him in a non-verbal summoning. Nathan blinked several times and came to. Winter pointed with her eyes at Zander and Kelly who had made their way by quite a lead down the great hall. Nathan sprinted after them while Winter remained in tow, protecting them from all directions, no matter her position in the marching order.

Nathan kept pace this time while he continued studying his surroundings. The great hall stretched fifty feet wide and hundreds of feet in length with offshoot hallways sprawling from the main hall. Similar to the doors along the corridors, more doors appeared that were also spaced and flanked to each other in unison. The passageways of the side halls and doorframes arched and then peaked into a sharp point, like an arrowhead. The borders had the same lettering, designs, and emblems sculpted into them as the other, though he intimately knew there was more meaning to them than décor. But unlike the rest of the cavern, the doors were constructed of dense wood and steel hinging and rivets, though they contained the same etching as the stone surfaces.

The beings residing there consisted mainly of vampires and a few other entities, including a couple of humans who appeared as somebodies of importance in the way they interacted with the other beings here; they were treated with dignity and respect. No one became dismissive of their conversations with them.

"Who are they?" Nathan asked Kelly.

"Diplomats," Kelly said over his shoulder. "Don't eavesdrop. It's considered a punishable violation here."

Nathan quickly faced forward, averting his eyes until they passed the group's conversation. He felt a little less inconspicuous when a few beings that came along their path stopped and stared at the group. A select number of them nodded and bowed their heads to Zander who returned the gesture.

They approached the end of the great hall where a set of double doors that towered over them by at least twenty feet were inset into the wall. Three Enforcers guarded the doors. Two flanked the doorway, while a third waited a few steps in front of the doors to greet them.

Their greeter was dressed more like a regal bandit than guard, his clothes were forest green and dark brown, made of some fine linen Nathan couldn't identify, with polished buttons and a beret fixed on his head. He brandished a sheathed saber with a hilt guard instead of a long sword dangling to his side. He sported a well-manicured mustache shaped into sharp points at the ends. He acknowledged the group with a sudden twisting of his body to move his cape from his shoulder to his back.

"Welcome. Of what business do you have with The Dark Temptress at her humble abode?" The vampire flashed a fanged smile as he bowed.

Winter stepped forward, "Enough with the theatrics, Clovis. You know they were summoned."

"One cannot be too cautious." Clovis rested his hand on his saber's hilt and waved a hand at Nathan's direction with flair and jest, "They might be imposters."

"Step aside." Winter took the combative stance Nathan had seen many times before, usually followed by Nathan having to pick himself off the ground in agony because he'd been slammed to the ground. Poor sod. Winter had taken it easy on him in practice. He half-hated to see what would happen when she didn't hold back.

"Ah, there she is. There's the fire I love to see. Yes, the fury of those eyes. They make me tingle in places unspeakable in polite society."

Winter stood her ground and glared, silent. But for some reason, Nathan became incensed and stomped forward past Winter, got so close to him that they could feel each other's exhaled breath, "So tell me, Sheriff of the Sherwood Forest, are you going to move or do I have to grab you by your gaudy facial hair and drag you out of the way?"

Clovis burst out laughing, looked over Nathan's

shoulder, squared off at him and said to Winter while glaring at Nathan in his own, sick amusement, "A new pet? This should be fun."

Clovis stepped back and unsheathed his weapon while Nathan followed suit. The two other guards stood at attention, unmoved by Clovis and his actions.

"I told you we don't have time for this. Move, or else." Winter placed her hand on the hilt of her sword. These actions brought a crowd to gather around the feuding group. No one interfered or dared to comment on the proceedings. Whatever the outcome, there would be consequences, and no one wanted to be drawn into this affair, even by association.

"Or else?" Clovis laughed harder than before.

"I fail to see the humor." Nathan could barely wait to tear into this fop, but he remained steady. He didn't want to attack first. Wait for the first blow, parry, and repost was his move against someone more skilled than he. That's what he'd been taught so far. Let them come in aggressive and overconfident. Plus, if he were perceived as the provoker, then he would be found in the wrongdoing, no matter if he was justified or not.

Clovis turned from amused to enraged, "Of course you wouldn't, you abomination. I'm going to carve you up while that coward of a mentor. . ."

Zander interrupted Clovis's diatribe with a wave of his hand, knocking Clovis ten feet through the air. He hit the ground like a sack of cement, his sword slid away another ten feet, "I warned you to never take my kindness for weakness."

Clovis sprang up, arched toward them, and hissed. The

two other guards held their post, unwilling to involve themselves in personal quarrels, though ready to intervene if the situation escalated beyond the adhered to law. Zander shook his head no but knew his warning would fall deaf upon the prideful vampire who practiced little to no impulse control when challenged.

Clovis leapt toward Zander, claws outstretched, baring teeth. All reacted and prepared for the aggressor's advance which included the guards stationed at the doors. Zander made a gesticulated motion with his hand and Clovis froze in the air, unable to move or speak in any fashion.

With Clovis suspended and helpless, Nathan marched over to his hovering prey, his blood still boiled in a blinding rage, taking him to a dark place where he freed his emotional deprivation. But more so, it impelled the beast stirring within him. He reached out to lay hands on his quarry, "Never taunt her again."

"Nathan!" Kelly yelled.

His hands covered the vampire's face, letting the inner power take hold. The life force flowed into Nathan who became a lightning rod of power, and the upwelling craved every essence of the vessel being drained. If Clovis could scream, he would have filled the corridors with the sounds of agony.

Zander knocked Nathan away with a gust of force. He bounced off a pillar to the ground, hard enough to quell the lusting energy stupor that nearly emptied his adversary. A crowd rushed over to the scrimmage and formed a semicircle perimeter around the scuffle. The onlookers dared not interfere once they discerned who was enmeshed in the incident. Winter and Zander, as well as the other guards, took control of the situation and gave statements to the Enforcers who arrived to deal with the aftermath. They determined judgment over the incapacitated defendant who had been found guilty according to vampire law. Clovis could appeal, but decisions were rarely overturned when decided with collaborated witness testimony.

When the ruckus subsided, Clovis was carried away to his fate and the crowd dispersed. Nathan, now recovered, asked, "What was that all about?"

Winter turned away, stomping off. Nathan watched her leave, and even though forewarned, his puzzled expression displayed his ignorance to the gravity of the situation.

Kelly poked him with the end of his shillelagh, "I could ask the same of you."

"I had to do something." Nathan felt a need to justify his actions. Though, as he spoke, his rationale sounded flimsy, even to him.

"Both of you escalated a minor altercation into an outright brawl. And for what? Your bravado, your desire for her?" Kelly spat out his detestation with all he could muster.

"You welcome your power to take away your reason, your control." Zander spoke matter-of-factly, "This will be your undoing lest you learn to command your mind and stalwart impetuous thoughts."

Nathan opened his mouth to protest but lowered his head when his shame for his conduct came as an epiphany. But then again, he'd just promised to mind his emotions not five minutes prior. Was he stupid? No, but he was reminded once more how dangerous he could become if he let his emotions dictate his actions. Plus, he had behaved like some kid with a crush, though he didn't connect the two fully for what it was. He glanced over at Winter who averted her disapproving stare away from him.

While Nathan licked his internal wounds, the great doors opened, and the two guards took their place in front of the procession with Zander and Kelly falling in behind. Before Nathan could step into place, Winter grabbed his shoulder, and from her position behind, spoke in his ear, "She will test you. Use your shields and avoid getting lost in her eyes or you might drown in her gaze."

"Winter, I . . ." Nathan's reluctant apology, or whatever he intended or unintended to say, was broken off as she shoved him forward in line and then took her spot in back.

Nathan followed the slow procession down the torch-lit, carpeted hall when he noticed that the hall and the little he could see from the road ahead didn't glow like the rest of the underground palace.

"Why isn't it glowing in here?" Nathan asked no one in particular.

Zander snorted, and without turning said, "The Dark Temptress prefers it. She has—certain tastes. You'll understand soon."

Nathan smiled, "Did you almost laugh? I'm shocked."

"Mind yourself." Zander's side of his mouth gave a slight curl up.

The lighthearted, brief banter eased the tenseness of the moment. He should have been nervous, but he didn't let the momentous event affect him since there was no use in concerning himself with the inevitable meeting he'd face in mere steps ahead. The entourage passed the threshold into the enormous, circular-domed ceiling to the similarly rounded throne room where the carpet continued from the hallway and stretched to a tall, imposing dais in the center. Black banners with emblems in dark red aligned the outer wall, staggered evenly between the candle holders with lit candles in them. To the right was a large bed adorned in black bedspreads and canopied with thin black veils that hung down the pillared bedposts. Though concealed in drapes, they were intended to only latently obscure the happenings within.

The dais took up much of the center of the room and consisted of marble that matched the flooring in the hall. It ascended twenty feet, with two plateaus staggered evenly between the set of steps from bottom and top. At its peak, the dais elevated to where a single throne sat, though its size couldn't be determined from their vantage point.

The two guards halted fifteen feet from the bottom step, moved aside and turned inward, an unspoken line not to be crossed unless permitted. As soon as the guards parted, Nathan noticed a cloaked figure in regal purple attire, a hood concealing the face, standing two steps from the top of the upper peak of the dais. Zander and Kelly bowed. Nathan imitated their actions, not knowing what protocol dictated, but he figured if he followed along that he couldn't go wrong or at least wouldn't insult such a powerful entity. He sensed her power emanating throughout the domed throne room. And even from the distance between them, the raw energy tickled his skin and goaded *his* power to arise. He struggled, wrestled this instinct into submission, and found shrewdness, instead of indiscretion or rash behavior, his best ally when confronted with adversarial situations. He planned on letting the more familiar, the more rational voices of reason, handle the details of their plight. What he *really* hoped for was to go unnoticed and keep his big mouth shut long enough to get through the meeting.

The being leapt from the imposing tower above and landed in a squatting position not but six feet in front of him. Her hood fell back as she raised her head and peered at them through the curtain of her long, naturally wavy black hair that shined like fine silk. Her violet eyes gleamed with the reflective shine that all creatures of the night possess. Her hair lay on and past her shoulders and parted to present a soft face with pronounced cheek bones and sultry eyes. She rose slowly and her cloak slid to the floor, revealing the slender yet curved being beneath the covering. Her black, floor-length Chiffon evening dress with a low cut V-neck accentuated her sumptuous cleavage and smooth skin. Her gown almost appeared to billow with a life of its own. Her eyes scrutinized and studied the group before her. Her royal-purple laced gloves matched her eye shadow. Deep purple lipstick colored her pouty lips which she left open just enough to show her fangs. Her delicate frame slithered toward them in a most eerie, yet seductive way.

Nathan felt power emanating from her, similar to the energy from the runes: alluring and destructive.

"Zander, it's been far too long." She smiled wide, with the kind of genuine expression one shows to dear friends and family.

"Your Majesty," Zander said as he bowed.

She slinked over to Kelly and her demeanor changed to

a more serious, menacing disposition, "Kelly."

Kelly bowed.

"I take it your Order has a vested interest in these happenings?" The chill from her voice could not have been colder.

"Yes they do, but that is not why I'm here," Kelly said.

She raised an eyebrow, "Continue."

"I'm here for my friend." Kelly looked over at Zander.

She gave an approving nod and her demeanor went back to a more pleasant tone.

Nathan stood still, his head low, hidden behind the forefront of the gathering in an unrealistic attempt at anonymity. His hopes soon came crashing down when her forced gaze met his from over Kelly's shoulder. She snaked between Kelly and Zander who parted, their faces not hiding their concern and confusion. They looked at each other and then back at the Dark Temptress and Nathan.

She came in close to Nathan, barely a breath away. She licked her lips with the tip of her tongue and looked into his eyes. He struggled not to display any kind of reaction but managed to stare into her seductive gaze without any outward expression. He had worked on this and it had paid dividends at this moment, but he didn't know how long he could maintain the ruse. Her power was so engaging, he wanted to slip into her arms and drown in her sultry dominion.

She smiled and circled him, sizing him up, "So this is your protégé?"

"Yes, your Highness," Zander said.

She came back in front of Nathan, this time pressing her body against his, one hand brushing the back of his head, "He looks nervous."

"I'm fine," Nathan managed to respond and keep control. Her touch not only stimulated his inner energy, but her touch, physical intimate touch, made him yearn for activities he hadn't experienced since his change. It made his lustful feelings rise, but also made him sad, and his heart shattered once more for the love he lost.

"No, you're not." She moved her hand down on his shoulder and placed the other on his chest, "I can feel your sorrow." She wrapped around him until their bodies were locked together with her leg pinning her pelvis against his, "Let me ease your pain." Her face was so close now, she breathed into his mouth while their foreheads set upon each other and their noses rubbed together. She peered into his eyes, "Do you want to accompany me to bed?"

Nathan said nothing. He held still while he sensed her power rise. A raging fire rose through her sensuous stare. A warm, inviting passion and fury beckoned him, but he had honed this energy before. He almost lost himself in the familiar blaze. It tore at reason, assured him tranquility came to those who abandoned control. His soul could reside in a place where his worries would dwindle into nothing but a dream long forgotten.

He built up his inner fortitude, and then glowered back into the source, exerting his will upon it. As soon as he pushed, it pushed back, and both joined in the clash of wills while gleaming into each other's thoughts. While she read through his history and how he had been molded into who he was until this day, *he* found an extensive history he could not fathom to read and remember in a lifetime. While he looked through her mind, he discovered the source of the rune's power were linked with the Dark Temptress, their energy was synonymous, one in the same, yet still separate from one another.

Before he could assimilate the truths he had learned, she gasped and broke her metaphysical bond as well as their embrace. She sped over to the edge of the dais, her back to them. Nathan looked back at Winter, not holding back the concern in his gaping expression. Zander turned to Nathan, "What have you done?"

The Dark Temptress responded for him, "Why would you allow him to bond with this place without knowing what he was doing and its dangers?!"

Zander turned back to her, she still faced away from them, "I told you he had a gift."

She spoke in a language unfamiliar to Nathan in which Zander answered. She spun around but only halfway and said in English, "The rest of you, leave us."

The group did as they were told while Zander stood his ground, apparently at her Majesty's demand.

"What language was that?" Nathan asked.

"Latin," Kelly said.

"Winter," the Dark Temptress prompted her Enforcer who turned around to address her, "I can see why you feel the way you do." She gave further instructions to her in another language that sounded different than the first.

Winter bowed and followed the group out. They waited for what seemed an exorbitant amount of time outside the double doors. They noticed several more guards lined around them, at the ready. They made no subtle or overt movements that appeared threatening. When Zander exited, he did so quickly and said, "Hurry."

He created a portal in front of him and stepped through. The rest rushed through before the pathway closed. They arrived back into Zander's living room. Without any word or warning, Zander knocked Nathan across the room, in the same fashion as he had done to Clovis, "Don't ever take my kindness for weakness ever again," he said.

Nathan got up, "What the hell?"

Kelly waved Nathan off and asked Zander, "What did she want?"

"She wanted to discuss what to do with him." Zander looked at Nathan as he said this, and not in a kind way.

"I take it she wasn't thrilled with what I'd done."

Zander sat down on the armrest of the couch, "You're too powerful for her to enthrall into submission. . ."

Nathan interrupted, "You mean I couldn't be raped."

"Nathan, don't," Kelly said.

"No, that's exactly why she got pissed." Nathan stepped forward.

"It's more complicated than that," Winter interjected.

Nathan glowered at her, as if betrayed.

"You used her power against her," Zander said. "She sees you as a threat, a possible rival. You know where her palace is, know how to use that power, and have shown her that you could defeat her given the right training or the wrong guidance. No one has ever been able to outright challenge her in hundreds of years. If someone were to get to you. . . " He let the thought fade into silence.

"That's absurd," Nathan said.

"Unbelievable." Zander shook his head.

"Look at it from her point of view," Kelly said,

"you've shown yourself to be impetuous, unpredictable, and at times, out of control. Mix that with the waning mortal feelings that still linger in your mind and that could spell disaster to us all."

"We warned you for a reason," Zander said. "You put me in a position where instead of vying for our stance against neutrality, I had to plea for your life."

Nathan collapsed on the couch, "So, what's the verdict?"

"She asked me what I thought about you." Zander moved over to the chair at the end of the coffee table and sat.

"And?" Nathan's impatient tone resounded in that one word.

"Nathan." Winter's soothing voice came through the building anger, and he settled down.

"I told her you were stubborn, that you were quick to react before contemplation, and your mortal ethics still hold sway with your decisions."

"I don't think that helped."

"And that you were loyal, courageous, and faithful to those you care for and love."

"You look as though she wasn't convinced."

"What did she say?" Kelly asked.

"She said, 'The same could be said of Demetrius back then,' " Zander sighed.

"She will never let that go," Kelly said.

"I informed her how you'd already rejected their offer and how far you've come with your training and that's probably why you were able to tap into her energy."

"Isn't that a bit of a stretch?" Nathan asked. "It was

more of an accident."

"I embellished." Zander waved a hand.

"I told you—vampire politics. Get used to them," Kelly said.

"And that line of crap worked?" Nathan asked.

"As far as she's concerned, you still have much to prove." Zander stood up. "Though she agrees we've been far too passive. We can proceed without hesitation."

"Where do we begin?" Kelly asked.

"Vampire politics, as you so elegantly put it. I have to contact certain individuals throughout the city. We still must maintain protocol. I will let the three of you know when I receive further intelligence." Zander grabbed various items from a drawer and put them in a leather carrying bag. Other things he stowed away in his pockets.

"Three of us?" Winter asked.

"Yes. You are to continue to train and watch over Nathan. I have further instructions from her Majesty, but I must convey them in confidence." He gestured toward his floor-level bedroom. He said something to her in a language Nathan couldn't understand and they went in the bedroom, closing the door behind them. Nathan wanted desperately to listen in but knew it wouldn't be wise. Besides, Zander probably had safeguards to protect from eavesdropping. No, he had to shake the habit of doing impulsive, self-centered things. It had nearly cost him his life on more than one occasion today. Why push the envelope?

"What language is that?" Nathan asked.

"You'd better start learning some of these languages if you're ever going to survive. And to answer your question, it's Gaulish." Kelly said.

"Isn't that an ancient Celtic language?"

"Bravo."

"So, is Winter. . ."

"Best to ask her yourself, don't you think?"

"Not without getting flipped to the ground or pushed across the room. I mean, what have I done to piss everyone off?"

"You still have a lot to learn about vampire power structure." Kelly sat on the edge of the couch and rubbed his hands together. Nathan saw a tension in Kelly he'd never seen before. "You see, you've done something that's only been accomplished by one other vampire, or any other being for that matter."

"I said no to sex. What's the big deal?"

"It's more than that. It's a negation, resistance to her power. You heard Zander when he said she could enthrall you, control you."

"Why is that such a threat? I am really having problems wrapping my head around this."

Kelly leaned back and rested his head against the cushion, "Vampires are a paranoid bunch, as you've seen."

"So I've noticed. And, I'm guessing, the only other vampire to resist her."

Kelly rolled his head toward Nathan, "Of course it's Zander. Did you have any doubt?"

It began to make sense, "She fears being overthrown by Zander? Ridiculous."

"Is it?" Kelly sat up and gave Nathan a stern look, "Say you and Zander either grow weary of submissive rule or decide to take sides with the Seditionists, the Dark

Temptress would find it difficult to hold onto her power structure. And since she controls the Council. . . " Kelly left Nathan to interpret the rest of the statement on his own.

Kelly and Zander looked over as the bedroom door opened and both Zander and Winter returned from their private conversation. Nathan gazed at Winter who wouldn't meet eye contact with him. She stood attentive to her surroundings, on guard, just as she did when they first met.

"I must take my leave," Zander announced to the room. "I don't know when I'll return. In the meantime, Nathan, practice your magick and combat here in my private area in the basement."

"Why didn't I practice there in the first place?' Nathan asked.

"We had to speed up your training, make you aware of your surroundings and how to use it to your advantage or protect you from it."

Nathan nodded, he couldn't argue. It made sense. He had learned quite a bit when earthly elements were involved.

"Kelly and Winter will attend to you while I'm gone." Zander began to spin his hand to create a portal.

"I can't leave?" Nathan asked.

"Only if they both escort you." The portal opened and Zander came over to Nathan, grabbed him by the shoulder and said, "It's about to get very dangerous for us all. Don't let your pride get the best of you."

Zander stepped one leg through the portal while Nathan warned, "Be careful."

Zander stopped but didn't look back, "I plan to. If not. . . " Zander simply stepped through the portal, leaving his statement unfinished as the portal closed behind him. Nathan turned around and caught Winter exiting the room to her designated place of rest up the stairs.

Nathan headed toward the stairs but Kelly grabbed his arm, "Let it go."

Nathan stopped. "What's going on? She won't even look at me."

Kelly released his grip, "She's a soldier. She has her orders. Don't make it harder than it is for her right now. She'll come around."

And with that, Kelly left for his quarters on the ground floor of the spacious house. Nathan had no urge to retire for the evening without an aide to assist him. He opened the hidden refrigerated compartment behind the table of expensive alcohol and pulled out a wine bottle. He poured the reddened liquid into a wine glass and smelled its aroma: a mixture of red wine and blood. He plopped onto the couch, leaned back, and sipped away the contents of the bottle until it ran dry. He fell into a deep slumber, contemplating the events of the day, reflecting how convoluted life had become since his change.

Jimmy Calvillo sat at the card table on a folding chair where the smoke from his cigar billowed and dissipated into the high ceiling of the Bigsby Foods warehouse where he had moved his central operations. His downtown office wasn't safe anymore, so he all but abandoned it, keeping just minimum operations going there in case someone planned a hit on him. Also, more space equaled more room between anyone entering, and he had increased the number of guards inside as well as increasing the number of lookouts around the building. He'd even paid off the local businesses surrounding the block to give him warnings if they saw anything suspicious from anyone, including law enforcement.

Nobody bothered Jimmy as he contemplated his next move, knowing their allegiance to him interlinked their fates. To move in on a connected guy, and a top earner at that, could be a death sentence if they failed. He knew his first move had to be eliminating the competition, then taking control of their expanding empire while not getting killed in the process. He puffed on his cigar while he mulled over ideas on how to accomplish this.

While he pondered these things, he heard the panting of someone running up to him, and he knew who it was before he saw them. Sal had beaded sweat coming down his forehead and face, and his undershirt soaked up the perspiration, leaving his button-down, powder blue shirt dry. He had run from an office up front to the middle of the warehouse to give him the news. Jimmy never cared to hear any news on the phone, preferring face to face, something he had learned from the older generation of the mob. And he'd seen too many guys get collared due to wire taps. His avoidance of technology had brought him this far. The old guard used to say that sometimes the old ways are the best ways. Who was he to argue?

When Sal reached the table, he was winded and could barely speak. He leaned forward, propping himself up with his arms against the back of a folding chair and panted. Jimmy waited for a minute and then gestured for him to take a seat while he caught his breath. Sal collapsed his huge frame into the chair, which creaked in protest of such a heavy person sitting down, and exhaled in relief. Jimmy stood up, poured an espresso from the nearby machine and placed it in front of the large man. Sal tipped the cup and consumed it like someone coming out of the desert for the first time in days.

"That hit the spot. Thanks." Sal put the empty cup down and he pounded on his chest.

"I thought your heart was going to explode when you came up here." Jimmy put out his cigar. He didn't want to add to Sal's problems. Most of the crew, including members of his former crew, didn't respect the big man, but they loved him all the same. The higher bosses thought more of him than that; he was loyal and showed respect to the bosses and always accomplished whatever task he was given. Jimmy was surprised when he was able to convince him to split off from Big Mike's crew, so he showed him the respect he deserved, regardless of what the other crew members thought of him.

"Me too." Sal rubbed his head and face with some unused napkins on the table from lunchtime.

"What do you have for me?"

"Lorenzo says our guest is ready to talk."

"This one survived?"

"Third time's a charm."

Jimmy and Sal walked through the maze of boxes and pallets to the back rooms and then up a floor. The metal steps clanged and echoed into the large space and dissipated into the cacophony of sounds of a busy warehouse. They reached a metal door behind which

235

muffled voices could be heard but not enough to understand. Two men manned each side of the door brandishing MP5 submachine guns. One of the guards slid the bolt across and unhinged it. He opened the thick, rusty monolith, creating an ear-piercing scraping of metal. Jimmy and Sal entered the room, though it was more like a solid metal cage. They stood just inside the doorway and watched as Lorenzo hovered over a man slouched and chained to a chair that faced away from the door. Lorenzo placed a gag back in the man's mouth before stepping away from him.

Lorenzo's sleeves were rolled up but hadn't been saved from all of the blood that accumulated on his fists and the blood splatters all over the room. He wiped off some of the remnants of drying liquid on his hands, using a blood-stained rag that wasn't much cleaner than his hands. Lorenzo approached Jimmy and stood between the two men that entered, Lorenzo facing Jimmy. Sal could see nothing but Lorenzo's back, except he stood slightly taller than the man blocking his view, allowing him to peer over the man's shoulder. This was definitely a sign of disrespect, but Sal kept his mouth closed. This wasn't the time or place to sort this out. That would come later.

"This one's ready." Lorenzo wiped his brow, but only managed to smear blood across his forehead.

"Thanks for showing some restraint," Jimmy said.

"The first two were stubborn."

Jimmy's mouth dropped, "You put your fist through the first guy's skull."

"I sometimes forget in the heat of the moment."

"Was this one tough to break?" Jimmy asked.

Lorenzo leaned in and whispered, "No, but he didn't beg or bargain for his life."

"Really?" Jimmy looked over at the man slumped over, put his hand on the back of Lorenzo's head and gave him a soft, approving slap on the cheek, "You've done great."

Jimmy went around and faced the man confined in the chair while the metal door dragged across the floor, leaving the two alone. The man's dirty face was streaked with sweat and blood while his discerning features began to swell and bruise. Blood spouted from his nostrils and coated everything from his upper lip down to his chin. The thick liquid dripped on the metal floor and reverberated on the surface like rain on a tin roof, creating a congealing puddle beneath the chair. His ragged clothes lay huddled in the corner, torn off him to further establish the lack of control the man had over the situation. To humiliate and break the man, prime him before he'd even been touched. They found naked men didn't have as much bravado as those still clothed.

Jimmy leaned down and looked the man in his eyes, "Are you ready to answer some questions?"

The defeated man nodded yes.

"Good. Then there's no need for this." Jimmy removed the thin rag tied tight in his mouth and ungagged him. "You've earned my respect. You took a beating like a man, and now you have an opportunity here to make things right."

The man struggled to keep his head upright as it drooped down and his eyes rolled upwards. Jimmy grabbed him by the chin and held his head up, "Hey, stay with me, or we'll have to start all over again. And I know you don't want Lorenzo to come in here, do ya?"

This drew the man's attention. He shook his head no, and held his head up as much as possible, though he couldn't hold it up all the way.

"All right, see? All better. Now we can have a conversation, man to man if you will." Jimmy squatted down, "I don't know about you, but I like to look someone straight in the eyes. How about you?"

The man shook his head yes.

"Of course you do. I could tell you're a smart man with integrity. And do you know why men like us do that? It's because the eyes don't lie. But you already knew that." Jimmy put his hand on the man's shoulder. The man flinched and began breathing heavily.

Jimmy did not react to this and continued, "You see there's many things one can do or say to try to deceive someone. But I believe, and I've debated this over the years, the eyes are truly the pathway to our souls. And every time we lie, a part of our soul dies just a little bit. I think that's why we have such a negative reaction to them. It hurts our souls. Wouldn't you agree?"

The man gave a quick nod and his face displayed the terror he could no longer suppress. Tears welled and dripped down his cheeks, intermingling with the blood, sweat, and dirt.

"That's good, that's good, because it's very important for you to believe me and to be honest with me."

The man snuffled as he shook his head, and though terrified, he continued to make direct eye contact.

"Now there's a reason I bring up honesty and it's

because your people haven't been so forthcoming with us."

The man began to hyperventilate, and shook and pulled against his chains, leaning away from his interrogator.

"Hey, shh, shh," Jimmy stroked his head, "calm down now. Just breathe."

Jimmy waited a moment for the man to slow his breath, "There, there, that's better. I don't want you to panic. And I don't blame you for being scared. Hell, I've been in your same predicament, and it isn't pretty. I just want you to be honest with me. No one is blaming anyone for anything."

Jimmy stood up and lit a cigar. He dropped the match in the pool of blood that made a sound of singeing when it hit the coagulated puddle. "We wouldn't be here if everyone were more open and honest with each other. Look, I'll tell you something not many know, that is, if you can keep a secret. Can you? I'm sorry, I never got your name."

"Dave," the man squeaked out, his throat dried, nothing but blood had drained down it for some time.

"Well Dave, I've been given quite a bit more influence here and am about to get even more influence soon, which means things are going to start changing for the better. That is, for everyone who plays ball. You'd like that, wouldn't you, Dave?"

"Yes."

"Good, that's good, Dave." Jimmy leaned down to Dave. "Tell me all about Dr. Half Moon."

Jimmy and Dave's conversation lasted at least half an hour, and then Sal and the guards heard someone pounding on the metal door. One of the guards opened the metal door where Jimmy stood in front of the doorway. Sal stepped in and said, "So did you get what you needed."

"I certainly did." Jimmy drew out his .45 pistol and shot Dave in back of the head. Blood sprayed from his forehead, the bullet killing him before he realized he'd been shot. He holstered his pistol and said to the guards and Lorenzo, "You can clean up this mess after lunch."

Jimmy and Sal stepped out of the room as the three entered the metal room and took on their were-rat forms. Sal shut the door in time for the muffled sounds of the rats gorging on the body.

"Wow, boss, you usually let the boys eat them while they're still alive." Sal relit Jimmy's cigar.

"Dave was a man of his word, never begged for his life, never lied to me. He earned my respect." Jimmy puffed on his cigar until it lit.

Sal closed his lighter, "I was wondering if, ya know, maybe I can become like you and them?"

"You mean a rat."

"Well, yeah."

"Oh Sal," Jimmy patted him on his shoulder, "we love you just the way you are. And besides," Jimmy patted Sal's stomach, "if you think you're hungry all the time now. . . "

Jimmy let the rest of the statement go unsaid. He walked toward the stairs, "Come on, Sal. I've got some directives for you to tell the boys."

"Okay, boss." Sal caught up, "What did that guy tell you?"

"Everything." Jimmy smiled as he puffed on his cigar, descending down the stairs, "And if this all plays out right, we'll have the leverage on everybody."

"So what do we do first?" Sal asked.

"Send the boys to pick up that doctor at the clinic and then we'll go from there."

"You got it."

When they got downstairs, Jimmy went out to lunch with one of his girlfriends. Sal was left at home base to make arrangements. But the first thing Sal did when he reached the office was to take out a cell phone and dial a number as he looked through the blinders, checking to see if anyone was around. No one was in sight when someone answered on the other end.

"It's me."

Someone on the other end of the phone asked a question.

"Dead Man's Land."

The conversation continued and he said, "No, they wasted him."

Sal listened intently to his instructions.

"Fuhgeddaboudit. I'll take care of it."

Sal hung up the phone, broke it in half, took out the battery and went to the warehouse's industrial furnace and incinerated the remnants of the phone.

Chapter Thirteen

Murray and Cooper no sooner pulled into the clinic's parking lot when several black SUVs boxed in their sedan, surrounding them. Eight men exited from two of the vehicles and approached the detectives. One had radioed in their captives while the others formed a ring around both door sides of the vehicle. The detectives sat still in their seats, awaiting instructions. They had no need to get upset. They had already planned their early arrival so that the ones in charge could display their show of force and then come back later without any further entanglements in the red tape that seemed to shroud this case from prying eyes.

Cooper turned off the ignition and continued to sit still, allowing the scenario to play out by the book. No weapons had been drawn, so aces to them. This had to look smooth, like they were going along with the program. If not, the powers that be would scrutinize their moves and follow them. They couldn't look like they totally relented without a fight but had to resist just enough to fool those in charge that they weren't going to do something stupid after their scolding. It was a fine line to walk, but Murray had it down to a science. Cooper had been military, so he knew the drill. What concerned them more was Deveraux. He might spoil their party. But Murray had a plan for that.

An agent on the driver's side knocked on the window

and presented his ID. Murray leaned forward as Cooper lowered the window, "Hello, agent. What can we do for you?"

"Can you step out of the car, please?" the agent asked.

"Certainly, but that didn't answer my question, now did it?" Murray put a bit of sarcasm to it, not laying it on too thick.

"That's fine."

Both men got out of their vehicle and Murray asked, "Are we under arrest?"

"No, sir."

"Yeah, right. Then why all of the men, like this?"

"You'll have to speak to your captain about that."

"So tell me, will we need our union representative?" Murray looked over at Cooper who moved his head in a nonchalant manner, while Murray lit a cigar and blew the smoke at the agent.

"I don't think that will be necessary, but if you feel like waiting longer for them. . . "

"Forget it." Murray nodded to Cooper who nodded back in acknowledgement. "Let's go."

The detectives were transported in separate SUVs back to the station. Cooper didn't converse with his escorts and stared out the vehicle. Murray, on the other hand, talked and talked until he could see the frustration in their face. So much for the steeled-eyed Feds and their famous stonewall of emotions. Murray even refused to put out his cigar before getting in, and it nearly developed into a physical altercation. When they finally gave in to his demand to smoke on the way there, he puffed on the cigar for just a moment, only to put it out on top of the leather seat in front of his, smiling as he did. No, the ride was tedious at best for the field agents.

When they arrived at the station and stepped off the elevator, every officer, plain clothed and uniformed, watched as the Feds paraded them like a *Most Wanted*. All went quiet as they passed. Whenever Murray or Cooper turned their head toward the group, most chose to break eye contact while others couldn't help but to stare.

The office blinds were already closed, signaling a private meeting, an ambush. Murray sauntered along as if he hadn't a care in the world, unfazed by the intimidation tactics they'd employed so far. Cooper followed behind, behaving in his usual, professional office mode. He almost appeared to march toward the office, ready to meet whatever head on.

Without knocking, Murray swung the door open so hard it slammed into the wall and rattled the office windows. He put his hands in his coat pockets and strolled in like it was his office. He stepped around the entire office with a slow and deliberate pace to show everyone he was closely sizing them up. Cooper followed in, not as cavalier as his partner, but on alert with his chin held high and his posture straight. He closed the door and stood next to the doorway, a flagrant demonstration on his part, indicating that he walked in here voluntarily but didn't trust what lie ahead.

Agents Martes and Loreto sat along the opposing wall to Deveraux's desk, Dubois leaned against the wall opposite of the office door while Fisher sat in a chair behind the desk next to Deveraux. It might have been their Captain's office, but everyone, including Deveraux whose long face showed he wasn't pleased with the situation, knew who was running the show here.

As the detectives suspected, they'd drawn the four culprits, the puppeteers out from behind their curtain of deniability and had come this much closer to exposing the truth. If they hadn't hit a nerve, uncovered something they wanted to keep hidden, they would have pulled the strings and never revealed their existence to them. For them to use such a blatant display of power meant they had them dead to rights. For what, they didn't know. And now they had to keep them beyond their reach and yet within sight, a delicate dance to be sure. Each would play their part.

"By all means, make yourself comfortable." Deveraux gestured to the empty chairs in front of the desk.

"I'd prefer to stand, sir." Cooper stood still, upright with his eyes forward.

"That's fine." Deveraux gave a polite, brief, and less than genuine smile considering the situation. Cooper might as well have flipped him off. But really, his attention feigned in on Murray who'd decided to sit on the corner of the desk where heaps of files were placed in tidy piles. Murray pulled one of the chairs over, the old wheels squeaking from compiled dirt and age, barely rolling. He plopped the files into the seat with indiscretion, a random page freeing itself from the pile. He pushed the chair back in place, dusted off his hands, and shrugged at Deveraux who could only close his eyes and sigh before saying anything more. Cooper straightened his neck upward and clenched in laughter that threatened to hedge up his throat and burst forth.

Deveraux shook his head, "Do you find all of your

shenanigans necessary?"

"With this present company," Murray gesture around the room, "yes, I do. Because this is a farce. You, I, everyone knows it."

"I grow weary of arguing with you." Deveraux rubbed his baggy eyes.

"Oh, I bet you are, but we haven't even started yet."

"You normally don't lay down the sarcasm so thick. What has gotten up in your craw?"

Murray despised when Deveraux displayed his Southern snobbery, but still, he did not take the bait. He knew they were going to attempt to pull them in and destroy their credibility, yet this seemed outright flagrant, even for his pompousness. Murray still didn't know where his Captain stood. Prudence dictated caution and distance. Regardless, Murray and Cooper had so far stuck to script, despite others' intentions and distrust filling the room to where one could choke on it.

"Why don't you halt with the big production and tell me what's going on?" Murray gazed over the four men.

Deveraux leaned forward in his reclining chair, "I'm attempting some discretion while addressing your questions to save everyone here ill will, but your insolent tone, your boorish manner with which you seek to browbeat everyone, has prevented me from such doings."

Murray looked heavenward and waved his hand in front of his face, "Your flowery prose won't eliminate the scent of horseshit coming out of your mouth."

Deveraux's voice increased in volume, somewhere between normal and yelling, as he scolded him, "Lower your tone or you will see what happens when my goodwill is tested beyond its measure."

"If I may, sir," Cooper intervened before the argument elevated, "everyone else, and that includes the entire building, knows what's happening here, but we don't. I believe we deserve that same courtesy regarding information."

Murry continued, "We've faced resistance since you assigned us this case. We didn't ask for it. But we damned well continued to do our job despite interference." He let that rationale resonate with the group. Deveraux opened his mouth to respond, but paused, contemplating their position. And instead of continuing their exchange of inflammatory remarks, he ceased that line of conversation and opened the discussion with all present.

Deveraux motioned to the man next to him, "This gentleman is Agent Fisher with the FBI, and the other gentleman over there is Agent Dubois with Interpol."

Murray pointed over his shoulder with his thumb, not even trying to turn and look behind him, "You forgot about Red One and Red Two back there."

The two men behind him laughed and then whispered to each other in another language. Murray knew immediately they spoke Italian. His contact with mobsters over the years gave him a rudimentary knowledge of the language.

Murray turned around, "Quindi sei Italiano."

"Very good," Agent Loreto said.

"They are of no concern to you, detective." Agent Fisher opened a piece of gum from its waxy paper wrapping and put it in his mouth, bringing the attention to him, "They're Agent Dubois' and the Bureau's to contend with."

Murray stood up, "How do you figure?"

"Sit down, Murray!" Deveraux yelled, and though uncharacteristic, it wasn't unheard of for him to reach the tipping point where the niceties of Southern hospitality went straight out the window.

"Captain, with all due respect, it's a legitimate concern." Cooper approached the desk. "Why is Interpol and the FBI involved in any local matter, and what does this have to do with us?"

"Let's settle down before this gets out of hand." And though presented as a plea to the group, Deveraux never broke eye contact with Murray.

"Hey, we're all on the same side here," Dubois said.

"Doesn't feel like it," Murray responded.

"We need the department's full cooperation if we're going to stop an international crime syndicate," Fisher said.

Murray swiveled his head back and forth between Dubois and Fisher, "In which absolves you from divulging any information."

"Gather all materials of your current investigation and hand them over to me," Deveraux commanded.

"You mean you're handing over the case to them, without as much as an objection?" Murray asked.

"Captain, you can't be serious." Cooper said.

"It's official." Deveraux's stern expression matched his voice, "And no, gentleman, you're handing over this case to me where I will coordinate the investigation with our combined resources."

"But who's heading the investigation then?" Murray asked.

"I believe Mr. Cooper could teach you about how rank works in a system since you have failed to grasp my explanation on the inner workings of the department." Deveraux turned to Cooper, "If you will kindly implement that task for me while you fetch those files."

Murray refused to digress into Deveraux's trap, "What about any further findings? You know you can't always sit on your hands and wait for the cavalry to come in every time discovery is made. What about time sensitive situations?"

"You report and wait for instructions," Fisher said.

"I'm talking to my captain right now, not you."

"On this, you are." Fisher raised his voice.

"You have no direct authority over me!" Murray screamed.

"Captain?" Cooper couldn't believe Deveraux let this go, in his office no less. What had happened to make the captain yield authority?

Fisher darted around the desk and stood so close to Murray he could smell his minty breath, "I could simply seize the files and charge you with obstruction."

Before anyone could do or say anything, there was a knock on the door, disrupting any further conversation.,

"I'm sorry, this is a closed meeting," Deveraux said.

As if invited, the door swung open, "Charged with obstruction? Harsh words to someone for simply doing their job. I think you're out of your depth on this one, Agent Fisher."

Deveraux stood up, "Ms. Davis, how may I help you?"

"I've been informed my services are needed here."

"Pardon me, I'm confused. No one to my knowledge

requested. . ."

"I'm their union representative, and at any disciplinary meeting I'm allowed, oh pardon me, required to be here. By the way, your department is supposed to allow the union advance notice so they are available for the member's service."

"My apologies, but there isn't a disciplinary meeting and so no violations. . ."

"Obstruction charges? Sounds like one, more like an ambush."

"We didn't intend to. . ."

"Didn't intend to? Oh Captain, how can you say that when your entire department, the entire precinct, had prior knowledge to this 'meeting' where two detectives are being threatened for doing their jobs?"

Fisher stepped to the side, "They've been uncooperative."

Murray turned around, "He means we're asking why we should hand over our case without an explanation."

Davis stepped to the side of the desk, "Tell me, Captain, wouldn't you question why you're handing over your case to another entity if you were in their shoes?"

"I have. And they've been informed that the case is a combined task force and that they will be informed on a need to know basis, but that's not what they're. . ."

"Are you referring to the news cast?"

"We haven't reached that part of the conversation."

"So, it is a disciplinary meeting. Tisk tisk."

"They spoke with the news about an ongoing investigation."

"And did they divulge anything the public didn't

already know?"

"No ma'am, they didn't. Still. . . "

"I'll make this simple for all of us, consider them warned, and I'll forget you violated union rules. Agreed?"

Deveraux sat down, "As long as they cooperate within the parameters of the investigation and turn in all materials of the case to me."

Ms. Davis looked at the detectives and all three shook their heads in agreement, "Sounds reasonable. I can always count on you to see reason."

"Thank you, Ms. Davis."

Davis scanned around at the other parties involved, "I take it no one else will attempt any violation of our agreement?"

"This is an inter-agency investigation. If we work together, we eliminate an international threat, and their hard work will get the credit it deserves. No one here wants to create friction between us," Dubois said.

Fisher unclenched his jaw, "As long as they abide by the agreement and share any information collected, including any future findings."

"Agreed." Davis outstretched her hand to Fisher who reluctantly shook her hand without eye contact.

Murray and Cooper walked out of the office followed by Davis.

"Ms. Davis?" Deveraux said.

Davis stuck her head back through the doorway, "Yes, Quinton?"

"Make sure your clients turn in the materials I requested."

"I'll have them delivered by the end of the day."

"Thank you, Ms. Davis."

"Always a pleasure."

Murray and Cooper pulled all of the superficial files from their desk, placed them in the internal agency mailbox, and sent the data files from their desk terminals to the Captain's e-mail.

Davis whispered, "The real files?"

"On my tablet," Cooper said. Murray didn't object to sharing information with her right now. He might dislike her underhanded tactics at times, but she was their lawyer on this one and wouldn't debate the ethics in what they would do with the data if the system wasn't going to play fair either.

"Make a copy for me." Davis slipped Cooper a stick drive. He banged out a copy and slid it back to her.

"For safekeeping?" Murray said.

"Yes, sir." She raised her eyes at him, and he nodded. Both understood what this really meant. They didn't need to verbalize the real danger going on here. Cooper thought he knew, but Murray and Davis knew for sure, and he trusted her more in that moment than he'd ever trusted any of the officers around them in this very room, not to mention the powers that be.

"Ms. Davis," Cooper broke the silent conversation between the two, "I didn't know you did union work."

"Oh, I believe in the need of unions and their protection of the plights that befall workers, including government workers." Davis looked back at Murray, waiting for a typical, sarcastic remark that normally would welcome a tirade of a discussion. Instead, Murray simply laughed.

Davis put a hand over her heart, "Something I said?"

"No, no. I appreciate what you've done for us. I won't say a thing," Murray assured.

"Why, George. I've never seen you speechless."

"Listen, I gave you a pass. Don't push it."

"My apologies, I couldn't help myself."

Cooper, who'd snickered this whole time, couldn't hold it in and laughed at Murray, "I thought only Laura could push his buttons so easily."

"Oh honey, if you knew this man's reputation with women," Davis joined in the mockery and laughter at Murray's expense. It became so loud that it drew attention in the squad room.

"Knock it off, people are watching." Murray wasn't amused.

Davis gained her composure, "One last thing, if you will come with me."

They accompanied her to her SUV where she pulled out a bag from the back. Murray opened it and examined the contents. Inside were two 12-gauge shotguns with stock and pistol grips, four boxes of shotgun shells, two ammo belts for shotgun shells, a box of .357 magnum shells, and two cell phones, probably burner phones.

"Why use these? We have our own," Murray said.

Davis didn't reply but dialed her cell phone, handing it to Murray. It was on speaker. Murray and Cooper already guessed who would answer on the other end of the line.

"I trust you approve of the weaponry provided for you," Big Mike said.

"The Benellis are great. Too bad they're useless to us. We're cops, not assassins," Murray said.

"And I pray you won't need them, but we all know you will. What's more important is you'll need the special ammo."

Cooper looked in the bag at the ammo while Murray continued, "Look Mike, I appreciate everything you've done for us, I really do. But the Feds have taken our case, and if we get caught using weapons you've provided for us," Murray paused, "I can't let you go down for something like this."

"I guarantee that won't happen."

"You think she's that good?"

"She is, but that's not the reason."

"Care to let me know what you have up your sleeve? Maybe just a peek?"

Cooper tapped Murray on the shoulder, revealing shotgun shells with silver buckshot and the .357 magnum shells with silver tipped hollow points. Then he showed him the box. Murray shrugged his shoulders.

Cooper intervened in the conversation, "Why do we have government issued ammo from a company that deals in weapon contracts with the Federal Government?"

Big Mike chuckled, "They're not the only ones who have friends in high places. Who do you think helped Senator Garcia with his campaign? The men who you met today are pulling strings you couldn't possibly fathom. We need to retaliate in kind."

"Oh, I agree with you on that last fact, but why the silver bullets?" Murray asked.

"You'll have to see it to believe it."

"Try me."

Mike sighed, "I've never asked you for anything

outright before. But I'm asking you now to trust me. All of us—you, me, Cooper—all of us are in danger."

"What's the catch here? I've never heard you so rattled."

"All I can tell you for now is that Jimmy Calvillo has a contract on the kid but wants the doctor taken alive. I'm only asking you to do your job, nothing that will get you in deeper that you are. Retrieve Dr. Half Moon and the young kid and take them to the precinct and arrange for them to be placed in protective custody. You do that, and I'll owe you one. For now though, all I can tell you is that Jimmy Calvillo has a contract on the kid but wants the doctor taken alive."

Murray knew how serious offers were. That meant Murray could ask him to do anything and he'd be obligated to do or act on that promise.

"I'll do it, and then I'll want some straight answers from you," Murray said.

"If this goes down, you'll see how big of a favor that is." Big Mike hung up and Murray gave the phone back to Davis.

Murray grabbed the bag, pulled out the .357 magnum shell, and began emptying his regular shells from his pistol and speed loaders. He smiled and said, "I guess I'm the Lone Ranger, but you're surely not Tonto."

"Who's the Lone Ranger?" Cooper asked. Davis laughed and Murray rolled his eyes.

"Just lock and load, soldier."

"Enough talking about it. Let's hit them now, all of them!" Jack stood up and threw his folding chair across the room. It hit the doorway into another room and the chair shattered into several twisted pieces. "They're taking us down and we're allowing them to push us around and take what rightly belongs to us all over again. Are we not a pack to be feared any longer?"

The pack responded in guttural agreement. Jack's word held weight being an Alpha that had joined the pack in his youth, right along with Fletcher.

Fletcher stood in front of the room with his arms crossed and allowed the pack their say in the matter. Truth be told, he took to heart their frustration, their rage, but he suppressed his passions for duty sake while also biding his time. He needed to come up with a strategy for an attack that would lead to victory while preserving as many lives as they could. Their numbers were few and he needed to save the pack from annihilation.

Fletcher stepped forward, "You're right. The time for discussions, debates, and treaties has ended. It's time for action. It's time for war."

The pack howled in concert, standing up and waving their fists in the air.

"We take back what's been taken and then some, tomorrow night, when the full moon is ours. We'll strike at once, at a coordinated time and rid the city of all the vermin. And as they taste their death, they will realize what retribution really means." Fletcher opened a beer and held it up, "But for now, drink and be merry, for tomorrow death will run with us into battle."

As the crowd dispersed for booze and debauchery,

Fletcher rallied the Alphas: Jack, Oliver, and Mason, for a quick overview of the battle plan.

"I see Julia recovered. Glad to have her back," Fletcher said.

"She's as tough as they come," Oliver replied.

"Good. You and Julia take Phil and Sam to the clinic and retrieve Kevin back here and the doctor to our safe house nearby. We need to secure her from our enemies until the fighting is all but over," Fletcher said.

"We're not hiding Kevin anymore?" Oliver asked.

"No, he's to hunt with us tomorrow and become a full member of the pack. He needs to hunt with our guidance before he suffers another unassisted change."

"Or a change forced on him, like last time," Mason said.

"Yes, never will we be subservient to anyone again," Fletcher promised. "Now Jack, I need you to gather the weapons. Also, while taking inventory of the weapons, make sure the walkie-talkies have new, charged batteries in them. We can't afford a repeat of what happened last time."

"I'm on it," Jack said.

"Mason will take point with the second group. Kevin will go with that group. Make sure he stays close. I don't want him going solo just yet, and he already has a target on his back."

"I'll keep him safe," Mason said.

"Jack is with me. Oliver, Julia, and Phil will scout the perimeters and be our point men." Fletcher turned to Oliver, "Retrieve the doctor and Kevin from the clinic just after it closes. Be careful."

"I don't plan on dying tonight," Oliver said. "Save a

cold one for me."

"Always, brother."

Sal ran across the warehouse floor, panting and sweating as he had done several times a day since joining with Jimmy. He reached the card table, out of breath as usual, where Jimmy had a cigar burning in the ashtray. His boss had seen him running and prepared an expresso at Sal's usual spot at the table. A towel had been recently placed there, available for the big man after his jaunts back and forth from the office. Sal panted and sat down to slow his breath.

"You look thinner." Jimmy placed the filled cup in front of Sal and placed one in his spot.

"Ten pounds." Sal wiped his forehead with the towel and draped it over the back of his neck.

"I'm going to have to call you Slim if you keep this up."

Both men blew the steam rising from the liquid inside, and Jimmy said and then Sal repeated, "Saluti."

Both men downed the cup of hot goodness and Sal said, "Good news. We've traced where that little wolf has been hiding."

"I knew we'd find him. Where is he?"

"He's been hiding out in the abandoned buildings by the clinic. Guess who's been helping him?"

"Well, the good doctor has made a fatal mistake. I want her precious puppy buried. Which building is he in?"

"That's the thing—no one knows. He changes

buildings every day except he goes to the clinic every night just after it closes."

Jimmy slammed his hands down on the table and smiled, "Perfect. Tell Joey to assemble a crew. I'm going to see to this personally."

"What about the doc?" Sal asked.

"We take her, make her tell us where the infant is and then bury her too. Anyone else there gets buried as well."

"Don't you think killing her will bring us some unwanted attention?"

Jimmy stood up, "Sal, I like you, but don't ever question my decision."

"I'm not, I'm just saying."

"And I heard what you said." Jimmy pulled out his pistol, "The decision is mine. I'll deal with whatever fallout comes. This isn't a matter of opinion or some damned debate."

"Okay, Jimmy," Sal held up his hands, "whatever you say."

"Good. Now get your rotund butt a moving and get me Joey."

With the incentive of not getting clipped, Sal sprinted down through the warehouse into the front office. He closed the office doors and blinds, took out a burner phone, and made a call before he called Joey, "He and Joey's crew is showing up tonight."

When Nathan made his way down into the lower-level practice room in Zander's house, Winter was already there, training at a speed Nathan had never seen before. She gave the four punching bags placed around her no quarter. Her fists and kicks came in a blur, the bags caving in as if they were made of soft cushions, her attacks landing with a force he'd never seen her display. She glanced over and continued to do damage to the bags, "You're late."

Nathan stepped closer, "After yesterday, it took a lot out of me. I'm not really in the mood. Do you think I can skip a day?"

Winter stopped punishing the bags and lunged toward Nathan, jumping forward and placing a flying kick to his chest. He flew across the room like a ragdoll and slammed into the wall. He bounced off the cracked, concrete surface and landed prone on the floor.

She walked over to him, and lifting him off the floor by his collar like a mother picks up her puppies, said, "Your enemies don't care if you're not in the mood."

Nathan got his bearings and steadied his gait. Winter walked a few steps away and turned, she charged at him again except this time she shoulder-blocked him. And again, he flew into the wall, slamming against it and sliding down into a sitting position. He stood, half bent over, his arms dangling at their sides.

Winter became enraged and threw three daggers at him. He deflected them with his shielding, but took no fighting posture, not even a defensive stance.

"Come on!" Winter yelled. "Fight!"

Nathan shook his head, refusing to give into her rage.

Winter rushed over to a punching bag and pounded on it in a blind fury until it dislodged from the ceiling and soared across the room, just as she sent him flying and the bag's inners burst open like a water balloon, scattering about.

"I'm not cleaning that up," Nathan said.

A grin crept up the side of her mouth, only to be batted down again by the maddened mood he found her in when he came downstairs. She turned away to remove her practice gloves.

"Hey," he put his hand on her shoulder to spin her around except she brushed it away with a backhand, "What's wrong?"

She turned to confront him, the pain behind the mask of aggression fooled no one, especially her, "You don't listen to me, you don't listen to Zander, or Kelly. And don't get me started about what you did to the most powerful ruler of our kind."

"You mean when she tried to roll my mind and sleep with me? What was I supposed to do, let her take me and do whatever she pleased?" Nathan's indignance bled through his reply.

"It would have made things way less complicated."

Nathan gasped in disbelief. He had no words that could express the way he felt about what she said without trying to make her understand how wrong that statement was to any human that had any shred of dignity, regardless of how gorgeous or powerful the Dark Temptress appeared. He doubted he could explain it in an entire lifetime if she didn't know how basic and necessary this was to human nature. It made part of his heart break for her and disappointed him, made him think less of her, and yet he still felt that certain something when he was simply near her.

"You have no idea what's transpired since you resisted the Dark Temptress's wiles, repelled her power, do you?" Winter asked.

"So? Who cares?"

"Everyone does. You don't understand how big this is. What most vampires follow, what dictates their position of rank, is their power and their power structure. If a vampire is seen as vulnerable, if they can't control an entity within their realm, their position is brought into question. There are a few things that can happen if this is brought to the attention of enough of our dominion. She can either display the power source as an obedient entity, someone can challenge her for her position, someone can attempt to take away the source of power away from her and control such entity, or what most vampires do with power they can't control or understand is they destroy the source of the problem. And don't think for one moment she won't destroy you if she believes you're a threat to her and her own."

"Is that what you're worried about?" Nathan scoffed. "That she'll kill me?"

"No, Nathan. If she wants you destroyed, I'll have to kill you."

"Oh, that sucks." Nathan never considered the one closest to him, the one who had been sworn to protect him, might have to kill him. He couldn't grasp it, contemplate the ramifications. His plate was full enough.

"Let's take a break. We need a moment. Lord knows I do." Nathan walked backwards toward the stairs, "I need a drink. What about you?"

"I don't know, Nathan, I . . . "

"Come on, just for a minute. I need a pick-me-up. I know you do after that display of, well, kicking my ass."

Winter shook her head and conceded. She followed Nathan upstairs and plopped down on the end of the couch. She didn't realize how tired she really was until she relaxed. He poured two glasses of reddened bliss into wine glasses, handed her one, and sat at the opposite end of the couch. He placed the bottle in between them on the coffee table.

At first they sipped their drinks in an uncomfortable silence. But Nathan couldn't stand the silence. It kept his mind on the thought of true death, the possibility of being damned. He couldn't stand it for another instant.

"How old are you?"

Winter nearly spat out the fluid in her mouth, "Nathan! Isn't it impolite to ask a lady such questions?"

Nathan turned in his seat toward her, "Yeah, but I don't know a thing about you. Where you're from, what you were like before you changed."

Winter turned toward him, "Most vampires would simply tell you they don't remember."

"Do they though?" Nathan shifted over, ever so slightly.

She looked up in thought and then brought her gaze back to him, tossing her hair aside, "Some things fade. I can't speak for all vampires. I believe they remember, but it's easier to forget."

"Because they lived so long?"

"Because it hurts to remember."

Both let the thought churn in their psyche for a second. Winter emptied her glass and Nathan quickly poured more into the glass and topped off his own.

"I can't help to ask," Winter paused, reluctant to finish her thought. "No, it's too personal, forget it."

"No, no, please. Ask me anything."

"All right," Winter bit her lip, then released it, licking where she bit but for only a minute and asked, "Why didn't you let the Dark Temptress take you to her bed? Is it because of, or partly because of, your wife?"

"No," Nathan stared into his glass, as if the answers would stream out of it without the pain, like some cornucopia of harrowing memories that seemed less sad than one remembers them, "I've accepted she's gone and that she wouldn't want me to fixate on what was rather than what could be. Though, it took a while for that to sink in, you know."

He attempted to look at her and smile, though he failed miserably. She nodded, and the silence began to fill the uncomfortable spaces again. But Nathan wouldn't have it, so he decided to be bold and asked, "Did you?"

"What? Sleep with her?"

"Yes. Oh yeah, and quickly too."

Nathan laughed, "Really?"

Winter laughed with him, "Oh, you think that's funny?"

Nathan turned his chiding a notch, "I don't mean any disrespect. I just can't imagine you succumbing so easily, is all."

"I wish. Though for a time, afterwards, I found it pleasurable, but . . . "

"First time with a woman?"

"Yeah, but that didn't bother me. I didn't feel exactly

violated or humiliated, but powerless. Yeah, that bugged me the most."

"Sorry, I didn't mean to bring up anything," Nathan's words fell short.

"It's okay. It isn't like I had a choice."

"Sounds like no one does."

Winter shifted forward, "No, not that. She changed me."

"Oh, she's your maker. Makes sense."

Winter brushed a strand of hair out of her face, "Lucky for you Zander doesn't fancy you."

Both laughed and drank a bit more until the bottle went dry.

Winter shook the empty bottle, "We have extended our break into a long brunch."

"We should get back to it then," Nathan went to stand.

"Wait." Winter paused and looked directly into his eyes, "You never answered my question."

"About?"

"The Dark Temptress."

"I think you know why."

And before anyone could say anything else, Kelly swung open the front door and rushed in, "Time to go."

"Did you find my son?" Nathan grabbed his gear.

"No, the person who knows is in peril. Quickly now."

Winter sprinted out the door with Nathan following soon after. As Kelly closed the door, he asked, "I smell blood and wine. What were you up to on the couch?"

"Very funny."

While in route to their hotel, Fisher received a call, and though brief, he almost seemed pleased with the news he heard. He hung up the phone, "Our sources panned out. The doctor has been aiding the young wolf the whole time but will be there with her after hours tonight so the pack can take him back to their temporary headquarters."

"Is the intel reliable?" Dubois asked.

"Between our men in the nest within the ruins around the clinic, the wiretap we have at the clinic, and the pack's headquarters, all roads point to an exchange tonight," Fisher said.

"How many are showing up?" Martes asked.

"Well, if the wolves are showing up in disputed territory, and the rats who've caught word of the exchange show up, then you're talking about at least ten to twenty lycanthropes." Fisher poured himself a drink from the vehicle's bar.

Dubois turned to Martes and Loreto, "Bring us the doctor. And if the infant's there, though doubtful, bring it to us. There's word she's hidden the infant on the reservation, but there's ways around that. Otherwise kill as many creatures as you can."

Fisher held his glass up to Martes and Loreto, "Happy hunting."

Chapter Fourteen

Murray and Cooper arrived that night armed with the weapons and special ammunition provided them from an unlikely source. And with all they had been through, and despite the implications, they were willing to give anything a chance if it provided them even the slightest advantage. Especially where Jimmy Calvillo was concerned. He'd earned a reputation of instability before his rise in rank. After his brother's murder, according to sources in the streets, he had gone on a warpath, killing anyone associated with or having information about Spinelli. If they could reach Kevin before Jimmy, they could at least save a life if not buy them time to connect Calvillo to one of his crimes. If they got to Kevin first, and though it was not a pleasant thought, they might be able to connect Jimmy to the deaths around Kevin or worse. Nothing ideal could come other than saving all involved. But that's the job: take the negative and turn it into something good, or at least something to work with for a conviction.

Cooper gripped his weapon two-handed, watching their surroundings for any activity. No one, not even an ambient sound made its presence known in the darkened parking lot. Not a good sign. In his experience, silence precedes an ambush. At this location within the city, no backup could reach them in any timely manner and there was no escape route except for the alleys. And as of late, venturing there in a darkened maze hadn't boded well for many.

Murray slung his shotgun over his shoulder as if he were hunting. He expected nothing more than a shootout, so he'd come mentally prepared, just like his days with the Gang Unit. They never went well. With his free hand, he buzzed the intercom outside the main entrance.

"I'm sorry, the clinic's closed," Dr. Half Moon said.

"It's Detective Murray. Open up."

"Can we talk in the morning, detective? It's been a long day."

"And it's about to get longer. Open up or I force my way in and arrest you for obstruction."

The door buzzed and Murray opened the glass door.

"Obstruction?" Cooper laughed.

"It worked for the Feds." Murray winked and entered with Cooper following, watching their tails while Murray swept the front and sides of their path.

They passed the open double doors into the clinic proper, and made their way down the hall, continuing at a slow, cautious pace, not letting any entryway go unchecked or any corner ignored. The buzz of the air system and hum of the half-lit florescent lights filled the empty facility with an ambient echo that would unnerve even the most battle hardened. It gnawed at the senses, making their trek down the hallways unsettling. They remained hyper aware, almost to the heights of paranoia. But there *were* things hidden in the night, seeking them, ready to pounce.

Soon, they came into earshot of a set of heeled shoes moving at a hurried pace toward them. They took to the ready but held their barrels low so no one would become a victim of friendly fire, though they were poised for action. Dr. Half Moon rounded the corner of a nearby four-way intersection of the hallway, and she yelled out, startled.

"Detectives," she put her hand on her chest, "you gave me a scare."

"Where's Kevin and what have you done with the infant?" Murray had no patience and there was no time to waste; they all were in grave danger.

Dr. Half Moon paused, "I don't . . . "

"There's no time," Cooper said.

Murray turned his head for a moment and thought he heard glass breaking behind them. Cooper reacted as well, "Listen, people are coming, and they're not going to ask. They're going to kill us all."

"I'm here, detectives." Kevin walked around the corner, shaking and sweating.

"Can't you see he's in pain?" the doctor said. "Only I and his people can keep him safe, help him control the change."

"Well, unless they're forcing their way through the front, they're not here," Cooper said.

"What change?" Murray asked.

"If you don't know then why do you have silver bullets?" the doctor asked.

"How did she. . .?" Cooper said.

"I can smell them from here," she said.

Murray snorted, "Oh come on."

Cooper shrugged, "Big Mike said you wouldn't believe it."

"Big Mike?" the doctor and Kevin stepped back as if

to run. "You're handing us over to the rats?"

"The rats?" Murray looked puzzled.

"We're taking you to the precinct," Cooper said.

"That won't help," the doctor said.

"Let's move." Murray got the group to round the corner and move down the hall but had to stop because Kevin rolled into a ball and shook violently.

"Hold on, Kevin." The doctor went to comfort Kevin, but Murray grabbed her by the arm.

Murray spoke through clenched teeth so as to not give away their position, "You better stop worrying about him and start talking. Why did you butcher the Brooks woman and take her child?"

"I saved that child! You haven't the slightest notion of what's going on here," the doctor said.

"Enlighten me then."

"There's a war going on and if they get a hold of him it might be the end of us all."

"Where's the baby now?"

The doctor hesitated then said, "The reservation."

"We have to get moving," Cooper said.

Dr. Half Moon helped Kevin get on his feet and threw his arm over her shoulder to assist him in walking.

"When we get to the back door, go for the car and then straight to the precinct," Murray said.

"Do you think we'll make it?" the doctor asked.

"I hope for our sake we do. Jimmy Calvillo wants you both dead, and he'll kill anyone who gets in his way."

Footsteps echoed louder and louder through the hallway from behind and seemed to get closer every second that passed. Finally, when Murray and Cooper knew they had no chance of outrunning them, they turned around, stepped backwards, and waved for the rest of the group to hide around the corner. The doctor pulled a snubnosed .38 Special revolver out of her lab coat pocket. Though the detectives saw it, they didn't object on the grounds they needed all the help they could get.

Jimmy, along with twelve of his crew, stomped down the hall, weapons in hand, including Jimmy who wielded a .45 pistol, "Why, hello detectives. I'm surprised to see you at such a late hour."

"I was in the neighborhood and needed an aspirin."

Jimmy laughed and stepped closer, "I know what you mean."

Murray and Cooper raised the barrels of their shotguns at him, but he wasn't fazed.

"When I get a pain, I can't ignore it or hope it goes away on its own." Jimmy went over and leaned on the wall.

"Sounds reasonable." Murray kept a blank face.

"It's best to," Jimmy inhaled deeply and exhaled, "take away the pain, eliminate what's bothering you."

"And what ails you now?"

"I'm glad you asked." Jimmy approached but three feet from Murray's barrel. "Excellent question indeed. What I want, what I need, is the good doctor and her patient, the young wolf."

"I'm sorry, but did you say the 'young wolf?'"

"Don't insult my intelligence, I . . . " Jimmy paused, his tense nature changed into amusement, "You really don't know, do you?"

Murray poked his shotgun at Jimmy, "I'll tell you what I do know, I'm taking these two in and no one is going to stand in my way, or I'll put them down without hesitation."

Jimmy laughed as he backed up to where his crew waited, "You may think you know what's going on, but you don't."

"I guess ignorance is bliss."

"Just walk away, Murray. I'll make it worth your while, for old time's sake."

"And I wouldn't live long enough to spend a dime of that money."

"You should have been one of us instead of a cop."

"Sorry to disappoint."

From the opposing hall where Jimmy stood, loud sounds came up the hallway. The noise was approaching quickly and increased in volume as it drew near. Cooper spun around and halted the advance of the four rushing up. Oliver, Julia, Phil, and Sam looked past the group in front of them to Jimmy and his crew.

"Ah, the wolves have come out to play," Jimmy said.

"Don't move," Cooper bellowed out his command to the four, who leaned forward but held their ground.

"We've come for Kevin. He's part of the pack," Oliver said

"Don't bother," Jimmy said, "he doesn't have any idea what you mean."

"Then why do I smell silver?" Phil said.

"That's exactly what I told them," Jimmy said.

Oliver pleaded to Murray, "I know you may not know or believe what's going on, but if we don't help him suppress his change, then things are going to get more out of control than they have already."

"Hey, no cutting in line!" Jimmy screamed. "I have

first dibs!"

"No one is taking anyone anywhere but to the station," Murray said.

"I can't allow that," Jimmy said.

"Me either," Oliver said.

Everyone froze, but only for a moment—as long as a heartbeat—and still that split second stretched out enough for everyone to react so they could survive the first volley of attacks.

Jimmy dodged left, firing at the three changed werewolves who jumped by Murray at unearthly speed. Murray fired at Jimmy, missing his intended target but his buckshot found two of Jimmy's crew who had filled the vacant space where Jimmy stood a moment prior. The two men went down, never to get back up. Cooper fired a shot that found no target. He blinked and Julia had changed into her half form and had Kevin and Dr. Half Moon by the hands. Cooper stared in shock.

"Help your partner," Julia growled at him.

Before Cooper could spin around, Murray screamed, "Jesus!"

The two detectives watched while three werewolves fought hand-to-hand with Jimmy's crew, who had transformed into were-rats.

After the initial shock faded, Murray said, "Escort the doctor and company out of here to some place safe."

"What are you going to do?" Cooper asked.

Murray spotted Jimmy in his half-form who also spotted Murray, "I've got Jimmy. Go."

Murray charged into the fray, his shotgun blazing a path toward Jimmy who went on the run, blind firing his pistol as he exited. His .45 went empty and he sprang into a blinding sprint toward the front door. Murray pursued, taking out another were-rat who had clung onto one of the wolves' back. Another wolf lay down along with several rats whose torn apart bodies were in the process of changing back into human forms. Murray swerved through the bodies in the hallway, hoping he'd catch a glimpse or a clue of where Jimmy had run off to.

Murray reached the shattered glass door and skimmed the area. He caught a glimpse of a silhouette of someone darting into one of several alley entrances. He didn't know if Jimmy moved through there, but he had to follow them. Luckily, he had a small flashlight he kept in his pocket but found wielding a shotgun as well as a light difficult if not impossible. So, he slung the shotgun over his shoulder and pulled out his .357 magnum to pursue a were-rat in the dark. It sounded like suicide to him, and yet he stepped through the threshold into the blackness.

Nathan, along with Zander, Kelly, and Winter, came upon the edge of the far side of the clinic's parking lot and peered around the area. They saw two groups venturing into the alleys with others in pursuit.

"Nathan, check the clinic while you two follow the larger group. I'll follow the two headed that way," Zander said as he motioned to where each group was directed to head out to. "Our mission is to recover the doctor. All else is secondary."

The group split up. Zander sped toward the two beings

while Nathan went to check out what had transpired in the clinic. Kelly and Winter were left to intercept the others.

It didn't take long to find the larger group, who were already engaged in battle. Three lifeless bodies of men were sprawled on the ground, presumably changed back to human form from their were-rat appearance. Off to the side, Dr. Half Moon knelt on the ground, clutching Kevin's body in her arms, the silver bladed dagger still embedded in his chest. She had lost all sense of what was happening around her as she wailed over the clamor of the fight not but a strike away from her. Julia remained in her half-wolf form, in combat with Agent Loreto who brandished silver bladed daggers.

Kelly split off to the left while Winter moved to the right to flank Loreto. After Winter moved into position, she charged into the fray, hoping to catch him unaware. Unfortunately, he spied the flanking attack, tumbled back from Julia, and sent a dagger to each attacker flanking him. One found Winter and pierced her shoulder, sending her plummeting to the ground. The other bounced off an energy shield Kelly had created and illuminated from his shillelagh.

"Get the doctor out of here!" Kelly yelled to Julia, who reacted without question. She grabbed the doctor, who didn't want to leave Kevin's body, threw her over her shoulder and ran off into the dark.

Loreto held out his hands, chanted, and beams of white energy shot out from his hands at Kelly, who shot out his own beam of bluish-energy wave that collided with the other. A thunderous clap spread through the air as both forms of energy clashed and became thin, fixed beams pushing its will upon the other, its center glared with neither gaining the advantage over the other until Kelly appeared to tire, weakened by the beam of light that had siphoned off of his power. By the time Kelly realized that Loreto had drawn in his energy and drained him, Kelly attempted to counter, but it was too late. Kelly went to his knees, and the wave of energy sapped all power from him. Loreto began to consume his life force.

While the two clashed, Winter pulled out the silver bladed dagger from her shoulder and called upon her vampiric power to recover from her wound so she could get back into the fight. When she managed to stand up, Loreto had pinned Kelly to the ground, draining the wizard of energy.

Cooper arrived, his shotgun drawn on Loreto, "Hands in the air!"

"You have no authority over me. Go home before you get hurt," Loreto said as he stopped his attack on Kelly and drew out his pistol. He turned his head in Winter's direction who had just gained her footing.

"Don't try it," Cooper warned the agent but knew he wouldn't listen.

Loreto raised his pistol and fired, missing his target. Cooper pulled the trigger and hit Loreto, knocking him to the pavement. But Loreto had not suffered a mortal injury and returned fire, striking Cooper square in the chest. Loreto stood, walked over to Cooper with a slow, arrogant approach to finish him off. Before Loreto reached him, his own dagger cut through the air, flying at him. He turned to shoot his attacker, only to drop his pistol from the impact of the dagger that drove deep to the hilt through his eye socket. The initial shock of trauma evaded him. He snorted in amusement at Winter who had given him the killing blow with his own dagger, then fell dead before his body fully collapsed on the ground.

Winter sprinted over to Kelly, "I'm so sorry."

"Don't be. My time has come," Kelly smiled. "Take care of him."

His final breath left his lips and he went limp. Winter closed Kelly's eyes and picked up his shillelagh. She mused over the weapon for a moment, an object that was as much of a part of him as his presence. She finished her brief mourning and darted off toward Zander's destination, thinking Nathan was safe, that the fight in the clinic had been done for some time and that he would stay where it was secure until someone arrived.

Murray ran through the brick and filth-laden maze, its stench hit the nostrils as pungent and full of dust and decay. He followed the path of Jimmy Calvillo's taunting-filled guidance. Murray rounded a corner, and there at the opposing edge of the dead end, Jimmy settled in with a human shield in his grasp, his pistol held to her head. Murray recognized his hostage, Pearl, and remembered her long and sad story of how she came to reside here. He didn't want her end to come like this.

He raised his .357 magnum, aiming for whatever vital target he could find on Jimmy's body. The most prevalent was the head, "It's over, Jimmy. Throw down your weapon and let her go."

Jimmy laughed, barely keeping composure. He seemed crazed and giddy and still as bloodthirsty as he'd ever seen him. Plus, how long had he been a were-rat, and did it effect his sanity? All of this combined didn't bode well for anyone, especially Pearl. "Do you think I came all this way through this trash heap just to give up? Surrender to you?"

Jimmy went into a fit of maniacal laughter that also fed his rage. He growled and snapped his jaws in Pearl's ears and made her cry, only making him laugh even harder.

"What do you want then?" Murray lowered his gun to his side. "No one else is here. You can tell me."

"What do I want? What do I want! I want blood! I want what I deserve!" Jimmy screamed as tears rolled down his eyes. Murray nodded. He let him talk, let him calm down. Best scenario for all parties involved would be for everyone to walk away, arrest him later with a SWAT team when he was unaware, catch him when he was more stable.

"Don't you think I should get a taste? I mean, after my brother," Jimmy's thoughts pierced his mind and the tears flowed freely with unsettling laughter.

"We all deserve it. Hell Jimmy, I'm looking to retire, hang up my spurs. Nothing has to happen here today." Murray hoped he could talk him down.

"No! No, it ends here tonight. With you and me."

"Why? It doesn't make sense."

"Because if I'm going out, I want it to be you."

"Don't put that on me."

"Better it being you than getting clipped."

Murray frowned, and knew he had lost the argument, that Jimmy's reason was sound, "Fair enough, but you let her go."

"She's a witness."

"At least let her stand to the side. She can't witness anything if she's dead."

Jimmy nodded and let her go, but Pearl stayed still, "No Murray, don't do it. He'll kill you and then eat you. It's what they do."

"Lady, you move or I'll plug you right in the back of the head and then feast on your corpse," Jimmy growled.

"It's okay." Murray motioned to Pearl to move to the side. She complied and grasped the wall, trying to make her body shrink into the brick structure around them. Both men lowered their pistols to their sides, waiting for the moment of truth.

"Any time you're ready," Murray said.

"On the count of . . . " Jimmy said.

Yeah, yeah, wait for the count of two and then the bad guy plugs you before the count of three. This wasn't the Wild West, and Murray wasn't waiting. And before the count of one came out of Jimmy's mouth, Murray shot from the hip, nailing Jimmy in the center of the neck. Jimmy held his wound that spewed blood like a faucet but managed to fire back at Murray before he could shoot again. The bullet hit Murray in the chest with such force it sent him to the ground, crumbling in a heap of pain. Jimmy lay motionless, bleeding out. Murray fell in and out of consciousness. In between the darkness, he saw two blurry figures engulfed in battle while flames and sparks of electricity illuminated the surrounding area. And then darkness claimed him for a deep slumber that only comes with serious damage.

Nathan awoke somewhere outside, his arms and legs bound with rope that had unearthly energy, making it stronger. He couldn't remember how he got here until his memories came flooding into his mind. He recollected his mission, heading into the clinic when he heard something flapping, almost making a whistling sound coming at him. He turned his head long enough to see a bola with silver coated chains and balls strike him, wrapping itself around his neck. The balls on the ends smacked him in the head, knocking him unconscious. He had been fastened to some kind of cement surface. He looked all around, and to the right, Zander had been pinned down in a similar fashion with the addition of being gagged. He gazed around some more at his surroundings, noticing the tombstones and foliage. Someone had brought them to the graveyard where he resided. In fact, the mausoleum in which he slept wasn't but a short distance behind them. That's when he spotted the man in a red suit reading from a book with gold inlay and gilding.

Nathan's limbs grew heavy. The bindings restrained not part but all of his limbs. His inner energy, his life force, rumbled inside and tore at his body like a confined animal attempting to claw to its freedom through a prison of flesh.

"What are you doing to me?" Nathan tried to get the man's attention who only ignored him and continued to read and chant from the text.

"What have I done wrong?" Nathan asked.

The man closed the book and stroked Nathan's head, "Nothing, my child. I'm undoing what has been done to you."

"I was told that was impossible."

"Are you a man of faith?" the man opened the book again.

"Yes."

"Then I must cleanse your soul to save you from damnation."

Zander managed to remove his gag, "Don't listen to him! He's preforming an exorcism! He's going to rip your soul away and destroy your body!"

He placed his hands on Nathan's chest and chanted while his phantasmal hands plowed through him, gripping onto his essence, yanking it, attempting to rip it from its corporeal form. Nathan gathered his power and resisted the energy pulling on him, but his energy source didn't want to resist the pull. The power that tugged on his energy felt warm and inviting. His energy wanted to bond on this different, brighter source of power and siphon its light into it and become one. His opposition to its pleas waned, and he found the glowing path to the source. This power welcomed his, urged a symbiotic melding. This differed from the struggles he felt where dark energies resided and fed upon each other. He drew from its purity, though he could distinguish his corporeal body wasn't suited to hone such energy.

Soon, his fight to maintain control and possession of his life force changed into the joining of energy with the man named Martes, sharing memories that fueled their power. He saw images of the things the man had done, the horrors of his actions and their self-justification. He had broken his sacred vow to protect the innocent.

Martes broke the physical and energy bind between them, rubbing the pain that scalded his arms, his mind racing. But the haunting deeds he had committed would not hide in the shadows of his psyche. They had been exposed.

"How could you?" Nathan asked. "You're a man of God."

"I am the instrument of God's vengeance, the protector of humankind. My soul is clean. What about yours?" Martes countered.

Nathan saw Winter sneaking up closer behind Martes. All he had to do was distract him until she got within striking distance, but Nathan had something more befitting for his punishment.

"Your soul is stained with the innocents murdered at your hands." Nathan's bindings fell off as if they were never tied and he instantly came to an upright position next to the slab he had been bound to. "You have sullied the Lord's name and now you will answer for your sins."

Martes had placed his sword nearby, leaning it on a tombstone. But when Nathan's power emitted around him, the sword responded to his call, its new master. The white-handled sword with a shiny silver hilt and blade unsheathed itself and flew into his grasp. The weapon revealed etched words along it: "Per Aspera Ad Astra."

Martes drew a dagger, ready for melee. By this time Winter had responded, drawing her own dagger, ready to attack. But Nathan had already called upon the weapon's power, and the overcast sky and darkness parted, sending a beam of blinding white light down upon Martes who burned in its purity, leaving him to scream and then silence as he turned to nothing but smoldering embers in a pile of ash. Nathan had to let go of the weapon, sheathing it with telekinesis. His palm had reddened from the power he wielded from the weapon and continued to burn long after he released the handle. The silver sheath had decorative crosses engraved on its outer side. He wanted to avert the crosses from his sight, so he turned it around to hide the inscribed symbols, though they didn't seem to bother him as much as Zander and Winter who were flinching from their sight.

Nathan felt a presence amongst them. He looked around, and all of nature ceased to move, except for Zander. He followed the scent of sulfur over to the burnt remains of Martes, and through the smoke he saw the transparent grey cloaked figure holding a scythe step forward and beckon the soul of Martes with a skeletal hand. The smoke drifted toward the deathly entity and formed into the haunting figure of Martes bound in thick chains, bent over by the burden of the chain's weight, his face pale and mouth gaped open, quivering as if to speak but his agony had taken his voice.

Nathan thought, *Why the chains?*

The cloaked figure replied in his thoughts, *The chains are built by the sins one crafts, link by link, while good deeds shed links of the chain. In the end, if one's deeds outweigh the chain, their spirit walks without burden. If not, the links remain, and only forgiveness can shed them.*

The two faded and time unfroze—as if no time had passed. Nathan looked over at Zander who merely nodded his acknowledgment of what he saw.

Winter came over and helped free Zander while Nathan secured the sword on his belt.

"How did you use that sword, let alone touch it?" Winter asked.

"What do you mean? You've had me wield magical weapons," Nathan said.

"It's a holy sword, a blessed weapon. You shouldn't be able to look at it or even its sheath, let alone call upon its power. It should have killed you," Zander said.

"Okay, but why does this guy have such a mighty weapon?" Nathan asked.

"He was an Inquisitor," Zander said.

"As in the Inquisition?"

"The same."

"I thought they only tortured people to convert them. Didn't they dissolve the group?"

"That's what most humans believe. The truth is they're the Vatican's secret police and hunters of the unnatural. Try to avoid them in the future."

Nathan nodded and then looked around, "Where's Kelly?"

Winter stepped forward, her head bowed as she presented Kelly's shillelagh to Nathan, "I'm sorry."

Nathan said nothing, took it gently from her hands, and looked the weapon up and down with admiration for the man who had owned it. Given how emotionally spent he'd become, and how the shock of the news hit him now, mourning his friend would have to wait another day. He walked away, the shillelagh resting on his shoulder like an umbrella.

Chapter Fifteen

Murray's eyes parted half-way. It felt like a chore to keep them open this much, let alone fully open. In an attempt to focus, he blinked, but the weight of his eyelids made them droop and blur his vision. Muffled voices and sounds faded in and out until the pain in his head subsided and allowed the function of hearing and sight to work properly. His vision cleared, and there was the face of an angel. The one who always had been there for him, no matter if he deserved her or not.

"I said you weren't permitted to die, old man." Laura kissed his hand and held it tight, their fingers interlocked.

"I'm glad I didn't disappoint," Murray's scratchy throat sounded as though he was chewing on rocks, his body ached all over, but he managed to lift his arm and wipe away a renegade tear from one of her eyes.

Barker knocked and then peeked in to see if he could enter. Laura waved him in and he stepped into the room, closing the door behind him. He had a somber expression on his face that wasn't hidden by the half-hearted smile he gave them.

Murray noticed this right away, "Don't look so glum. I'm not dead yet."

"I'm sure Fitzgerald will be upset." Barker's attempt at

humor didn't play well as Murray's face went serious, shaking his head no.

Murray tried to sidestep the faux pas, "That's why I've always worn a vest."

Laura's disapproval became evident in her glare at the two men, then she locked eyes on Murray, "You haven't been conscious for five minutes and you're already up to something."

"Whatever do you mean? I couldn't have done anything." Murray wanted to smile but dismissed the thought as soon as it came to him.

Laura's suspicious gaze trailed back to Barker, her frustration and question emanating in one word, "Ernie?"

Barker hesitated over his words, as if he didn't trust his own explanation, "It isn't anything that he's done, necessarily."

"Do I have to call your mama?" Laura asked.

Barker turned to Murray, his hands in the air, and then turned back to Laura who'd stood up by now and had her arms crossed, "Murray is listed on the squad's dead pool."

"What?" she turned to Murray.

"His name has been on it for three years," Barker squeaked out.

Laura's mouth dropped open and her hands went to her hips, "Are you serious?"

Murray moved around on the bed, "It's just a jab at my age."

"No, it's not!" Laura protested. She'd gone through this with him before.

"Calm down, will you? We can discuss this later."

"Oh, like I've never heard that before. Tell me, when

exactly will that be?"

"After this case, when I retire."

Barker and Laura went silent. A grave look fell upon them.

"I've been thinking about it for a while now but thought Cooper should know my intentions beforehand."

Laura sat back down by Murray and gripped his hand.

"What's going on?" Murray turned to Laura, "I thought you'd be happy."

Barker intervened, "There's someone here to see you. I didn't want to let them in right away, until you both had your time together."

"Let them in." Murray had no idea who waited in the hall, several people who couldn't believe he survived had come to see him, he supposed.

The door creaked open and Sylvia Brewer stood in the doorway in her blue and grey sweats with the hoodie that hid her undone hair and bare face revealing lines of tears she'd shed. Barker shut the door when Brewer managed to enter. Laura went over and hugged her. Brewer lowered her face into Laura's shoulder and muffled cries filled all in the room with sorrow, for Murray realized Cooper had died. His sadness matched Brewer's for but a moment, then transformed into vengeance.

Murray turned to Ernie, "Tell me what they know."

Both men exchanged brief summations of what occurred, minus the supernatural aspects. Barker reported the police had summed up the attack as an attempted kidnapping of Dr. Half Moon. The police intervened and saved the doctor who was being kept in a safe place while Cooper died in the line of duty fighting members of the

Calvillo family, and that Murray had been credited as taking down the ringleader.

"So, the department is spinning this thing into something positive," Murray said.

"Did you expect anything else?" Barker asked.

When the men finished, Murray noticed Laura and Brewer over by a laptop, sitting very cozy, whispering to each other and then glancing over to him and then the screen, "What's going on over there?"

"I don't believe it. No matter how many times I see it, I don't believe it." Laura looked at Murray with a look of condolence and sadness.

Brewer handed the laptop over to Murray and hit play, "Cooper wore a body cam and piped it into my laptop in case something happened to you guys."

Barker watched, "Is this for real?"

"Unfortunately. But who would believe us? That's why we got hosed every time we tried to move the investigation forward," Murray said. "Did they find the body cam on him?"

"I actually did," Barker said. "I didn't know what had been filmed, but I'd been instructed to give it to Ms. Davis."

"Why did Davis want the body cam?"

"Because Bill wanted her to have it," Brewer said. "And he asked us to help expose this if you both had died. She has a copy, just in case."

"Well, I'm not dead."

"But you need help," Brewer said.

Murray looked at Laura, "How did you get involved in all of this?"

"I consult with the station on the tech side and they bring me things they can't account for, prove real, or if something is fake footage. When Sylvia gave it to me . . . " Laura's voice trailed off.

"Spinelli told me I would have to see it, that I'd never believe it unless I saw it for myself," Murray started laughing.

All looked at Murray and Laura asked, "What's so funny?"

"He also told me once I figured out who was blocking our investigation that I'd retire because of all the dirt we'd exposed."

"Don't quit," Brewer said as he stared outside the window.

"If I pursue this, if *we* pursue this, things may not turn out the way you think they will." Murray held his head down and shook it.

"You'll never forgive yourself if you walk away," Laura said.

Murray stared at her in shock. He expected she'd say the opposite.

"We've got your back," Barker said.

"Are you sure?" Murray addressed everyone in the room, "You're risking your careers, your lives. If you're that hell-bent on taking them down, I'll take the risk. I've already lost a friend and don't want to lose anyone else."

Brewer walked over to the bed, tears flowing, not from grief, but from a boiling rage, "Right before I came here, I had to identify his body. If anyone had told me when Bill and I got engaged that a week later I would be burying my fiancé, I would have taken him and run away to the ends of the world to cheat death."

All remained silent and then she continued, rubbing her engagement ring with her thumb and index finger, "But now, I'd give up everything to watch the bastards who killed my love burn."

Murray smiled, as if he'd been given permission to finish this on his terms, "You're damn right we will."

Zander slammed the receiver of his phone down and for a rare moment, let his frustration show. Winter and Nathan sat on the couch, their rage and sadness had passed into numbness, their win seemed more like a loss. Nathan's attention kept drifting off to the shillelagh propped next to the coat rack by the door. The loss of Kelly hadn't truly set in but the sadness had already given way to memorable moments. He hadn't known him long, but the impact he made on his life would stay with him.

"They have your child." Zander leaned on the small table where the phone sat, his back was all he allowed them, though they sensed his controlled vexation radiate.

"The Seditionists?" Nathan jutted up, "How?"

"All we know is they attacked the reservation and the tribe's power couldn't hold them back," Zander said.

Nathan paced behind the couch, "So, what now?"

"With all that is happening in the city, a war is inevitable, which is good for us."

"Who are our allies, who do we trust?"

Zander turned around, his neutral demeanor back, "No one for now. I'm waiting for a call from Spinelli to broker a deal."

"I won't trade my boy." Nathan became defensive, a slight tone of anger.

"Not at all. It's imperative we get him back."

"At first you wanted to forget about him. And now you're willing to risk a deal with the rats in a war? What makes my kid so important?"

"It's time he knew," Winter intervened.

"And what do you think Her Majesty would say about divulging such information?" Zander asked her.

"She's pragmatic. Any information shared that gives her an advantage to win a war, gain power and notoriety, is encouraged." Winter crossed her legs and leaned back against the nest of couch pillows she positioned around her.

Zander gestured to Nathan, "Please, sit."

Nathan complied, anxious to hear the reason.

"When your vampiric power was tapped, it awoke your dormant bloodline power and sent ripples of its energy outward. How far, we do not know for sure. We can surmise it reached the borders of town."

"And so, everyone in town knows." Nathan paused, "Did you know this would happen?"

"I suspected."

"Then why pretend, why the ruse?"

"We didn't know who you would align with."

"But technically, you're my master."

"Sometimes one's greatest foes are the ones you're closest to."

Nathan rubbed his hands together, "And so, my child has my abilities?"

"Not your vampiric, but yes, anyone of your

bloodline's power will rise."

"How soon will they manifest?"

"For your son, soon," Winter said. "That's why all parties show interest. He can be trained at an early age, and the younger they are, the easier it is to indoctrinate them."

"You seem to know a lot about this," Nathan said.

"It's part of my job, to gather information."

Zander's cell phone rang and he stepped into the other room where Winter followed him and closed the door. Nathan had concerns with his son gaining power at such a young age and feared the power might corrupt him. No wonder Zander and Kelly were apprehensive to tell him the harsh truth of his son's place in both the mortal and immortal world. Being human had enough perils in it to deal with, let alone to walk between both existences and not get lost in its pull toward desire and damnation.

Chapter Sixteen

Murray burst through the elevator doors, not even waiting for them to fully slide open. His shotgun rested on his shoulder as he plowed a path to Deveraux's office, with Brewer and Barker tagging along behind him. Laura had departed the group to meet with Davis and disclosed information to her pertinent to the case. Barker had acquired—more like commandeered—the weapons Murray and Cooper had used from the evidence storage. And since he was committing a crime obtaining these for Murray, he decided he might as well procure the other shotgun. All agreed confronting Deveraux wasn't the smartest move on their part, but it was the fastest way and gave them the advantage of surprise.

Murray swung the door open with unneeded force where he found Deveraux on the phone, taken aback by such a brash entrance by Murray and his entourage that followed. Barker closed the door and peeked out the blinds, though their loud entrance caught everyone's attention and could prove folly for them.

"No more being kept in the dark, no more of this need to know crap. Start talking." Murray didn't mince words. He lowered the shotgun off his shoulder and gripped the weapon with two hands.

Deveraux ended his call, "Murray, I know things look

dire. . . "

Murray cut off his Captain's attempt at appeasement with the blast of a shotgun just over Deveraux's head. Pieces of the wall and dust fell on the captain as he rocked back, in shock and fear.

"Jesus!" Deveraux yelled. The sound of gunfire brought the entire floor to his doorway with their weapons drawn. Barker dismissed it as a misfire. The other officers looked at Deveraux, all covered in dust, who confirmed the story with a nod and a wave of his hand. When the crowd dispersed, Barker shut the door, "Should I even bother closing it?"

Murray kept his steel eyes and clenched jaw on Deveraux, "That depends on what comes out of his mouth next."

"If you'll allow me." Brewer put her hand on Murray's forearm, that calming touch that women give to a man for them to relent, signaling it was her turn. Murray eased the grip on his weapon, slung the shotgun over his shoulder, and then took a step back.

Brewer stepped forward, pulled out the tablet and hit play on the video, placing it in front of Deveraux who scarcely watched any of the footage but set his eyes on Brewer's eyes, welling up with tears for the hundredth time. "You sent them on a suicide mission, sent them unprepared to deal with the very things you knew they wouldn't survive."

"I told them to stop the investigation."

"Shhh!" Brewer wouldn't allow him to talk himself out of this one. "And you involved foreign assassins to ensure they were eliminated while in the line of duty."

"That wasn't what they were here to do."

Brewer ignored his attempts to dissuade her, "You helped orchestrate an international conspiracy with foreign governmental entities, attempting to cover up a world most people consider fairy tales. I have enough proof here, along with what Cooper and Murray collected, to send you away into the deepest, blackest holes for life."

"No one will ever believe you, about the monsters."

Brewer leaned forward, her finger in his face, "It doesn't matter what the conspiracy is about. All the public has to know is that you conspired with foreign agents and that Americans died as a result. You'll be the politician's scapegoat, considered a traitor to his country. You'll never see the light of day. And you've played politics long enough to know I'm correct in my assessment."

"What do you want?" Normally, Deveraux played it cool. He had dead eyes along with a monotone voice, but not this time. Sounding defeated, he tossed the pen in his hand across his desk and leaned to the side with his hands folded to his face.

"The truth," Brewer commanded.

Deveraux sighed, "I had no choice in what occurred. Between downtown, the Federal and foreign governmental entities, I had no power, even within my own department."

"So, the government knows?" Barker asked.

Deveraux laughed, "Not only do they know, they coordinate within a governing system latently guised as secret meetings between leaders."

"Including the creatures?" Murray asked.

"It's called The Assembly. This is where all leaders of every type from every nation gather and discuss laws and other issues, with the same forums and intentions of human governing parties."

"How are you a part of it?"

"Every larger branch of law enforcement and military leadership know, have access to a data base, and have special response units to deal with uncontrolled activity."

"And so they have the power to take over local jurisdiction?"

"If they need to suppress the local populace from their activities, then yes."

Brewer interrupted, "You said there was some kind of database. Do you have access to it?"

Deveraux shifted in his chair, "Listen, I believe I've shared more than enough pertinent, classified information here."

"Oh no you don't. Cooper's blood is on your hands, not mine. If you want to make it right, you give us access." Murray's shotgun lowered onto the desk, its muzzle pointed at Deveraux."

"Are you sure? Once you see this, you'll never look at the world the same way again."

"Our lives are already not the same." Brewer looked the Captain directly in the eyes and showed him what all this subterfuge had brought her, "What would you do if you were me?"

Without any further discussion, Deveraux led the group down into the sub-basement where only the warehouse service elevator and a set of emergency stairs went further down. The group got off the elevator to transfer to the service elevator. Deveraux had to contact the sub-floor and request transport down.

"If this city's database wasn't in this building, we'd have no access," Deveraux said.

"Lucky for you we do have access," Murray said.

When the elevator arrived, a worker came up and Deveraux had to sign them in with a keypad for permission. When they got reached the sub-level, they entered a room with many paper files, boxes, and file cabinets that towered above them all, set up in rows marked in numeric code. They went through the main pathway to a desk centered in the room where Deveraux requested a key from the clerk. Murray recognized some of the old folks, from retired cops to clerk staff who handled the secured files here, including the head clerk, Danny Simms, who retired from vice a good ten years ago.

"So, retirement just wasn't your speed." Murray said to Simms.

"George, I see you've stepped up your game, entered the world where the big boys play," Simms said.

"Not me," Murray said, "I'm just visiting."

Simms's expression went dour, "Nobody just visits this world, trust me."

"I always have." Murray shook his hand. "You should get out sometime, and we can have a drink."

"Well, I certainly know where to find you," Simms said. "Say hello to Laura."

"Definitely."

Deveraux went over to a panel next to a benign wooden door, placed his key into the slot and turned it. The wall next to the door slid aside and displayed a room where old data bank terminals and new tech towers stood in rows. Off to the side, desks with workstations awaited them. All four settled into a station. Meanwhile, Deveraux explained the war that had brewed up between the ruling groups of creatures in the city. Their main objective, for a reason unknown to the human authorities, was to battle for possession of Nathan Brooks' child.

"I'm sure the Brooks are rolling over in their graves knowing their child is being tossed around like a hot potato," Murray said.

Deveraux typed into a menu on Murray's station and clicked on a heading, "I don't believe you get the gist of what's happening around here."

All parties gathered around Murray's screen and witnessed their findings.

"Nathan Brooks? A vampire?" Murray shook his head.

"Didn't the body go missing?" Brewer said.

"How did you know?" Barker said.

"I'm a reporter. It's what I do." Brewer said.

"I just don't understand how you can keep any of this a secret."

"People won't and don't believe it, even if they see it," Deveraux said. "I'm from the south. It's an unsaid truth these things exist. Sometimes families will pass down a story about how they had a brush with the unnatural."

"Sounds like you have a family story," Brewer said.

"I suppose I could tell you, now that you won't think me mad for passing down such tales." Deveraux brushed his mustache with his fingers. "When my mother was young, her family would love to take the occasional evening trip on Bourbon Street. While walking along one night, she noticed a man who didn't move right, he swerved in and out of the congested sidewalk of people with an odd smoothness that she described as breathtaking. She stared at the man, couldn't keep her eyes off of him. That's when he turned with the shiny eyes of the nocturnal, smiled at the little girl, tipped his hat and disappeared into the crowd. Many years later, while on Bourbon Street, she came across the same man, and though he wore more modern wear, he hadn't aged. Again, she couldn't help but to stare, as if the child within her surfaced and took all adult sense of survival away, and the man once again turned. At first, his expression was that of an animal, the predator hunting, and then he stared at her with no expression as to ponder why she had not done anything but stare at him, frozen in the moment. And as if a memory of something long forgotten hit him with joyous delight, he smiled at her and held his hand up to her childhood height. She nodded her head yes, confirming his memory. He then tipped an imaginary hat and disappeared into the night."

When the group finished, they left the sub-basement by elevator to go back to Deveraux's office. When they stepped off the elevator into the squad room, they were met with bustling activity that seemed more like chaos.

"Captain," Evans ran up to the group, "we've been looking everywhere for you."

Deveraux cut Evans off, "Why is everyone running around like they have no sense?"

The organ pipes filled the church with a reverent hymn as the funeral procession made its way down the center aisle to the rounded alter dais where the priest chanted the opening prayer, blessing Angelo Spinelli's casket with holy water, placing the pall on it.

And while this occurred, what remained of the Calvillo crew gathered in a back room in the Bigsby warehouse to discuss new leadership and how to proceed. Soon after the meeting commenced, Sal and three others entered the room with machine guns and cut down every single man and were-rat in the room. When the carnage ended, the four ditched their guns amongst the dead, soaked the room with gasoline, and lit the place on the way out. As the four sped away, Sal looked in the rearview mirror and saw nothing but smoke coming from the building from several blocks down the road.

Later in the funeral, after the priest read the Gospel and gave his sermon to the assembled about life, death, and spirituality, Mike Spinelli was welcomed up to the pulpit and delivered a touching speech concerning his brother and how his presence in his daily life made him a better man.

During the sermon, the wolves, excluding the members guarding Dr. Half Moon, gathered at their headquarters in the city and prepared for the planned assaults that night. They assured themselves they had the right plan at the right time, but the wolves stalked their prey too long, and their hesitation to act became their downfall. The front and back doors exploded, followed with machine gun fire engulfing their building as the trapped could do nothing but run and duck enemy fire from every direction. And when the barrage ceased, and only a few wounded withstood the bombardment, they changed into their wolf forms and charged their enemies, ready for hand-to-hand combat with their attackers, only to be riddled with another salvo of bullets, ending their uprising before it ever began.

When the communion hymn commenced, all rose, and the ushers guided the congregation row by row from their pews, so those who took part in the acceptance of the Eucharist could form a line down the center and side aisles.

At the same time, a special SWAT team raided the Seditionist vampire's brood, destroying most of the vampires while they slept, though the high-ranking vampires and their Enforcers had managed to slip away. The team estimated they had wiped out ninety percent of the creatures residing there. The team torched and demolished the building with explosives laced with silver dust, and reported to the news and the on-looking populace they had taken out a large drug factory involving an international drug ring.

The recessional hymn rang out from the organ and through the speakers in the church while the casket and priest led the congregation on their slow march out to the vehicles that would head to the cemetery. Meanwhile, Fisher and Dubois rode in the SUV toward the Field Office to report on the loss of the two foreign agents.

"How will we justify Martes and Loreto's actions?" Dubois had the most to lose since he had been placed in charge of the agents through Interpol.

"We don't," Fisher said.

"Easy for you to say."

"We tell them their agents went rogue. And since we had no prior knowledge of their actions, there's nothing we could have done. They're dead. We control the narrative."

An explosion from underneath the vehicle interrupted their conversation, shook the vehicle into a roll, and engulfed it in flames. A secondary detonation tore the vehicle apart, sending flames and scorching metal in the air. The military grade explosives placed under the engine and the gas tank guaranteed no survival from the wreck.

When the sermon at the graveyard concluded, Noodles whispered to Big Mike, "It's done."

Chapter Seventeen

Murray showed up at Big Mike's apartment after the funeral, as requested. He asked Murray for backup, to leave his cop sensibilities at home, and to bring the armory. He'd resupply him with silver rounds. And despite the carnage that raged over the city earlier, this war wasn't over. Deveraux contacted the powers that gave him the official capacity to get involved in the scrimmage. On the other hand, Barker had been assigned to the special SWAT team who stood at the ready if Spinelli failed in eliminating the threat to the city. The powers that be presumed one entity of inhuman remain as a dominate group and should be allowed to reign within their realm due to the natural order of things. But that the top tier ruler, those who had influence over the inhuman beings, would be human.

Murray rang the doorbell, never expecting who opened the door.

"Hello, George." Ms. Davis was dressed in a teal nightgown. It didn't hide much.

"Really?" Murray averted his gaze as he entered.

Davis closed the door and went behind the bar, "What's the matter? From what I hear, it isn't like you've never been with a black woman before."

Murray slumped into a chair facing away, "Some things you can't unsee, okay?"

She poured three scotch on the rocks, "I kind of like seeing you like this, uncomfortable and squirming. Actually, I find it rather satisfying."

Big Mike came from the bedroom, his Thompson machine gun in hand, "I thought I asked you to play nice."

"I only play nice with you, sometimes." Davis handed him a drink.

Murray glanced over his shoulder, only to see the two kissing, "You could have done that before I got here."

"Have fun you two." Davis strutted back into the bedroom, her drink in hand while she waved goodbye to Murray.

Murray shook his head as Mike brought over his drink. Both men charged it down their throats.

"Another?" Mike headed toward the bar.

"Absolutely." Murray followed Mike's lead.

Mike poured another round.

"Why did they allow you to conduct that bloodbath you've strewn across town?" Murray slammed down his drink in one tilt of the glass.

"Are you asking me as a cop?" Mike drank his glass and poured them another round.

"I think we're beyond that. I'm here with downtown's blessing. I just want to know how you have carte blanche."

"Simple answer is I'm human. I've convinced the Feds to hand me over a billion dollars-plus in grants for renovations to the city, but only if I take control," Mike said.

Murray nodded, "So, you have a license to kill."

"Look at their point of view. Can you imagine this city falling into the hands of non-humans?"

"I can relate."

"If I run things, the government's happy, KC is happy, and the money flows in like water."

"That's what it's really about: the money."

Big Mike put the glass up to his lips and laughed, "It's always about the money."

Both finished off their drinks and gathered their gear, loading their weapons and strapping them on. Soon, Noodles came to pick them up.

"Hey," Murray said to Noodles, "did you know Mike was involved with Davis?"

"Don't get me started," Noodles said.

"Why not?" Mike asked. "She's attractive, powerful, and we can be honest with each other without the other relationship burdens or commitments."

"Ah, a friendly friend." Murray nodded to Noodles, "How convenient."

"That's enough with busting my balls. What about you?" Mike said. "I could write a book on how not to keep a lady, based on your experience."

Noodles smiled, "I'd read that."

Noodles pulled up in the clinic parking lot at the opposite end toward the edge of No Man's Land. The other vehicles following them parked and all got out of their vehicles and armed themselves. In addition to weapons and ammunition, Mike had provided them with armor vests they strapped on before placing their weapons on their bodies.

"This is what we are fighting for, this land," Mike said.

"It's an abandoned district loaded with homeless," Murray said.

"You don't get it?" Mike nodded his head and chuckled. "When we develop this part of town, the homeless will have jobs or a better place to stay, and the economy will thrive with youth coming here for entertainment and consumption. Trust me, in five years, you won't recognize the place, I guarantee."

"But first we need to fight *who* for it?" Murray asked.

"The Seditionists, bad vampires not on our side. They're behind everything. And they have the advantage."

"Of course they do. They're vampires." Murray's sarcasm overtly bled through.

"No, no, you don't understand. They have the infant."

"Brooks' child?"

"They want to trade him for control of the city."

"We can't let them have either." Murray didn't know the significance of the baby, but it didn't sound like anything good would come of letting vampires have a baby.

Noodles nudged Big Mike with his shoulder, "Here come the wolves."

When Oliver and his pack came running up, Oliver changed back to his human form and said to Mike, "I'm sure you've heard by now they have the child."

"What happened?" Big Mike asked.

"While you went on a rampage, Radomir stormed the reservation and took the child. If you hadn't killed off most of the pack, they might not have succeeded," Oliver grunted the last part of the explanation.

"Fletcher wanted me dead," Big Mike replied.

"On that I can agree."

"Listen," Big Mike wrapped his arm around him, "when this is all over, I'm going to give you a big slice of territory, a business to run it out of, and a promise to protect one another from any harm. Think of it as an investment for the future, guaranteed."

"We still need to have a serious discussion afterward. You left only ten of us alive."

"That's about all I started out with, a crew of relatives and friends. Sometimes you have to tear out the overgrowth so you can start anew."

Just before the conversation escalated, a swirling circle of sparkling energy formed from out of nowhere and opened up. Two men and a woman stepped through, and though they appeared human, their pale, chilling presence could be felt from a distance away. Murray averted direct line of sight with their eyes, knowing full well that a vampire could hypnotize mere mortals with their gaze. The three approached Murray who recognized Nathan. Murray's caution turned to disbelief.

"Nathan Brooks." Murray usually could muster up something to say to just about anyone, but this was an extremely rare exception.

"Detective, I've heard you did much to help my family. Thank you." Nathan said.

Out of habit, Murray stuck out his hand to shake, but Big Mike caught his wrist, "Not a good idea."

Big Mike yelled out to the assembled, "Okay, gather around. We're all here, despite our differences, to stop a tyrannical group of conquerors who will stop at nothing to take our city. And then more cities will fall under their rule and expose us to the world, and then all will turn on us. We must save not only ourselves, but everyone else, beginning here and now."

"And what of the child? Will you take control of him and us as well as the city?" Phil grunted. "Why should we help you take the missing piece of power from your enemy when you had a part in destroying my people?"

Nathan rose up, pushing Big Mike to the side, "No one gets to claim the child. He is my son."

Zander put his hand on Nathan's shoulder, patting it, "Mr. Spinelli is right. We have all lost loved ones at each other's hands, but the enemy who's orchestrated the recent bloodshed awaits us. And what he offers is obedience or destruction."

Damien, one of the wolf pack spoke up, "If he's so powerful, why not join him?"

"Then go," Big Mike said, "see how subservience suits you."

"You may go if you wish, and you might live long enough to regret it," Zander said.

Oliver shoved Damien to the side, "This bickering is pointless! We fight today and discuss peace in victory! Who's with us?"

All the lycanthropes agreed, grunting in unison.

The group marched to the agreed meeting place within the maze of buildings to a clearing that was walled by crumbling brick buildings. The Seditionists had positioned themselves at the best vantage points of higher ground and were encircling the area where the group entered. Once they entered, there was no turning back, no choice but to fight for survival. Though their numbers had been depleted, the strong of the group endured and had made ready for battle.

Zander and Big Mike stepped forward with Nathan and Winter close by, Zander and Murray covering Big Mike's back. Demetrius came forward to meet them half-way with Radomir and Jade just behind him.

"Hello, old friend." Demetrius's voice came off as somber, almost sad, though no one else picked up on this except the long-lived vampires present.

"It's been a long time," Zander nodded.

"Over a hundred years. It's a shame, meeting like this, under these circumstances."

"It is a shame." Zander folded his hands in front of him.

"Have you considered my offer?"

"We have."

"And?"

"Where is the child?"

"Dismissive as usual," Demetrius scoffed.

"He's here!" Radomir yelled and turned everyone's attention to another vampire standing on an elevated pile of rubble. The vampire cradled the child. Radomir glided over to him and took the child into his arms.

"Satisfied?" Demetrius said.

Zander nodded and then gazed over at Nathan who had somehow kept his composure.

"You never answered my question," Demetrius observed, "but that's how you do things. Manipulate. Manipulate."

In the midst of the conversation, Murray whispered to Big Mike, "Shouldn't you intercede?"

"And miss this drama? You can't make up stuff this juicy," Big Mike laughed.

"What are you going on about?" Zander let his puzzled expression show, upsetting Demetrius who raised his voice an octave.

"Why did you leave my side?"

"We've discussed this. It was *you* who left, not me."

"No, you don't get to change the subject as well as the happenings of the past." Demetrius let his anger, his power, spill over and all felt a tingling sensation over their bodies. His steel mind, his sheer will intermixed with woe showed how focused he could become. But his armor had a weakness in it, and that weakness turned out to be Zander.

A moment passed as Zander simply looked at Demetrius without responding.

Demetrius continued, "You stuck your nose into scrolls for over a hundred years, for what? To become a lesser being? The Zander I knew would have welcomed new power, not shunned it or sought to reverse it. You're the cause of all of this."

"We all changed that day. When we marched into the Red Hand's lair and became infected. I looked for a cure. You just read the scrolls and became indoctrinated and left to conquer the world. I refused, and you and your horde left to do what you do best—spread bloodshed."

"Infected?" Demetrius stepped in closer to Zander, baring his fangs, "It's the greatest treasure I'd ever collected as a Warlord. With this blessing, I will never kneel to lesser men again."

"Those who lust for power are never sated."

"As opposed to rot under one's foot." Demetrius drew

out his sword. "Remember when we had our twin swords crafted and then you had them enchanted?"

"Enchanted in the breath of a dragon, yes I remember it well."

"Only for you, years later, to throw your sword down at my feet before you abandoned us. Do you know how long I mourned for you?" Demetrius's lip quivered. "As if you died because that's the only way I could keep from being torn apart inside?" Demetrius's breath became heavy. "Do you know how much pain I endured in that one act of defiance?" A stream of tears ran down Demetrius's cheeks, his face changing from a sea of sorrow into a storm of fury.

"You can rattle on with empty words to justify your bloodlust all you like, but I know the truth."

Demetrius discarded any attempt of concealing the wrath that only fractured love can bring. He raised his sword over his head and swung downward as to split Zander in two, only to miss when Zander used an invisible force of energy to push Demetrius backwards. His boots drug in the dirt but he never lost his footing. The intended blow cut into the earth, billowing dust filled the air. Zander drew his sword at the ready, sparking the others to attack as both sides clashed with their weapons and claws.

Big Mike and Murray managed to get to an edge of the battle and stood back to back, taking shots whenever they could. They had to be mindful of friendly fire, though Murray didn't hold as stringent to minimizing collateral damage as Big Mike did.

"If your old man could see us now!" Murray yelled over his shoulder to Big Mike.

"No doubt!" Big Mike fired on a vampire who'd

overpowered one of the wolves, saving him. The half-formed werewolf jutted his head around to see who'd downed the vampire all over him and paused briefly before rejoining the melee.

Winter had engaged with three Seditionist Enforcers, the blades of their weapons clattered together with the sound that only bladed weapons make when forced upon each other, colliding and sparking in breathtaking speeds. She had brought a lot of attention her way, in particular the Enforcers, since she'd dispensed through four opposing vampires in no time at all. Nathan separated from Winter and Zander at the beginning of the conflict and pursued those who held his child captive. Winter despised being separated so far from Nathan. But she had her hands full, and with so many attacks coming her way, it would have been detrimental in this situation to fight and protect him at the same time.

When Nathan reached the vantage point where Radomir still stood caressing his child, a familiar vampire blocked his path, his weapon ready. Nathan couldn't help but worry about his son's safety and what lay beyond for them both, regardless of the outcome.

"You didn't think I'd miss the party, did you?" Clovis bowed.

Nathan pulled out the shillelagh, "What a pleasant surprise. I thought they'd punish or maybe even kill you."

"They did. I was shed of my title and banished. But my new family has welcomed me with open arms. Shall we dance?"

"But of course." Nathan swung his club and it smashed upon his opponent's sword, their weapons clanged together with the dull sound produced from the violent connection between wood and metal.

Nathan began the first wave of assaults as the aggressor, swinging the shillelagh in down strokes so his weapon might crush his opponent with overpowering blows that would bring his enemy to his knees. Clovis was too seasoned of a warrior to succumb to such a simplistic assail. He dodged and parried the attacks, triangulated his stance so Nathan could never bring down the debilitating force that wore on someone bombarded with wallops from a bludgeoning weapon.

Clovis moved with precision, outflanking the foray of his enemy who was dead set on being relentless in their offense. This played right into his preferred fighting style where his fencing took precedence. He would allow his enemy to wear down through attrition, take the aggressive stance, and then bleed them until they had nothing left but to kneel in defeat for the killing blow.

Nathan had allowed his emotions to dictate his reckless behavior, channeling his inner demons into an obedient weapon at his command. He came to his senses and suppressed his primal instincts. He halted his reckless behavior and circled his rival to measure their strategies in which Clovis had done the same.

"I'm impressed," Clovis said. "For a minute I thought you were nothing but a rabid dog who didn't know any better. I see not only passion but wisdom in your fighting."

Nathan lunged then faded back, testing his response while studying his attack method. "Stand down. My quarrel isn't with you."

"I beg to differ. You humiliated me, caused me to lose

rank and my family. I cannot stand for that. I must reclaim my honor from the one who stole it from me."

"Is your honor worth losing your life?"

"You've not been a vampire long. You'll never understand, even if you survive me."

Across the battlefield, Oliver and three other wolves, all in half-were form to take advantage of their claws and mobility, tore their way through lower ranking vampires to get to Radomir, their smug adversary who had been the thorn in the wolves' side since the last war between the pack and their brood. They wanted to ensure Radomir wouldn't evade justice for his betrayal and breaking of the peace treaty.

Two vampires engaged them, both concentrating on taking down the massive alpha wolf. One vampire was armed with a dagger, another with his claws. Oliver growled and readied himself for their simultaneous charge. Both sprang into action with flying lunges and swipes, only to sever and pierce nothing but air. Their target dodged their strikes and took advantage of his place in between them, digging his claws into them as they passed by. Both assailants crumbled to the ground. Only the vampire brandishing the dagger survived to counter, the other suffered a fatal claw strike pierced through the heart, ripping the organ in two. Oliver didn't wait for the recovering vampire to recoup, charging him as he stood up. The vampire sensed the oncoming attack and tried to thrust his dagger into the wolf, but he plunged his weapon into his enemies' shoulder, hitting nothing vital or maiming his attacker enough to make him rethink continuing his onslaught. And despite the wound, Oliver grabbed the vampire's neck and bit into his skull, crushing bone and tearing through brain and flesh with his teeth until the vampire went limp in his clutches. Oliver threw the body aside and howled out in victory.

Zander swung his sword with a downward thrust, his weapon clashed against Demetrius' sword. He parried the attempt with ease and countered with a looping side swipe. Zander riposted the side slashes with a thrusting jut of his blade that ended the exchange. Both backed away a few steps, studying each other's movement, anticipating their next move. Combat in sword fighting meant more than hacking one's opponent to pieces; the art of sword play taught strategy and patience. And like anything learned and mastered, the reflexive response becomes second nature, whether intended as an offensive or defensive action. They both searched for a weakness and had not found it. Sometimes it took a while to feel them out. Other times one side would tire, become overly aggressive, or simply make an error. They had to be sharp and exploit the situation once it emerged. The opportunity might not come again.

"After all of these years, I thought you'd be out of practice," Demetrius said as he encircled Zander with a quickened pace, ready to try a new strategy and go fully offensive at a blinding pace.

"You've underestimated me again," Zander responded

as he readied his sword in one hand while calling upon an energy ball of plasma in the other, launching it at Demetrius, disrupting his plans. The energy attack nearly hit its target, though he gave up his footing to avoid the volley. He landed face first into the dirt, and by the time he turned around, Zander had his sword at his throat. Demetrius sat back for a minute and laughed at his folly.

"Well, that was unexpected," Demetrius said as he remained seated.

Zander lowered his weapon and stepped back to allow Demetrius to get up, "I'm surprised you didn't expect that from me."

"I told you if your sword work ever got on par with your magick you would be unstoppable."

"But don't you remember my response? When that day comes, I won't need to fight."

Demetrius stood, dusting himself off, "We are who we are. Don't deny yourself of your talents, of your skills."

"You've never understood me. One cannot keep on fighting until he's faced his greatest adversary—himself."

"You can lie to yourself all you want. We aren't just warriors. We're vampires. You cannot deny our very nature."

Zander sighed, "Don't you see this is pointless? We can't continue on like this. Let us come to a truce, some kind of settlement where both of us can come to an agreement that won't intervene with the other."

"Even if I agreed with you, there's no way I can turn back now."

Zander's demeanor and voice took on a grave tone, "What did you do? Who are you allied with?"

Demetrius gave him a nefarious grin, "I told you I would never kneel before lesser men. I gave my sword to the most powerful amongst us. Their cause is my cause now."

"You don't mean . . . "

Demetrius interrupted him, "The Fallen shall rise again."

Zander let his dread show and whispered, "The Great Culling."

"I need you with me my friend, along with your student and the child. If not, I must eliminate any threat or face their retribution also."

Zander's rage stirred, his eyes glowed at the threat as dark clouds quickly formed and rolled. He raised his hand, formed a fist, and brought it downward. Lightning struck from above, aimed at Demetrius who dove out of the way but was hit by the edges of the called lightning, its painful searing leaving burn marks. He yelled in agony as it electrified his body.

When Zander prepared to bring down another bolt from above, Rowland dove from the cloud of dust and slashed sideways at Zander, injuring his left arm. He stepped back, honing his power to allow the wound to heal while nullifying the pain so that he could continue to fight. Zander called upon his weapon to ignite and engulf his blade in flame. Rowland hesitated with his follow up to his melee, weighing the risks while measuring his chances. Demetrius stepped forward with the slightest of limps, ignited his sword, and waved off, "Watch my back. He's mine."

When Oliver reached his destination, he found Horace awaiting him. He twirled his gladeus in one hand while an amulet dangled from the other. Oliver knew right away what the amulet could do to the lesser of his kind. The pack had already presumed Kevin was under the control of some kind of magick, though they didn't know for certain the origin until Horace deliberately displayed the device.

The amulet glowed with the color of moonbeams, for such devices are bestowed their power in a moonbeam and the blood of a wolf to draw the desired effect. The three wolves behind Oliver shook and howled with uncontrolled spastic tremors. When their uninhibited movements ceased, their eyes glowed with the whitish tinges the amulet gave off. They surrounded Oliver and their obedience became unhindered of thought and only answered to the amulet holder's dominion over them. Oliver released his power and struggled in a desperate effort to gain sway back upon his compromised pack members. But his efforts came to no avail as the wolves arranged themselves into a triangulated formation where they could lunge at their leader without constraints of space. They leapt at their intended with concurrent precision, though Oliver had managed to dodge and block their claws and bites, but he knew he couldn't maintain a total defensive stance and survive. He maneuvered from the center of their assault and situated himself so he could take them on one by one, or at least prevent getting mauled by all three wolves at the same time. The three formed a line and crept up on him, snarling and snapping their jaws. Their tactic wasn't as coordinated as before since they'd become skewed from their controller's line of sight. And before the group could pounce on him in a strategic manner, Oliver jumped on one of the wolves, stomping him under foot, his paw smashed his head into the terrain, knocking him unconscious. The other two lunged at Oliver, which proved useless as he batted both down hard into the earth. Another wolf lay unconscious while the last rose up, shook his head, and charged back into the fray and met his end when Oliver caught him by the head and ripped it from his body when the wolf attempted to bite the large alpha in a last ditch effort.

Oliver turned his attention toward Horace who smiled at the wolf and continued to twirl his gladeus, pacing back and forth in anticipation.

"Bravo!" Radomir said from his view on the hill. "I'm sorry I can't stay for the finale, but I wish you the best of luck."

With that, Radomir spun and dissipated from sight, leaving Horace and Oliver face to face. Horace bowed to the wolf leader in a mocking manner and howled in the air. Oliver's fury triggered his power which he emanated across the scrimmage. Julia's skin tickled when his power washed over her, she smelled his scent and the rage he spread throughout. She feared he'd lost control in the thralls of combat, his mind unbridled. She defeated her opponent in a rapid succession and sped off to her beloved to come to his aid.

Big Mike pulled the trigger and his machine gun clicked empty. He dropped his weapon without hesitation in a fluid movement such as SWAT members change weapons. He grabbed his .45 Caliber handgun and stepped back, reluctant to go through his ammo like he did with his machine gun. Murray noticed the switch in weapons, taking note of his supply of shotgun shells coming close to depleted.

"I'm almost out," Murray said.

Both men headed to a nearby mound of rock debris and ducked behind. Big Mike took out his phone and shouted something to Murray, but he couldn't hear over the explosive magical battle being waged.

"What?" Murray yelled at Big Mike, though they were a meter from each other.

"We've got help coming."

"How long?"

"Minutes away. Let's keep low and wait."

"I've heard that way too often." Murray rose up and settled into a spot on top of the mound. Big Mike shook his head and followed. While they had an almost clear vantage point from up high, it exposed their position. Dust hid them from the sight of others. This did skew their vision, but the smoke and dust passed by in no time.

"If we can get a clear shot at the leader, we should take it," Murray said.

"Agreed," Big Mike said. "What we haven't factored in is when we shoot, hit or miss, we'll have a mess of vampires all over us."

"Then let's make every shot count."

"Dad had you pegged."

"Oh?"

"He said you were really a gangster who happened to

have a badge."

"I should argue with you about that."

"But you can't."

"Let's just say I won't and leave it at that."

Big Mike chuckled, "Fine by me."

As the battle between Nathan and Clovis continued, both had learned much about each other's particular style of fighting but had not been able to exploit their findings. The combat trudged on, neither side relenting. But Nathan feared Clovis, due to his years of experience in swordplay, would eventually discover a way to defeat him. He had to find a way to beat him through deception and magick. He considered a surprise attack or a blatant salvo of energy attacks but that seemed too much of a gamble. No, he needed to bring him in close, play into his ego and advantage. That's when his brilliant, dangerous plan formed in his mind.

He concentrated, tapped into his power while he utilized his sorcerer's skills as well as his vampiric abilities, while not exposing the ruse. Once an image of what he intended formed in his mind, he prepared to enact it.

He feigned impatience for a while, and then he displayed frustration. When he was certain Clovis bought into his charade, he yelled out in fury, charging toward the vampire, erratically swinging his shillelagh in reckless abandon at the prepared enemy across from him. Clovis stepped aside, parried the charge, and countered with a quick stroke to Nathan's upper arm—the one he wielded his weapon with—which he extended and left exposed. Nathan lost his grip on the clubbed weapon and it slid out of his hand, landing in the dirt at Clovis' feet. He cradled the freshly-wounded appendage with his left hand and hissed at his opponent as he paced around in agony, possibly looking for an escape route. Clovis kicked the weapon far to the side and walked over to his victim with his sword down at his side.

"Your impatience defeated you," Clovis said as he continued to advance closer. Nathan stood still, looking around like a cornered rabbit. "No one is coming to help you. We are vampires. We don't beg or plead for mercy."

Clovis stopped within less than arm's length and pointed his sword under Nathan's chin, pulled him in but a breath's distance apart, "Don't fret about Winter. I'll be gentle, though she deserves something more stringent."

"I will let her know." Nathan smiled at Clovis, who felt strange, suddenly weakened. He couldn't maintain a hold of his sword as his arm drooped to the side. His blade fell, stabbed into the ground in an upright position. His legs went to jelly and found it difficult to keep balance. He swayed as if inebriated. He felt his strength, his life force being drained from his body. And though too late to act, he realized his fatal error.

The illusion of Nathan's injured arm faded, and he had a grasp on his foe, bleeding him of his life's essence as before, except this time no one was there to stop him from sapping him dry, no one to rescue him. Clovis' last cognizant thought was how his own words came to haunt him before the pain encompassed all rational thought and tolerance. Soon after, Nathan let the wrinkled, sunken-in corpse out of his grasp, falling and shattering into a pile of brittle pieces upon the earth.

Demetrius walked toward Zander with Rowland just behind him, confident in their new-found advantage over the conjurer, but halted their forward progress as a sense of dread came over them. Rowland spun, raising his sword just in time to block Winter's leaping attack from above. She came down with a hard impact that nearly drove Rowland into the ground. She didn't relent and pressed the assault while Rowland took on a defensive stance, still reeling from the sudden attack and barrage of strikes that followed.

Though injured, Zander summoned his magick to contain the damage to his arm so it could heal while fighting, though this eliminated his ability to conjure energy weapons. He stepped forward, sword raised in a readied posture. Demetrius crossed his sword with his old friend's weapon, his heart filled with pride, for their fighting spirits hadn't waned since they were mortal and young, ready to face death without hesitation. This is what his soul yearned for: a battle in which he might lose. It had been many years since he'd experienced the battle shakes, and his hands couldn't stop trembling. This nostalgia of sorts energized him and his power radiated, sending a shockwave over the entire campaign field. An icy chill ran over all those present, immobilizing everyone momentarily, all but Zander. He shielded, deflecting any assault on his mind and body. It took no concentration on his part. He naturally did this as a part of both his sorcerer and vampiric power.

Zander chose a defensive counter strike approach to begin, and stood vigilant, awaiting Demetrius's first strike. Both remained still, knowing this confrontation could not end with both left standing.

Soon, Demetrius commenced the first move with an angled strike followed with a flowing placement to block the counterattack. Their flaming blades hissed and crackled in the air, their swords pressed together again. They had both studied under the same sword master, their patterns of attacks, parries, and blocks mirrored an image of two Samurai locked into a never-ending duel where neither had gained an edge over the other.

Horace and Oliver charged each other with blinding speed, knocking other combatants who impeded their skirmish out of their path. When Oliver drew close, he dove with both front claws extended. Horace countered by diving low, slashing the wolf's inner left thigh as they passed one another. The cut went deep, the blade had been crafted of an alloy of silver and steel—like most creatures of the night brandished—so the wound would heal slowly, if at all. Oliver's movement became hindered and impaired his fighting abilities. This made him rethink his tactics. He had to bring the vampire close, toe-to-toe, so he'd have a fighting chance.

"What's the matter? Can't face me in a straight-up fight?" Oliver had to somehow antagonize his opponent enough to make him give up his advantage.

Horace winked at him, jogging forward, twirling his gladeus and picking up speed upon his approach. He rushed past the wolf who nearly surmised his path, but his claws missed while the vampire scored another wound to his enemy on his inner bicep. Horace spun his weapon in celebration, blood flung from the blade, inciting euphoria in the vampire who then licked the blade and smacked his lips. Oliver grew more angry and growled at Horace, and made an imprudent leap at the arrogant rival, missing his intended target and landing prone in the dirt. Horace took advantage of the defenseless wolf and stepped on his back, pinning him down. He spun the sword in his hand into a backward grip, plunging the blade downward through the top of the wolf's head, killing him instantly.

Julia had arrived at the moment of her husband's demise. She howled in agony as she sprinted at the vampire responsible for his death. Horace stood for a moment, basking in his victory for too long, for when he caught Julia charging in the corner of his eye, he pulled his sword from the defeated wolf's head at the same time she pounced on him, before he could react in a defensive manner. His sword went flying into the air, lost to him as his sense of direction had been thrown askew in the scuffle. The two ended up on the ground with her on top of the vampire, pinning him down so he couldn't move. Her claws dug into his shoulders. He grimaced in pain while baring his fangs at her. Her tears rained down on her husband's killer, and within seven breaths, she decided what to do. Her jaws went for his throat and she clamped down and bit through the vampire's neck, severing it in two. Horace's head rolled away. She did it without remorse for her enemy had showed no mercy to her husband. His actions demanded pack retribution, and had come swift, without rebuttal or debate. She sat next to her husband's body that had changed back into human form. She pulled him up next to her, hugging him while crying in anguish. Misery emanated from her and all of the remaining wolves felt the sadness of their loss.

Winter and Rowland encircled one another, clashing swords as well as hand-to-hand assaults on each other. The speed of their attacks couldn't be fully tracked by the human eye. After some time of testing the combatant, Winter found an opening. Rowland tended to sometimes extend his lunges too far, and he had repeated that mistake one too many times. He lunged forward and left himself vulnerable. She spun and brought her sword around, slicing him down his back. He stumbled then fell to his knees, his sword barely in his grasp. He swiped with a blind counterattack but instead launched his sword from his grip, sailing out of reach. As he attempted his futile venture, Winter spun her sword in a reverse grip and thrust it backwards into her opponent's chest, right through the heart. She turned around as a dagger buried itself into her chest. She fell to her knees but maintained a defensive posture with her sword. Radomir stood there with the child cradled in his arms, delighted his ambush had worked.

Meanwhile, Demetrius gained the edge in the fight and pressed the skirmish as the aggressor. Zander backpedaled and lost his footing, landing on the gravel he slipped on, sitting upright. Demetrius raised his sword to strike down his adversary, not risking victory over chivalry of dueling, except he lowered his arm involuntarily. It drooped down in pain, and his sword fell down and extinguished itself. Murray had gotten off an accurate shot with his .357 Magnum but had only injured the leader. Nathan had been fighting his way back through to Winter and Zander and spotted Winter who appeared to be gravely hurt. He tried to maneuver past two vampires without engaging them, but they seemed dead set on taking him on. His wrath built and his power responded. He reached out with his claws and pulled outward as if he were prying elevator doors open. His energy stretched out, piercing the vampires and ripping them apart.

Radomir caressed the child, smiling and glancing at Winter in self-gloating when Jade approached him, "My Lord, hand me the child so you can finish her off."

His eyes lit up as he handed her the infant. She grabbed ahold of the baby, bowed and stepped aside. Radomir looked down at his prey, extended his claws and stepped forward. When he took his first step, Ivan appeared behind him, and in one stroke of his sword, chopped off his legs at the knees. He screamed in agony, dropping to the ground, looking at the removed limbs and remaining stubs in terror and pain.

Jade shouted over to Demetrius, who turned just in time to witness the removal of Radomir's legs. While Demetrius remained distracted, Jade rushed over to him, the child still cradled in her arms. She looked into her leader's eyes, "I told you you'd rue your decision."

Jade had already unsheathed her dagger while she spoke to Demetrius. She plunged her dagger into his heart and twisted the blade. Demetrius collapsed to his knees, and before he could do or say anything more, she stabbed him through his eye—hilt deep—ending him. He fell to her feet and she kicked his body for just desserts. Ancelot ordered all of the vampires to stand down. Jade had made a deal prior with Big Mike for a truce amongst all parties involved to form a united coalition that benefitted every species upon the death of Demetrius.

Zander immediately dashed over to Winter to give aid. He removed the dagger from her chest and used his energy to stave off the damage in an attempt to let her body heal. Big Mike and Murray brought emergency services over too, though it seemed no help could be given to her now. Zander kept her alive as long as possible so Nathan could say his farewells.

When Nathan approached the group surrounding Winter, Jade stepped forward, handing him his child, "Here is your son. Perhaps you should let the government entities raise him. They will continue to pursue you until you give him up."

"Jade," Big Mike grabbed her arm.

Jade stopped, looked at Big Mike and nodded, and then said to Nathan, "I'm so sorry."

Jade walked away and the crowd parted for the shell-shocked vampire. Nathan knelt down next to Winter and took her by the hand. Winter looked up at Nathan as a tear streamed from her eyes. She tried to speak but her head went limp. Zander stopped using his power and closed her eyes.

Nathan peered into his son's eyes. The child had his face and dark hair but Rachael's soft glowing eyes. The prophetic echoes of all he'd seen and all he'd endured rushed through his mind, and he fully understood all. He'd lost long before things came to pass, for fate had aligned itself against him from the beginning. The epiphany struck him like a sledgehammer to the gut. And still without uncertainty, his resolution held true from its inception, even in this moment of sorrow. His final consideration on the matter didn't require any deliberation or compromise and transcended any reason or logic. He knew a selfish decision would cause many to suffer and align themselves against him.

Nathan walked to Murray and placed his baby in Murray's arms, "Raise him, keep him safe.

Murray held the dark-haired baby boy, dumbfounded for a moment, and when the impact of the responsibility hit him, Murray said, "Don't worry. We'll protect him. What's his name?"

"Aiden. Rachael always liked that name."

Nathan went back to Winter's body and a cold sadness enveloped him. He squatted down and cradled her, stroking a few strands of her hair and whispered regret in her ear. He raised his gaze from her to the haunting presence of the grey-cloaked entity before him. All others except Zander, Viggo, Ancelot, and Jade stood frozen in time.

"You can't have her," Nathan yelled as he stood.

The entity held out a skeletal hand, laying claim to Winter.

"Can he really communicate with reapers?" Ancelot asked Zander.

"Yes," Zander said.

"Incredible," Viggo said.

"I refuse to give her to you." Nathan glided into the air.

Zander realized what Nathan intended to do, and this frightened him, "Nathaniel, wait!"

Zander's plea fell on deaf ears and Nathan's inconsolable heart would not hear any of it. Death had cheated him, so he would cheat death. He arrived at his home in the graveyard and placed her on the slab and concentrated, calling upon his power. He conjured the powers of necromancy, and dark clouds swirled into a whirlwind of purple energies of death that crackled in the night air. Zander arrived, realizing he had come too late. The power built until it teemed over and then, before it burst, Nathan poured the energy into Winter. Its dark radiance enveloped her and erupted in a thunderous sonic boom and then dissipated.

Winter rose into a sitting position from the slab, her back arched, her mouth and eyes opened wide. The forces set upon her were that of something unnatural, surfacing from the depths of a place unknown to her, forgotten and unbearably torn through the fabric of existence.

She twisted her body toward Nathan who stroked her cheek and brushed aside an untamed strand of hair from her face. Her mouth remained open, gaped in shock, and a single tear streamed down her face as she whispered, "What have you done?"

To Be Continued...

About the Author:

Steven Turk is a nurse that specializes in the care of the physically and intellectually disabled. A father of three sons, and husband to his beautiful, intelligent wife, he is a life-long resident of Topeka, Kansas. *Bound by Blood* is his first novel.

~ Coming Soon ~

Book 2 in the Blood Begotten Series:

DEAD OF WINTER

"LIKE" **STEVEN TURK AUTHOR** ON FACEBOOK AND WE WILL FACEBOOK MESSAGE YOU THE FIRST CHAPTER OF *DEAD OF WINTER*.

Flint Hills Publishing
WWW.FLINTHILLSPUBLISHING.COM

Made in the USA
Monee, IL
27 April 2024

57613370R00196